THE DANCING FACE

About the Author

Mike Phillips was born in Guyana, but grew up in London. He worked for the BBC as a journalist and broadcaster on television programmes including *The Late Show* and *Omnibus*, before becoming a lecturer in media studies at the University of Westminster. He has written many critically acclaimed crime novels, including *Blood Rights*, which was adapted for BBC television; *The Late Candidate*, winner of the Crime Writers' Association Macallan Silver Dagger for Fiction; *Point of Darkness*; *An Image to Die For*; *A Shadow of Myself*; and *Kind of Union*. He co-wrote *Windrush: The Irresistible Rise of Multi-racial Britain* to accompany the BBC television series, and an essay collection, *London Crossings: A Biography of Black Britain* (2001).

Appointed the first Cross Cultural Curator for the Tate Galleries in 2005, Mike also wrote for the *Guardian* and after leaving Tate was employed as Cultural Director (Cultuurmakelaar) for the town of Tilburg in the Netherlands. Subsequently he worked as a freelance curator, notably with the Belgian artist Koen Vanmechelen, organizing exhibitions in Brussels, Venice, London and Los Angeles. His public service includes trusteeships of the National Heritage Memorial Fund and the Heritage Lottery Fund. Most recently, he served as an independent adviser to Inspector of Constabulary Wendy Williams's *Windrush Lessons Learned Review* for the Home Office.

THE DANCING FACE

Mike Phillips

With a new introduction by
Bernardine Evaristo

PENGUIN BOOKS

PENGUIN BOOKS

UK | USA | Canada | Ireland | Australia
India | New Zealand | South Africa

Penguin Books is part of the Penguin Random House group of companies
whose addresses can be found at global.penguinrandomhouse.com.

First published by HarperCollins 1997
First published with a new introduction by Penguin Books 2021
001

Set in 11.6/15pt Fournier MT Std
Typeset by Jouve (UK), Milton Keynes
Printed and bound in Great Britain by Clays Ltd, Elcograf S.p.A.

The authorized representative in the EEA is Penguin Random House Ireland,
Morrison Chambers, 32 Nassau Street, Dublin D02 YH68

A CIP catalogue record for this book is available from the British Library

ISBN: 978-0-241-48267-4

www.greenpenguin.co.uk

This book is for Kip, in the hope that it will help
him in the struggle he is about to encounter.

My thanks to Kwesi, for his suggestions, research
and his help in focusing my mind on the experiences
which lie behind the story.

Thanks also to Julia, Antonia ('Madame' B), Onnikatchie
Wambu, John Akomfrah, Donu Kogbara, Linda Bellos,
and all the others who offered encouragement,
suggestions and argued the issues with me.

Introduction

Black Britain: Writing Back is a new series I've curated with my publisher, Hamish Hamilton, at Penguin Random House. Our ambition is to correct historic bias in British publishing and bring a wealth of lost writing back into circulation. While many of us continue to lobby for the publishing industry to become more inclusive and representative of our society, this project looks back to the past in order to resurrect texts that will help reconfigure black British literary history.

The books included in the series are my personal choices, determined by my literary values and how I perceive the cultural context and significance of the books. The series is not to be regarded as an attempt to be definitive or to create a canon. Canons are by their very nature hierarchical and have traditionally been constructed by the prevailing white orthodoxies of academia. Black British writers rarely appear on these reading lists, are rarely taught to new generations of readers and unless they become commercial successes, their legacy very quickly disappears.

My aim is to present a body of work illustrating a variety of preoccupations and genres that offer important and diverse black British perspectives. Good books withstand the test of time, even if they are of their time. I am very excited to introduce these books to new readers who will discover their riches.

Mike Phillips arrived in Britain from Guyana as a child and has lived in London ever since. He began his career as a BBC journalist and broadcaster, before becoming a full-time writer. Between 1982 and 2005, he published thirteen books including several crime fiction novels, most notably the Sam Dean series, featuring a black British journalist-turned-detective who made his groundbreaking entry in *Blood Rights* (1989), tasked with tracking down the missing daughter of a Tory MP. Back then, all Conservative MPs were white, by the way. This was swiftly followed by *The Late Candidate* (1990) and *Point of Darkness* (1994), until he departed our consciousness in *An Image to Die For* (1995). I remember the BBC television adaptation of *Blood Rights* in 1990 starring Brian Bovell, a well-known actor from the black theatre scene. It was astonishing to see a serious television drama written by and starring black British creatives. We hoped it marked the beginning of a breakthrough, but sadly it would take another twenty years before a black man played the sole, lead detective in a British crime drama – Idris Elba as Luther in the eponymous BBC series, launched in 2010.

Crime fiction, with its tendency to focus on the more formulaic mechanics of storytelling, usually has a bad rep in literary circles, but it's a hugely diverse genre. The hard-boiled detective sleuths of Walter Mosley's novels, arguably America's foremost African American crime writer, are quite different to the legal thriller, with John Grisham as its most famous proponent. Also, a big shout-out to British writer Nicola Williams, whose legal thriller *Without Prejudice* (1997), with a black woman barrister as protagonist, we've republished in this series. Val McDermid was one of the first crime writers to put women in the driving seat in crime fiction, bursting on to the scene with a socialist, lesbian, feminist journalist-turned-detective in *Report for Murder* (1987). Then there's Lee Child, whose Jack Reacher thrillers are a global phenomenon. More recently, Jacob Ross, a very literary writer, introduced us to a rare Caribbean manifestation of the genre, the 'Digger' Digson quartet of mysteries, the latest being *Black Rain Falling* (2020).

Crime fiction will always have human fallibility and culpability, as well as moral philosophy, at its core, albeit communicated with varying degrees of sophistication, and the form is perfectly suited to thrashing out arguments around law versus justice. With *Blood Rights*, Phillips took the genre into then unchartered territory as he swam through the murky waters between Britain and the African diaspora. His novels vibrate with the tension between power and privilege, with characters who exemplify the most ruthless and desperate aspects of human behaviour. From upper-class white enclaves to multicultural metropolitan districts, he maps out a fictional territory pertinent to the black British landscapes with subtextual ruminations on manhood in relationship to family, fatherhood, community and nationhood. In his 2000 novel *A Shadow of Myself*, he takes the reader across to Eastern Europe and into the lives of two mixed-race men, strangers, who seem to share a Ghanaian father, Kofi, who had studied in Russia in the fifties. One brother, a filmmaker, grew up in

London, the other was raised in East Berlin by his Russian mother. The novel stirs up a potent mix of politics, subterfuge, mystery and criminal activity.

The Dancing Face exemplifies the best of Phillips's vigorous writing while manifesting the ongoing discussion and demands around reparations and the restitution of African artefacts lodged in British institutions: objects procured through theft, the spoils of war, exploitation. Characteristically, this controversial issue, which speaks to Britain's expeditionary, missionary and colonial history, is cleverly refracted through a thrilling storyline, that is, the *re*-theft of one such Beninois mask, about to be included in an 'Africa on Tour' exhibition. The two protagonists, Gus and his younger brother Danny, are from humble origins. Danny is a bright and keen university student while Gus, who holds a PhD in West African history, is frustrated at the ineptitude of the Committee for Reparations to Africa to which he belongs, considering it 'part of the circus of minority demands which floated on the outer fringes of British politics . . . To these people direct action meant waving a banner in the street, and he had finally left when he worked out that no matter how many official asses they kissed, and no matter how many column inches were lavished on the cause, nothing would change.'

The characters are, variously, deceptive, dangerous, foolhardy; their motives and behaviour clash with sometimes disastrous consequences. There is a price to pay for avariciousness, and even the most idealistic individuals are stymied by their own weaknesses. Rereading this novel I was taken back to the black arts bougie scene of the nineties, recognizable to those of us who swirled around it, such as the mention of an art gallery in Finsbury Park, clearly modelled on what used to be the Black-Art Gallery on Seven Sisters Road, where Gus meets the public-school-educated Nigerian millionaire Okigbo, who has his own reasons for getting his hands on a talismanic mask made for the Oba of Benin. A lot has been packed into this novel written twenty-five years ago, yet far from feeling like a period piece, its politics are completely contemporary.

It's a shame that after *Blood Rights*, none of Phillips's crime novels made the transition on to the screen. They are still so ripe for it. It's not too late. His other books range from *Community Work and Racism* (1982); a collection of short stories, *Smell of the Coast and Other Stories* (1987); to the doorstopper *Windrush: The Irresistible Rise of Multi-racial Britain* (1998), co-written with his brother, Trevor Phillips, and one of the earliest, most substantial books capturing the generation of Caribbean immigrants who arrived in Britain from the forties onwards, and their descendants. The writer Andrea Levy acknowledged the influence of this mighty tome on her breakthrough novel *Small Island* (2004), about the Windrush generation.

Any timeline of black British literary history worth its salt needs to include the oeuvre of Mike Phillips, whose novels are both page-turners and intellectual investigations into important social and political issues. He forged new fictional pathways at a time when mountainous obstacles made it incredibly difficult to break through. We need to remember the pioneers. All later generations follow in their footsteps.

Chapter One

From where Gus was sitting the thing in Rodney's hand looked like a gun.

'What is that?' Gus asked quickly. The metal surfaces in the confined space of the van amplified his voice, making the question louder and more assertive than he'd intended.

'What's it look like?' Rodney said.

He stuffed it in the waistband of his jeans, zipped up his jacket and put the helmet on.

'I don't want anyone hurt,' Gus told him. 'Leave it behind. There's only a girl and an old bloke in there.'

Behind Rodney, Baz grunted, a muffled booming sound. Already armoured in leather, his face concealed by dark glasses and a cyclist's mask, he was crouching by the rear window peering out at the pavement.

'Nobody's going to get hurt,' Rodney said, grinning. 'It's only a replica.'

'Leave it behind anyway.'

Rodney stopped what he was doing, turned round and

looked at Gus, the strap of the helmet dangling down past his chin.

'I leave it behind,' he said, 'how do you reckon I'm going to get their attention?'

Gus didn't reply because he hadn't thought about it. When they'd discussed this part of the plan, Rodney had simply said that he and Baz would go in and deal with the security guard. Together they constituted such a formidable physical presence that it hadn't occurred to Gus that they'd use a gun.

'No problem,' Rodney said, 'they see the gun, they just do what you say. Otherwise, you might have to beat the shit out of some stroppy old git. Don't worry. It's okay.'

'If you want to talk about this some more,' Baz said, 'I'll relax and get me sandwiches out. Just let me know. Fuck.'

Rodney turned round, fastening up his helmet.

'Come on then,' he said.

They'd been sitting at the parking meter in front of the building for more than an hour, watching the comings and goings. It was impossible to see inside, because the plate glass of the shop-front had been replaced by a solid wall, decorated by the logo of the university and, below it, the title of the department, Art and Design, but Gus knew exactly how it was laid out and what was happening there. For instance, the street door opened on to a small tiled hallway, at the end of which was a locked door with a window of reinforced glass, through which the security guard could view visitors before letting them in.

There would only be one man on duty, because they changed shifts at eight, and the two night men, who were tall and young, had been replaced by a balding middle-aged geezer with bow legs. Gus knew this would happen in precisely the way that it did because he had watched it, sitting opposite in his car, several times during the previous week. An hour later the receptionist would arrive, to be followed, shortly after, by the red-haired assistant curator. The curator himself, the boss, wouldn't turn up until mid morning, and sometimes he didn't show till the afternoon, unless there was a special consignment whose unloading he wanted to supervise. Business would usually end at about five when the receptionist and the assistant curator went home and the security guard locked the doors to wait for the night shift to arrive. Gus had it sussed.

At first he had planned to go in after midnight when everything was quiet and dark. That was before Eleanor attended the launch party, chatted up the curator, and found out about the security system which went into operation at night. In contrast it would be child's play to get in and out during the day. He had chosen this particular Monday because he knew that the curator would be absent, delivering a speech at a conference. In normal circumstances his assistant would have been in the building by now, but during the early hours of the morning Rodney had gone up to Shepherds Bush and slashed the tyres of his Fiat. That would slow him down, Gus thought, by at least an hour, and that was enough. He permitted himself a glimmer of pride at the thoroughness of his planning, but it vanished abruptly when he remembered the gun. It was the unexpected angle which always screwed things up.

Inside the building Liz's day had just begun. She followed the same routine every day. First she put the coffee on, then she collected and sorted the letters and faxes. Then she listened to the phone messages, checked the e-mail, made notes and prepared memos for action. After this lot she was usually ready for a cup of coffee with old Bert, the security guard. She liked it best when Dr Leonard was safely out of the way, attending one of his conferences or giving a speech somewhere. Otherwise he'd be appearing suddenly, with a list of unpredictable requirements, letters to be written immediately, phone numbers to look up and all the rest of it. It wasn't that she minded the work. It was his fussy manner she couldn't stand. She disliked also the feeling that he saw her as a mere secretary. She had got the job, she thought, because of her degree in art history, and working on this project was her first step on the ladder of museum administration. But, instead of treating her as a potential colleague, Leonard behaved as if the ability to type and file letters was her most important quality. William, the assistant curator, was a different matter. She liked William, but he hardly ever asked her to do anything. Instead, he'd switch on his computer upstairs and disappear into it for hours on end.

Both of the curators had their offices on the first floor. The rest of it, like the whole of the second floor, was used for storing the stream of exhibits which had been arriving for the last month. The building had previously been a showroom belonging to one of the public utilities, but, since the industry had been privatized, the site had been closed down and leased to the Arts Council while the company waited for a suitable buyer. Subsequently it had been loaned to the university and Dr Leonard had captured it in a series of complex departmental negotiations as the headquarters for his touring exhibition of African sculpture. As Leonard pointed out in all the memos he wrote while laying the groundwork for his coup, the site might have been built for his purpose, since one of its features was a cul de sac at the back, which offered every convenience for the loading and unloading of large items. As he predicted, this entrance turned out to be invaluable, because, as the date of the exhibition approached, the rate at which the items arrived had speeded up. On some days, there were crates and messengers turning up practically every hour.

As a result Liz had no suspicion when the buzzer went and the messenger announced himself. 'Messenger for Africa on Tour,' the voice said through the intercom, and she pressed the button which opened the street door without hesitation. As usual, Bert went to take a look through the glass. Standing by her desk with a sheaf of letters in her hand, Liz could see, over his shoulder, that there were two messengers waiting, helmeted and masked as they usually were. It was odd for two of them to arrive at once and Liz found herself thinking about the waste of resources that this represented. It wasn't just the cost of having two men delivering two small parcels that one of them could have carried comfortably, there was also the increase in traffic and pollution on the roads. This was the sort of speculation she found entertaining, and she was making a rough calculation of how much the exhibition was contributing to the deterioration of the environment in London, when Bert staggered backwards and fell, almost at her feet. Her first idea was that he had stumbled on the carpet, then, almost in the same instant, she realized that she'd seen one of the messengers give him a violent push. She raised her head to shout at the man, but when she saw that he was pointing a gun straight at her the sound seemed to stick somewhere in her throat and what emerged was a sort of strangled croak.

'Take his keys and unlock the back door,' the man said.

'What do you want?' Liz asked.

Later she wondered about her nerve in talking back to the man, who towered above her, threatening her with a gun, the lowered visor of his helmet giving him the menacing look of an alien spaceman. At the time, she told William that afternoon, it wasn't a question of nerve. She opened her mouth and the words came out, like a dream.

'There's no money here,' she said. 'Only the petty cash. This isn't a shop or anything. It's part of the university. We don't have anything valuable.' A thought struck her. 'Do you want the computers?'

'Shut the fuck up,' the man said quietly. 'Take his keys and unlock the back door.'

Bert was already holding out the keys.

'Just do exactly what he tells you,' he said.

He sounded serious, but composed, as if all this was normal and predictable, and she took the keys from him slowly.

'Move,' the man shouted suddenly, making her jump.

She turned round then, and began walking into the corridor which led to the entrance at the back. The messenger, she couldn't tell which one, walked behind her, one hand holding her firmly by the base of the neck. At first she twitched a couple of times, trying to shake his hand off, but his grip only grew tighter. He didn't speak.

As they walked through the small loading bay to the back door, Liz had begun thinking about what she might do, and she wondered whether she could trick him into letting her operate the alarm, but, as if the man read her thoughts, his pressure on her neck increased, and she told herself that it wasn't worth it, especially with Bert lying in there with a gun pointing at him.

After she'd turned the key in the lock, the man pulled on the handle so that the sliding doors opened by a foot or so, and she saw the side of a black transit van blocking the way. He drew her back from the opening then, and another man appeared in the gap and squeezed through, pulling the doors closed once he was in. He was a little shorter than the other two but not by much, wearing a flat cap drawn down over his forehead, dark glasses, and a scarf over his chin and mouth. Even so she could tell he was a black man, like the others.

This was all she had time to see before the pressure on her neck turned her round and the man pushed her back through the loading bay into the corridor. She imagined that they were going back to the reception area. Instead, they stopped halfway down the corridor and she felt her hands being pulled behind her back. A sudden spurt of fear spiked through her, and she opened her mouth to scream, but, as she did so, a hand clamped itself over her face, muffling the sounds. Immediately she began, involuntarily, to struggle, fighting to release her hands, to break away and run. But the men were too strong for her to do more than twist her body from side to side, and in a moment, her hands were tied behind her back with what felt like the wire that came wrapped round the crates. Up to that point she hadn't noticed that they were opposite the door of the cupboard where the cleaners kept their mops and buckets, and she felt an immediate flood of relief when she understood that all they were going to do was shut her in there. Thank God, she thought, as the door slammed shut. For a couple of seconds she leaned against it, savouring the miracle of her escape, then something moved in the dark and this time she screamed for real. Then she heard Bert's voice, saying her name quietly. 'Liz, Liz.'

Chapter Two

Gus found the crate on the first floor. It had been opened, so he didn't have to search about among the boxes looking for the catalogue number Eleanor had given him. It was sitting, in pride of place, on a cleared space in the middle of the floor, the other boxes lined up in a semicircle round it. In that position, it looked as if it was already an exhibit, propped up inside the frame of the wooden box, the side of the crate lying flat in front of it.

The room was dim, the light from the windows at the front shaded by the boxes piled round the walls. In the dark the mask seemed to be shining. It was an oval-shaped face with holes for the eyes, and firm, curved lips. The expression was one of calm dominance, as if this face knew that it would be gazing out forever at a crowd of subjects. This face, Gus thought, knew its own value. He already knew that it was made of gold, and most of its surface was as smooth as he'd expected, but there were veined, cracked patches on the cheeks and around the rim. It was smaller, too, than he'd thought it would be: less than two feet long, and about half that across.

Gus got to his knees to take a good look, then it struck him that it must have been colder in the room than he'd realized, because he shivered as if a chill draught had swept over the back of his neck. Automatically he wrapped his arms round his chest, feeling the goosebumps crawling over his skin. In a second the sensation, whatever it was, had gone, but it left a kind of aura round his nerves which he couldn't quite put his finger on, like the memory of something which he hadn't actually experienced. The taste of a smell. A ghost in the mouth.

'Come on then,' Rodney said behind him. 'Is that it?'

He bent over Gus, peering into the box. Gus got to his feet hurriedly. In that moment there was something unpleasantly intrusive about Rodney's presence, and, in any case, he hadn't intended that anyone else should see it. In a sense it didn't matter because Rodney already knew what it was and roughly what it looked like, but, although this was an idea he dismissed whenever it occurred to him, Gus had a feeling at the back of his mind that there was a sort of dangerous and transforming power about the mask itself.

They took it through the back and loaded it into the van without difficulty. As they went past the cupboard he heard a sort of scurrying sound and he took another look to check that there was enough of a crack under the door to let the air in. It was actually a flimsy door and he calculated that if the assistant curator didn't arrive soon they'd manage to force their way out within the next couple of hours.

Back in the van he drove soberly towards Euston Road, slotting into the rush hour-traffic. Behind him Rodney and Baz were talking in quiet monosyllables, but Gus felt as if his head was floating somewhere above the roof of the van, the feeling of elation so strong in him that he couldn't focus on what they were saying, and he hardly heard. He'd expected them to be noisier, more boisterous at this point, but he could see how chuffed they were from the grins on their faces, and he had the sense that they were looking at him with a new respect. As they drove into the tunnel near Euston, Rodney patted him on the back.

'All right then, Gus?'

After Euston Station he turned off and stopped in a side road to let Rodney and Baz out as they'd arranged. He parked carefully at a vacant meter, switched off the engine, then reached into his pocket and gave Rodney the envelope which contained the money. Rodney opened and riffled through the notes, counting quickly. Fifteen hundred pounds, in fifty-pound notes.

'It's all there,' Gus told him.

'I know that,' Rodney said, but he didn't stop counting.

When he'd finished, he tucked the money into the pocket of his jeans and motioned to Baz, who slid the side door of the van open and got out. Rodney made to follow him, then he paused and looked back at Gus.

'What do you reckon that thing's worth?' he asked. 'Million?'

'No way, man,' Gus said. His answer was automatic, but the truth was that he had no idea what the thing was worth and the question gave him an uneasy feeling which was intensified by the sceptical look on Rodney's face. Rodney believed in what they were doing, Gus thought, but that kind of money might tempt anyone.

'Well, I don't really know,' he continued. 'It only has a value if it goes on the market, and that will never happen now.'

Rodney nodded, but Gus noticed something cross his face, a sort of sneer, before he turned and got out of the van. In a second he walked past the driver's window, rapping lightly on it as he went, saying goodbye.

Gus watched the two boys as they strolled towards the corner. From behind they looked almost identical. Two black boys, heads shaven almost to the skin, somewhere in their early twenties. Rodney was the taller and slighter, a couple of shades darker than Baz. That was it.

When they'd moved out of sight, Gus went to work. If his guess was right he still had an hour or more. He crawled into the back, levered open the crate and took the mask out. He laid a square of foam on top, folded two sheets of cardboard round it to make a flat shape, and then wrapped it in brown paper. He finished the package off with string, and laid it on the floor next to the driver's seat. The remaining litter of the packing case and motorbike helmets he covered with a tarpaulin, before hauling himself back into the front and driving off again.

While he was completing these tasks his mind was preoccupied with Rodney. Baz didn't worry him, because Baz was, so to speak, merely hired help, and he had no doubt that he would simply follow Rodney's lead. Rodney was the problem. Always the unexpected, Gus thought. Nothing had happened yet, of course, but he had a nasty feeling that it would soon enough, and it was the look on Rodney's face as he stepped out of the van which had created this disturbing train of thought. He'd had a mocking and furtive expression which Gus hadn't seen before, and which set up an apprehensive jangling in his head.

As it happened, he'd thought of Rodney as a partner up until that point and trusted him accordingly. In fact it had been Rodney who made the first approach, and after his final meeting with the committee he might have given it all up if it hadn't been for Rodney. It had actually started out as one of the most dispiriting evenings of his life. The truth was that when he'd joined the Committee for Reparations to Africa, he had, in a sense, been acting against his better judgement, and he'd grown progressively disillusioned with their activities. Even so, it had taken that last pointless gathering to finally make up his mind.

The meeting had been held at the chairperson's house in Tulse Hill. The turnout was good, about half a dozen seated at the big round table in the dining room which led out on to the back garden. Gus had attended meetings and sat on a variety of committees with all of them over a number of years, the only exception being Rodney, who had been a student when they'd last met. Gus had been told that he'd dropped out of his degree course, and was slightly surprised by the fact that, when he joined the group, Rodney was already a member. When he mentioned, in passing, that he already knew Rodney, the chairperson had looked pleased. Rodney represented, she remarked with an air of some satisfaction, the youthful element.

On the occasion of his last meeting Gus had found himself sitting opposite Rodney. Behind him the walls next to the French windows were studded with pictures of the chairperson, Janice, a former dancer and actress, shaking hands with famous people.

She was still beautiful, but nowadays her hair was seeded with grey, and, instead of the smile of broad seduction, her expression was one of resolute control, appropriate for a woman who was consultant to a government department and sat on a number of quangoes.

The meeting had been a special one, called to discuss the long-term arrangements for holding a vigil outside the various sites of the Africa on Tour exhibition. 'Wherever they go in the country,' Janice said grimly, 'we should be there.'

Gus had already made up his mind to oppose the whole affair. Demonstrations and vigils were pointless, he told them. The only result, he said angrily, would be a few minutes on the air being patronized by a succession of young white women with microphones. If they wanted to do anything, he ended by telling them, it should be something dramatic and unorthodox, something that would scare the shit out of the establishment and the media. Anything else was a waste of time.

The first objection came, as he knew it would, in a long and rambling speech from Ras Oswald, the gist of which was that violence or the provocation that violence offered was to be avoided. What was needed, he mumbled, was a period of peaceful meditation and prayer, after which Jah Rastaferai would show the way. He was followed by Susie Prescott, a poet who had just returned from a British Council tour of the USA. She was tired of the macho bullshit she'd heard from Gus, she said. She proposed, instead, a vigil of women, which would draw in radical white women and, by utilizing women's solidarity, rival Greenham in its effect. By the time she'd finished there were tense and angry vibes twanging through the room, and Janice stepped in to calm things down. She had received, she told them, a reply to her letter to the Heritage Secretary, suggesting a meeting with an official at the Ministry to discuss the issue, and perhaps it would be better to delay discussion of their plans until after that date.

Gus had heard enough.

'You can do what you like,' he said. 'I don't want to be involved any more. I resign.'

He got up and began walking out.

'That's not the attitude, Gus,' he heard Janice calling out behind him. 'Come back. Let's discuss this.'

He didn't bother to reply or even hesitate, but as he crossed the gravel at the front of the house, he heard the door open and foot-steps crunching after him. At first he thought that Janice must have adjourned the meeting and come out to persuade him, but when he turned round it was Rodney.

'You're right, man,' Rodney told him. 'I resigned too. Them talking shit.'

It was clear that Rodney was using language which demon-strated his solidarity and disgust, and, as they walked down Brixton Hill together, the boy listened and nodded his agreement while Gus elaborated on why the committee was a complete waste of time. After this they met a couple of times, and Gus soon understood that Rodney's anger and commitment was equal to his own. On the second occasion he outlined the plan that had come to him, in a flash, on that evening while he was storming out of Janice's house. Rodney greeted the idea with unqualified and reassuring enthusiasm, and, suddenly, it was real.

Rodney had suggested bringing in Baz. Baz had some experience with this kind of thing, Rodney said, and he'd be cool. The only problem was that he'd want money, up front or as soon as the job was done. The important thing, Rodney continued persuasively, was that they couldn't go around recruiting people who would do it out of conviction, because a single refusal would mean that there was someone around who knew all their plans. Baz, on the other hand, would do the business, and if he was properly paid would keep his mouth shut forever. Sweet. What made it safe and certain was the fact that in Baz's world a youth who became known as an informer couldn't expect to live happily, or long. Besides all that, Rodney knew Baz, and knew he was cool. Convinced, Gus agreed. It made sense. His only problem was finding the money, and once he'd met the Nigerian that turned out not to be a problem at all. On the other hand, looking back, Gus knew that this was the point at which his relationship with Rodney had changed. It was subtle, nothing he could pin down, a matter of the odd sarcasm. After Baz came in, he also had the feeling that Rodney was closer to the other boy, and that it was they who were the true partners in the venture, while he stood somewhere on the outside looking in.

It had been a mistake also, he realized later, to tell Rodney that he had a patron who was coming up with the money. He had kept the name to himself, as he'd promised the Nigerian, but once Rodney knew that Gus had a backer he had begun to hint that, like Baz, he deserved some reward. After all, he said, he was taking the same risks, and if things went wrong his life could be ruined. Gus saw the justice in that and he agreed to pay Rodney what he had left after he'd covered his expenses. Now, it struck him that he'd made all the wrong moves.

As he wheeled the van carefully round King's Cross, he thought about the look he'd seen passing across Rodney's face, and it occurred to him that, instead of satisfying the boy's need for cash by dropping him a bung, he had merely whetted an appetite which might prove impossible to satisfy.

Chapter Three

Gus was not easily intimidated, but the first time that he had come close to the Nigerian he'd felt distinctly uncomfortable. It wasn't a feeling he could pin down with any precision. It was simply that there was something about the man which troubled him, as if Okigbo had a solid physical aura with which he could reach out and touch you.

Perhaps it was his size. Gus was easily six foot tall and a bit, but Okigbo towered above him by at least a head, and he had broad, solid shoulders which tapered down to the waist and hips of an athlete. Gus couldn't guess his age. He had no softness around the middle, but his thick neck and his steady, penetrating eyes seemed to be saying that he was a man with the power and experience which came from having been around for a lot longer than Gus's thirty years.

'I understand,' Okigbo had said. 'How much money do you want?'

The question startled Gus. He'd only been in the room a few minutes, since coming up in the lift with one of the bodyguards.

Gus hadn't seen the man before, but, dressed in a neat dark suit, and surrounded by an aura of polite and impenetrable menace, he seemed identical to the other bodyguards who were always hovering a few paces behind Okigbo. Outside the lift the bodyguard had searched him for weapons, running practised hands lightly over his back, up his legs and between his thighs. Only then had he allowed Gus to enter. As it happened, the door didn't lead into a room at all. Gus had found himself in a hallway which was the entrance to the apartment that Okigbo occupied. Gus had no idea how big it was, but on the first occasion he visited he had guessed, from the number of doors he could see, that it was easily the size of a large suburban house. At the end of the hallway the door opened into a large sitting room. The furniture consisted of a couple of sofas, a big round table and a sideboard, all of it in leather and light wood. Gus imagined that these were standard fittings for a furnished apartment of this kind, but someone had spread lengths of cloth over most of it — kente, adinkara, adire — the garish dark and light African colours giving the whole room an exotic gleam, which somehow seemed fake, as if the sitting room had been dressed up for a special sale of outlandish curios.

Dr Okigbo was lying back on a sofa in the far corner. His expression was serious and withdrawn and he didn't get up or offer Gus a drink or a coffee or a cup of tea. Instead he asked whether Gus had got the mask. When Gus said yes, he smiled, sprang to his feet, walked over to the window and looked out, then turned and asked about the money. For a moment Gus was confused. This wasn't how he'd intended it to go. He'd intended to tell Okigbo something about how it was done — not every detail, but enough to justify what he'd spent. Then he'd planned to open negotiations about the funds he needed to set up the rest of the operation.

Okigbo's mouth twisted sarcastically, as if he knew what was running through Gus's mind.

'Let me tell you something, my friend,' Okigbo said. 'I am not the local council or the Gulbenkian Foundation or the Prince's Trust or any of those other things you're accustomed to fooling around with. I'm not an accountant. I keep an accountant because I don't want to waste my time looking over my shoulder. I know money. I grew up playing with piles of cash like you played with mud. I have an MBA from Harvard. I know business. I know what you did and what it's worth. You don't have to give me accounts. We made a deal. Back in Nigeria I make a deal with a man and he cheats me I'll have him killed.'

Gus fumbled around in his mind for a reply. The trouble was that he couldn't tell whether or not Okigbo was joking. He knew enough to understand that Okigbo was no pussycat, and he'd heard more than enough stories about what went on in West Africa to know that whatever he imagined could be true. This was the crunch, he thought, and he sat up straighter and squared his shoulders, but before he could say anything Okigbo swung away from the window and looked intently at him. When the Nigerian did this his eyes seemed to open wider and bulge a little. Suddenly he laughed, and pointed his finger at Gus.

'Don't worry,' he said, still laughing. 'I won't kill you. I only do that if I feel in a very bad mood. Besides, I trust you, my brother.'

For a moment Gus felt a spark of relief, then it struck him that Okigbo had managed to threaten and reassure him in the same sentence. In the back of his mind a surge of self-congratulation glowed. How right he had been to get the mask away, out of London.

There was a tentative rapping on the door, and Okigbo barked out a couple of words Gus didn't understand. The door swung open and a woman came in. She was wearing a black veil and a long black robe and she was carrying a tray which contained a bottle, two glasses, a pair of silver tongs and a pitcher full of ice cubes.

Okigbo pointed to the table without speaking, and she went over to it, put the tray down, bowed to each of them in turn, then turned and left. As the door swung shut behind her, Gus looked away from it to see Okigbo watching him with an amused expression.

'Aha,' Okigbo said. 'No one, I don't care who he is, can resist a Somali woman.'

Gus remembered that while the woman was in the room he hadn't been able to take his eyes off her. She had been tall and thin and graceful, like a model swathed in black silk. When she came into the room it was as if something mysterious and romantic had entered. He wondered whether she was Okigbo's wife.

Okigbo dropped ice cubes into the glasses, filled them with whisky and handed one to Gus.

'What was your father?' Okigbo asked. 'Where did he come from?'

'He came from the Eastern Caribbean.'

The truth was that Gus wasn't sure, because his English mother sometimes used to get confused about which Caribbean island his father had come from, and for a long time he hadn't been interested in pinning it down, then when he wanted to she was dead and it was all too late.

'I think he must have been Yoruba,' Okigbo said. 'I can see it. You are built like a Yoruba. I know many West Indians, and some of them are perfectly Yoruba. I think your father must have been one of them. That makes us brothers.'

Gus knew how unlikely this was. 'I thought,' he said, giving his voice a deliberate dryness, 'that Okigbo was an Ibo name.'

A frown crossed Okigbo's face, a quick spasm of irritation. 'My father was Ibo, but my mother was Yoruba. A woman of great strength.'

Gus nodded in acknowledgement, but he felt a tiny spark of triumph at having penetrated the African's surface.

'When can I see this thing?' Okigbo asked abruptly.

'The mask?'

Okigbo's mood seemed to change suddenly. His face twisted in irritation.

'Yes. The mask. The Dancing Face of the great Oba. This is what I want to see.'

Gus hesitated, pulling together the arguments he would have to use. The difficulty was that the issue had nothing to do with the logic of his intentions. What counted here was the power of the imagery he could create.

'This isn't a simple theft,' he said. 'It's a mystery. Years ago there was a racehorse named Shergar. You've heard of it?'

If Okigbo felt patronized he didn't show it. Instead he inclined his head in acknowledgement, his eyes fixed on Gus.

'It's been in the news for all these years because it was a mystery. This is the same, except that it's more important. Think about it. An object no one much has ever heard about but which is said to have great value suddenly disappears. What is it? Who would do such a thing? How many millions would it fetch? No one can find it. The longer it stays out of sight, the more intriguing, the more theories and arguments emerge. All the speculation will centre on the issue of African art, on the manipulation and dispossession of Africa by the Europeans, because that's the meaning of the thing itself.' He paused, wondering whether he'd said enough. 'The point is that it has disappeared. That's what it's all about. If I could, I'd forget where it is myself. From your point of view, for your own protection, it's best if you don't know where it is.'

Unexpectedly, Okigbo grinned.

'Thank you,' he said. Then he leaned forward, the grin vanishing to be replaced by a frown. His eyes swivelled, as if in thought, before they focused on Gus again.

'That's very interesting,' he said. 'But, forgive me, you're speaking as an academic theorist.' He held up his hand to forestall Gus's protest. 'I don't mean that what you're saying isn't true. I'm sure it is. But you're missing something. Your plan comes out of a European imagination. It reduces everything to abstractions. When a European looks at the dancing mask, if he's intelligent or educated, that is, he sees art. That is something separate from the reality of life. A thing to be appreciated or valued, or whatever the fuck Europeans do when they encounter what they call beauty.'

Gus blinked, staggered by the contempt in Okigbo's voice when he said this. The Nigerian smiled again, as if he knew what Gus was thinking.

'When I think of this thing, I'm confronting the part of my life which is entwined with my feeling for my father and his father and for all the ancestors who have given life to my family and to my nation. It speaks of my dreams, of all the things we have done and felt in the past, and all the things we will do and feel in the future. It's not art to be looked at and admired. It is a spirit.' He paused, studying Gus. 'You understand the Christian doctrine of transubstantiation? This is the spirit which is transformed into substance by the power of faith.' He paused again. 'That is the real mystery. That is why I want to see and touch it.'

He stopped speaking, leaned back in his chair and looked at the ceiling.

'You already know that,' he said. From under the lids his eyes glinted at Gus. 'In other circumstances I would be offended at your assumption that my interest was mere curiosity. But, as it happens, I've been wondering what you were intending to do with it after it's served your purpose. My father believed that all men were in the grip of a precise destiny. Perhaps your fate is to return this thing to where it came from.'

Gus had been struggling to conceal his astonishment. He was familiar with the beliefs that Okigbo had been uttering. That wasn't it. What startled Gus was the fact that none of this fitted his image of Okigbo, which was that of a sophisticated and cynical playboy. Hearing him express his attachment to traditional African beliefs was as much of a shock as if one of his Marxist friends had suddenly confessed to being an evangelical Christian. All along he'd had the feeling that Okigbo was sceptical about the politics of what he was doing – it was the main reason he had for not trusting the Nigerian – but the implications of what he'd just heard left him floundering.

'I'm not interested in what happens to it,' Gus said, hoping that he'd responded quickly enough to hide his uncertainty. 'Not as such. I appreciate that it has a far greater significance, but I intend to take one thing at a time, and having it means we can focus international attention on challenging the Europeans to compensate Africa for all the loot they took out of the continent.'

The phrases tumbled out of his mouth with a practised fluency, and his voice rose, ringing in the confines of the room. Okigbo nodded seriously, as if he accepted the dominance of Gus's passion.

'When I came to you,' Gus continued, lowering his voice. 'I told you that was what it was all about. I'm not a thief. This is an opportunity to do something big, and I'm not going to risk blowing it. Not even for you. Not when we've come this far.'

'Okay,' Okigbo said, raising his hands in a gesture of surrender. 'I understand that. This is why I'm financing you. But you have to trust me. All I want is to see it. When can I see it? Today, tomorrow? When? Just you and me.'

'I don't know,' Gus said. He had determined to resist this pressure while he was on his way to the hotel, but now he found himself wavering.

'My brother,' Okigbo said. 'We are both Yoruba.'

He put his hand inside his jacket and took out a thick envelope. He opened it and leaned forward to show Gus the contents. It was full of fifty-pound notes.

'Here is a thousand pounds,' Okigbo said. 'I had my bank send this over today for you. This is an expression of my faith and trust. Take it. But don't tell me that I can't see this thing.'

'Let things cool down,' Gus said eventually. 'A couple of days. Then I'll get in touch.' He stretched his hand out to take the envelope, then he halted it in mid air. He wanted the money, he knew, but not at the price of letting Okigbo think that he had agreed. 'But no promises. It depends on the situation.'

He took hold of the envelope with the tips of his fingers then, but Okigbo didn't let go for a few seconds, letting Gus tug at it, his bulging brown eyes staring straight ahead. Then he opened his hand, and nodded.

'A couple of days, my brother.'

Chapter Four

Danny hadn't yet received the parcel sent by his brother Gus, and even if he had, he wouldn't have known what to make of it. Gus never wrote, not even a postcard. Usually he telephoned, and towards the end of term Danny would start expecting a call from him, asking when he was coming down to London for a visit.

On the other hand, on a morning like this, halfway through one of the dullest classes he'd ever attended, the end of term seemed very far away. Even Flegenhauer looked bored. Danny could tell by the way that he ran his hand over his thinning blond hair and pursed his lips that he was struggling to maintain his concentration. Karen had been reading her paper on Peter the Great's foreign policy for the last twenty minutes, and she hadn't yet said anything that couldn't have been extracted from the standard textbooks. This hadn't surprised Danny, or anyone else in the group, and they'd all been prepared to be bored. After all, they knew what was coming because, say what you like about Karen, she was well organized, and each of the six students at the seminar had a couple of primly typed sheets of A4 in front of them which contained a summary of her paper, followed by a numbered list of her main arguments together with a short bibliography.

As it happened, her efficiency didn't count for much with Fleggy. As all the students knew, Flegenhauer had spent more than a year in an East German prison, and after his release he'd had to support himself by hustling on the black market. It wasn't until the Berlin Wall came down that he'd been able to reconstruct his research and start publishing again. So if there was one thing you could bet on, Danny thought, it had to be the fact that Flegenhauer would fail to be impressed by Karen's suburban tidiness. In any case, the layout of her paper was beside the point, because everyone also knew that Flegenhauer's real work was focused on ethnicity and nationalism in the Baltic states. Danny doubted that Flegenhauer cared about Peter at all, and if he did, it was because of the Tsar's impact on the region around the Baltic, an aspect of the history which Karen's paper had completely ignored.

Danny dropped his pen, picked it up, and, trying to look as if he was taking notes, began doodling. He might have given himself a break by pretending to go to the loo, but one of the other students had been gone for the last five minutes and there was an unspoken consensus by which the members of the seminar restricted their absences to one at a time. He'd have to wait.

Suddenly Danny's mobile phone began ringing. Karen had launched into a digression on the state of the roads in eighteenth-century Russia, and she'd just used the word 'communications' when she was interrupted by the electronic warbling. Her irritation was compounded by the ripple of laughter which ran round the group, and she gave Danny an angry glare. He shrugged and she dropped her eyes, searching for the right place on her page of printed notes. Simone, the student sitting beside her, winked at Danny and he smiled back.

In normal circumstances he'd have been more apologetic, but he was feeling a little aggrieved about the direction that the seminars had so far taken. Danny's main reason for signing up to attend this seminar group had been the chance to talk with Flegenhauer about European ethnicity and nationalism, the subject in which he intended to specialize. It was also the one area of history that Danny had studied in any detail, even though his interest had been more or less accidental. At school he'd been the only black boy staying on for the sixth-form exams, and he'd spent a year retaking his GCSEs, so he was already a year and a bit older than the rest of the class. From the beginning he had what the headmaster described, in private, as a chip on his shoulder. Whenever the classroom discussions touched on Africa or African politics, he'd found himself listening, mute and raging, to a litany of ignorant opinions about tribalism and about the violence and naivety of African politics. By the middle of the first term he'd had enough. The final week of history lessons had been set aside for a discussion of democracy. Danny knew what was coming, so he'd scoured the newspapers at the weekend, and on Monday he walked into the school carrying a sheaf of newspapers featuring huge photographs of Bosnian refugees, dead bodies in the snow, and limbless children. Before Miss Hudson could start the session he had walked to the front of the class, held up the newspapers so everyone could see, and then begun to distribute the pile along the nearest desks. 'Before you start going on about

Zulus, and the ANC, and massacres in Rwanda, take a look at what a bunch of Europeans are doing to each other,' he shouted.

It was as if he'd dropped a bomb. Miss Hudson gave him a stern look and told him to sit down. She was a tall, gangling, sandy sort of woman, and for the rest of the day she treated him with an apprehensive caution, as if he might explode without warning. The class itself was unusually quiet and subdued for most of the morning, but as the day wore on Danny's classmates began breaking out in sarcasms and, in some cases, expressions of outright anger. At the end of the day Miss Hudson summoned him into the room she shared with a couple of other teachers and asked him whether he had a problem. That was only the start of it. Over the next few days Danny found that with one sentence he had gained himself a reputation which oscillated around the claim that he was a dangerous black militant, and came to rest on the conviction that he was a difficult, unstable character. The floodgates had opened. Wherever and whenever, it seemed, that he showed himself during the breaks or before and after school, various kids to whom he'd hardly ever spoken were approaching him to begin pointless arguments about the O. J. Simpson case, about Mike Tyson, about Louis Farrakhan and the Nation of Islam, about the fatwa against Salman Rushdie.

Danny had tried to hold his ground. His problem with these encounters was that he hadn't thought very much about such people, and, although the news about their activities had interested him, he didn't care very much about what had been happening to them. So the intense anger and hostility his white schoolmates seemed to feel towards these figures, and by implication himself, surprised and almost paralysed him. At the end of the second day, as Danny walked towards the schoolgates, someone called out, 'Ojay, Ojay!' By now he was half prepared and, pasting a superior smile on his face, he walked on as if he hadn't heard, but as he climbed on the bus he was boiling with rage. The term ended the next day, but after all this Danny knew he had to find a way of defending himself.

Over the holiday period he read everything he could find about tribal conflicts in Europe. He read about the Hundred Years War and the Thirty Years War, he read about the massacres of Jews and Huguenots, he read about the Magyars, the Bulgars, the Croats, the Slavs, the Serbs, he read about the relentless ebb and flow of violent imperial expansion and resistance, he read about the endless formation and reformation of nations, all of them accompanied by a great washing of blood, he read about the advance and retreat of religious movements, about the immolation of witches, about the torture and exile of nonconformists. At the beginning he smiled and hugged himself with delight at the ammunition he was gathering. Then a kind of horror at the unrelenting cruelty of it all settled in his mind. By that time, however, he'd read enough to begin cutting a dash in his history classes. The first person to notice was the head of history, Mr Turner. He was a specialist on eighteenth-century Britain and a seasoned professional, so he had been aware of Danny's presence in the sixth-form intake. The fact was unusual, but Mr Turner hadn't seen it as requiring any special attention, because one look at Danny's file had told him all he needed to know. The boy was mixed race, the product of several different foster homes. After twenty years in the school it was obvious to Mr Turner that Danny was part of a group of pupils from whom he defended himself with an amused and sympathetic cynicism. Underprivileged, aggressive, no hope and no prospects. The thing was to get them through the class with the minimum of fuss.

On the first day of the new term, however, Danny astonished him by coming out with a brief and largely correct account of William of Orange's political alliances before his accession to the English throne. In the staff room afterwards, Mr Turner told his colleagues that the boy had actually been reading and remembering what he read. With Danny's background in mind, Mr Turner assumed this meant that he was both exceptional and exceptionally ambitious. Over the next two years Danny became a star, his increasingly detailed forays into East European history treated with a proud indulgence by the history teachers. At the end of the course he wrote a prize-winning essay on European ethnicity and its role in the origins of the First World War, and went off to university in what amounted to a blaze of glory.

He'd been excited to find that Flegenhauer was to be one of his tutors. Flegenhauer was the real thing, but apart from a couple of lectures in the first year he hadn't had a chance to speak to the man until the start of this series of seminars, and he'd hurried to the first session anticipating a long debate about what had happened to European nationalism behind the Iron Curtain. Instead, Danny had found himself sitting through a rambling paper on the Crusades, delivered by John, a balding monk from East Anglia, whose real interest was the break-up of the Byzantine empire. Karen's session had sounded more promising, but now Danny was bored, and as far as he could tell, so was everyone else in the group. The warbling of the telephone was a perfect excuse. Instead of switching it off, he got up, grabbed his bag, gestured in apology to Flegenhauer, and hurried out of the room.

In the corridor he leaned against the wall and pressed the button. It was Little Osman.

'Wanker,' Danny said. 'You rang me in the middle of my seminar, man.'

The protest was a ritual which sprang from Danny's observation that if he didn't object to Osman's behaviour matters would get much worse, and, as usual, Little Osman seemed completely unworried by accusation or abuse. He avoided most of the classes for which he was registered, and he regarded Danny's insistence on regular attendance as an amiable eccentricity.

'Don't worry about the seminar,' Little Osman growled in his ear. 'We got some trouble.'

Danny straightened up, pushing himself away from the wall. This sounded as if it was going to be bad news about the business, although Danny still found it difficult to think of it as a business, especially when he thought about how it had started, sitting around with Osman one night in the second-floor kitchen in Mitsubishi Hall. This was in the early hours of Sunday morning, and most of the students they knew were away, either tripping back home or raving it up in the nearest big city. Neither Danny nor Osman had a home to which they could go and, stuck on the campus at the weekend, they had plenty of time to talk about the deficiencies of the university's social life. The problem, they agreed, was that there was nothing to do. The raves in town were full of schoolkids zonked out on speed and E, while the union bar was infested with rugby-playing public-school maniacs zonked out on beer and E.

'What it wants', Osman said, 'is something really cool. Like clubs in London.'

That was the beginning. At first it was meant to be a one-off. Danny had a vision of how it could be. The craze for giant raves had more or less come to an end, and most people he knew were bored with heavy metal and acid house. When you were trying to live a normal life, like getting up in the morning for lectures, most of that stuff was too heavy or too weird. What would work, he told Osman, was a kind of postmodern approach. 'What?' Osman said. A mixture, Danny told him, featuring the best of the old traditional music, like from the eighties, plus the new, like from today. Three floors, house music on one level, then rock bands on the next, and down on the lowest floor, blues and soul.

The next day they printed up some business cards with the name of the company, Cool One, in W H Smith, and started finding out how much it would take to rent one of the clubs in town for an evening. The prices for the weekend trade were horrifying, but eventually they made a deal for an evening during the week at a club in the city centre. It cost marginally less than the overdraft that the bank was giving students that year, and when Danny and Osman put their resources together they found that they had enough to make the advance payment that the owner of the club wanted. The outlay left both of them penniless, and by the evening of the event Danny was beginning to think that he might have made a big mistake. As it turned out he had nothing to worry about. Osman had exerted himself, handing out flyers to every student in the town, and the crowd was so enormous that, towards midnight, there were queues lined up waiting to get in. Cool One was a success, and after Danny had paid off the DJs and the bouncers, the partners still had a couple of hundred left between them. At the end, as they packed up to go home, the manager had asked when they would be running their next club night. Danny hadn't thought about it, but he knew better than to hang about when opportunity beckoned. 'Same time next month,' he said quickly.

That had been a couple of months ago, and things had gone so smoothly that Danny had forgotten that they could also go badly wrong. Osman's words, and the tone in which he'd said them, gave him a sinking feeling.

'What kinda trouble?' Danny muttered into the phone.

'I don't wanna talk about it right now,' Osman said. 'Meet me lunchtime.'

Danny went back to his seminar in an irritable mood. Karen had apparently ground to a halt, and Flegenhauer was discussing some point she'd made about Peter's Baltic fleet, but Danny was barely listening. Somewhere in his head he kept hearing the echo of Osman's voice. He could only guess at what kind of trouble had turned up, and he knew that it wouldn't have been any use asking. Even in the most ordinary circumstances Osman refused to say anything important on the mobile phone, so his caginess wasn't necessarily a pointer to the size of the problem. On the other hand, there'd been something about the seriousness of his tone which told Danny that this time his partner wasn't exaggerating.

The end of the session came as a relief, and he was halfway down the corridor, picking up speed on the way to the lift, before he remembered that he'd been intending to hang around and talk to Simone. She was a mature student, at least twenty-seven years old, who had previously worked in some branch of the Civil Service. She was also in her second year, but Flegenhauer's class was the first time Danny had encountered her, and after he'd taken in the long legs, curly brown hair and the wicked smile she gave him from time to time, he was hooked. The fact that she was six years older, a woman of experience, made her even more alluring, and since this seminar was the only class where their paths crossed, Danny had been priming himself to chat her up and ask her out. The phone call had also ruined that prospect, so by the time Danny got to the car park at St Osric's, the hall of residence where Osman usually parked his transit van, he was seething with resentment.

There were a couple of girls chatting to Osman, who was leaning against the open door of the van, and they moved off as Danny approached. He noticed that they were clutching bundles of flyers, which lightened his mood a little. Osman was good at persuading the tastiest first-year women to go around publicizing Cool One's events, and when Danny thought about it, he had to acknowledge that without his partner's energy and sociability their business would hardly have become the success that it was. The trick was that Osman had never displayed any of Danny's inhibition when it came to dealing with the public-school-educated white kids who surrounded them, probably because he'd attended a famous public school himself. That was where he'd become known as Little Osman, which was nothing to do with his size (he was actually well over six feet tall and big with it), but because one of the older pupils was a Sudanese boy, also named Osman, and the nickname had been the handiest way of distinguishing between them. Oddly enough, this was the only story Osman had ever told about his experience at the school. Danny once asked him why, but he'd simply shrugged and said it had been one of the most boring and frustrating periods of his life, so there was nothing to say. Danny hadn't pressed him any further, but he had the feeling that his partner was hiding something, partly because Osman didn't mind talking about other aspects of his life. His father had qualified as a lawyer in London, and practised for several years before being offered an important government post back in Nigeria. By then Osman, who'd been born in Bristol, was already eight years old, and instead of taking him with them, his parents had put him in boarding school. During the vacations he stayed with an elderly white couple in Bath, and until he was eighteen only saw his family at intervals of two or three years when they visited Britain. At first it seemed to Osman that he'd been abandoned, but later on, he told Danny, he came to see that his parents thought what they'd done had been the best thing for him. Even so, the first thing he did on leaving school was to head for Lagos. Defying his father's insistence that he should begin a course of study in Europe, he'd joined the army. Thanks to his father's position, and his foreign education, he'd enlisted as an officer, but after a few years 'stuck in the bush' he'd had enough. By then, he'd come to terms with his childhood anger about being left behind and, funnily enough, he said, he'd missed England. He'd missed the strange, soft drizzling of rain, the pearlescent light at twilight, and the springy grass of green fields. It was as simple as that.

Listening to all this, Danny suspected that there was a lot more to tell, but he knew that if Osman didn't want to talk there was no way of getting it out of him. It was an attitude Danny understood well enough, but there were times when he had the uneasy sense that he didn't know as much as he should have about his partner.

'We got to kick some ass,' Osman said abruptly.

'What you on about?'

Osman swung open the driver's door, and settled himself behind the wheel. Danny walked over to the other side and got in beside him.

'I went in the union this morning,' Osman said. 'They've got a package waiting for you. It came to the union. No address. Just your name. Big package. Heavy.'

Distracted, Danny thought about it.

'That'd be my brother probably. He doesn't have my address since I moved.'

He'd moved into a bedsitter a few weeks previously, but he regarded the arrangement as strictly temporary so he hadn't written to Gus to tell him the new address. His guess was that it had to be some kind of present, and, in that case, the only person who might have sent it would be Gus. For a moment, he wondered whether it was an anniversary he'd forgotten, or whether Gus had bought him some books. That would be just like him, he thought. Suddenly, he realized that Osman hadn't answered his question.

'Is that what you wanted to see me about?'

'Of course not,' Osman growled.

'So what is it?'

'That asshole DJ.'

'Which one?'

After they started booking DJs, they'd come to the conclusion that they were all assholes.

'Doctor Spin.'

Osman growled the name out with a contempt which surprised Danny. Doctor Spin had been a student at the university some years before they arrived. He came from an anonymous conurbation on the fringes of the South coast and, bored out of his skull by two years of being a hardworking sixth-former, he'd thrown himself like an eager young seal into the flow of urban student life, which to Doctor Spin meant booze, drugs and rock music. Academic pursuits came very low down on his list of priorities, and after a year when he was seldom seen in any of the classrooms, he failed every subject in the first-year exams. They let him repeat the first year and he squeezed into the second, but when they threw him out after another year, he had grown into the persona of the dopehead DJ Doctor Spin. No one could remember his real name any more, but he was a fixture at most of the local raves, which were largely frequented by students, and he'd been Danny's first choice for hosting the acid house section at Cool One's club nights.

'Doctor Spin.' Danny repeated the name to make sure. 'What's he done?'

Osman grunted angrily.

'It's not so much what he's done,' he said. His voice rumbled in the confines of the van. He reached behind the seat and came up with a couple of bottles of his favourite drink, a herbal concoction with a bitter, flowery taste. Danny would have preferred squash or orange juice, something straightforward, but Osman swore that his special brew was the secret ingredient in the diet of Olympic champions, and he refused to tolerate any other kind of liquid refreshment.

'It's not so much what he's done,' he said again, 'it's what he is, which is a serious dickhead.'

Danny gestured his assent. He couldn't guess what was coming, but he knew that it would be useless to try and hurry it up. Trying to calm his impatience he looked round into the back of the transit. It had a weird neatness which Osman said was institutional habit, but the look of the van made Danny feel disorientated, a little uneasy, as if a performance artist, aiming for effect, had put it together. Along one side was a row of cardboard boxes filled with books. They were arranged in alphabetical order, each box labelled with big, black letters. At the back Osman had stacked a folding table and a couple of camp chairs, and hanging above them was the lamp he used when he wanted enough light by which to read. On the floor was a faded Axminster, and piled behind the seat were Osman's sleeping bag, his bottles of drink, and a box containing fruit, carrots and celery sticks. The entire effect was like being in an eccentric sitting room, which was precisely what it was meant to be, because Osman lived in the van. He'd spent the first two terms in St Osric's, then he'd moved out, bought the van, stuck it in the car park and continued using the facilities at the hall of residence as if he still had a room on one of the corridors. The beauty of it, he told Danny, was that he had practically no living expenses, it was not much smaller than most student accommodation, and he had all the mobility anyone could want. Danny had to agree that it all made sense, and after a while he forgot his first impression, which was that Osman had gone stark, raving mad.

'I should have known', Osman said, 'the first time I saw that car of his. Bullshit Escort with Doctor Spin printed across the windscreen. And that ain't good enough for him. He's got Doctor Spin 'cross the sides and the back too. What kind of shit is that? It's like a stereo on wheels. Everybody's got to know he's a fucking DJ. I was down the city centre last week and I hear this music in the distance. Like it's about ten in the morning you can hear him coming. I knew it was him. Nobody else. Announcing himself. Like he's black or something.'

Danny grunted. Now Osman had said more or less everything there was to say about Spin maybe he'd get to the point.

'On top of that,' Osman said with a spurt of renewed energy, 'he's only sitting in the most conspicuous piece of shit in the whole town, making more than enough noise to wake up a dead man, and he's sucking on some disgusting little roll-up spliff, so when the cops stop him, he can outwit them by eating it or sticking it up his ass, then he can go round telling his idiot friends about his exciting morning and how clever he's been. Dickhead.'

Danny guessed it was time to intervene.

'So what's he done?'

Osman shook his head and clicked his tongue angrily.

'Selling White Dove. We have to talk to him.'

'Selling White Dove?' Danny's tone was incredulous. This accusation was the last thing he expected. It didn't make sense. After all, everyone who did E also sold it or gave it to someone else, and the same charge could have been levelled at half the students who came to their club nights. 'What are you on about? They're all doing it.'

Osman sighed loudly. 'This is different.' He paused for a moment, as if deciding what to say. Then he came out with it. 'Dave came over this morning.'

'City Centre Dave?'

Osman nodded, almost reluctantly, as if confirming a piece of bad news, which, in a way, this was, since City Centre Dave – so called because no one ever saw him anywhere else – was one of the most notorious bouncers operating among the city's clutch of clubs and pubs. The nuttiest ravers on the scene calmed down when they saw Dave. He had that effect on all the clubbers even though no one had ever seen him raise a fist in anger. On the other hand, fearsome rumours circulated about his past exploits and his capacity for violence when roused. Boxing was his game, and there were rumours that he had crippled a man in the ring, that he had been an enforcer for East End promoters, that he had the temperament of a human Rottweiler. Most of it might have been lies, but Dave was more than six feet tall and had shoulders wide enough to brush against both sides of a narrow doorway. Add to this the fact that he was a black man with features so blunt and battered that they might have been carved in stone, and none of the kids who turned up in the city centre were mad enough to take the risk of testing his reputation. As a result Dave's crew of bouncers was in constant demand.

'I didn't know he ever got over this side of town,' Danny said. He didn't ask why Dave had bothered because he knew the answer. Osman sometimes worked for the crew on a part-time basis, driving them around and occasionally standing on the door when there was a man short. Dave was proud of the fact that Osman was a student, because it proved, as he told the club owners, that his employees were sophisticated security specialists, instead of a bunch of thickos in dinner jackets.

It hadn't been a long story, Osman told Danny. Dave was a man of few words. He had known that Doctor Spin was out of his skull most of the time and that he was mixed up with some funny people, but he'd taken no notice because it was none of his business as long as there was no trouble in the club. In the last month, however, everything had changed. A few weeks back some young mug had come out of one of the local clubs and collapsed, laid out by White Dove, alcohol and whatever other substances she'd managed to lay her hands on during the evening. Since then she'd been lying in a coma at the city-centre hospital. By coincidence, her mother was a well-known local magistrate, so the publicity had been enormous. Under pressure from the local establishment and the papers, the cops had exerted themselves to an unusual extent, threatening small-time dealers, conducting random searches, and setting up undercover teams to penetrate the club scene.

At the beginning, Dave's police contacts had told him about what was going on, and he'd been grateful for the warning because it showed that they thought of him as being on the right side. In fact it made very little difference to how he ran things. Dave was straight down the line. His bouncers searched anyone who raised their suspicions for concealed weapons, but it was impossible to exclude every kid with a tab of E in his pocket. It was also necessary to make allowances for at least one recognized dealer, working for the local network. The big players respected each other's territories and, unless there was a power struggle going on, they would usually be represented by a single dealer whose operations would be discreet enough to avoid embarrassing the bouncers. Only one kind of clubgoer faced a total ban from Dave's clubs. These were the young chancers who'd scored enough E to turn on a thousand kids, and had begun touring the clubs in an attempt either to set up their own permanent sales network, or simply make a pile out of the stock they had in hand.

These newcomers were always trouble, attracting the attention of the police, or poisoning their customers with the incredible concoctions which were sometimes unloaded on them. In comparison, the professional dealers were simply part of the furniture. From time to time they might be selling rubbish, like flour laced with speed or even aspirin, but the kids never seemed to notice, swallowing whatever they doled out and rushing off to dance the night away.

All this made life fairly easy for Dave, which was the way he liked it. Doctor Spin was something else altogether. Until recently he'd hardly caused a ripple on the surface of the bouncer's attention, but from the beginning of the police crackdown his behaviour had changed. The first symptom was his new girlfriend, Cynthia.

She was in her early twenties, a tight, tall, pale-faced woman with black hair teased into spikes, and there'd been a mild sensation when she appeared carrying some of Spin's equipment. The only women Spin had been seen with, so far, were dopey-looking first-year students. In contrast, this woman seemed brighter, more attractive than anyone would have expected. But in a short while the curiosity about her died down and she began making friends with the bouncers and the regulars. Some of them tried it on with her without getting anywhere, so it seemed she was only interested in Spin. In fact, she was more or less straight: a secretary who worked for a big firm in the city centre. This was the reason, she said, why she was always buying various kinds of dope in quantities which were larger than the average. She was doing a favour for her nine-to-five friends.

Everyone liked Cynthia, so Dave was more than shocked when he heard, 'on the grapevine', that she was an undercover policewoman. He didn't say who 'the grapevine' was, but Osman had a shrewd idea that it was one of his police mates. The alternative was that Dave was so familiar with the network of cops who worked in drugs and vice that he'd recognized her. The story was that Spin had been caught with a bundle of blow in his car and had got himself off the hook by agreeing to infiltrate Cynthia into the milieu of clubs and dealers. She had done her work well and, after only a few weeks, she was probably in a position to put the finger on a good half of the town's dealers.

'What's all that got to do with us?' Danny said. 'Everybody knows we don't do drugs.'

That was his first line of defence against any problems with cops or dealers. He had never had anything to do with their business. This was more out of habit than the result of a conscious strategy. Years before, when he'd been living in the group home, one of the boys on the floor below had died of an overdose. He hadn't seen the body, because they'd hustled it out while the younger kids were still at school, and the boy had only been there a couple of weeks, so none of them went to the funeral. Even so, in Danny's imagination he could still remember the dead boy, his eyes hollow and staring, his skin waxy and yellow. For a long time he'd been afraid to go to sleep in the dark. He couldn't get out of his mind the thought of the boy lying downstairs, a ragged tide of poison dragging him down into the darkness.

On the day of the funeral all the kids in the house were on edge and touchy. By some coincidence, Gus had turned up that afternoon and was waiting in the sitting room when Danny walked in from school. When he told his brother what had happened, Gus took him down to McDonalds for a milkshake. On the way they talked about drugs. Or rather, it was Gus who talked while Danny listened. He was already fourteen, and it was time, Gus said, that he understood these things. That white boy, Gus told him, had wasted his life, but it wouldn't matter to anyone except his family, if he had one. It was different for us, Gus went on, and at this point he grabbed Danny's arm, turned him round and stared him in the face.

'We don't have anything except each other,' Gus said intensely. 'If we want a life we have to make it for ourselves. Fuck yourself up with drugs and even if you don't die, you're messing up your chance to make it.'

Danny agreed obediently, but Gus wasn't finished. 'If you

waste your life,' Gus said, 'it affects everybody like you, every-body born black, especially mixed-race people like us, because that's what the whites want to see. You screw yourself up and it just proves what they believe about you.

'You've got to understand that,' Gus grated, staring into his eyes. 'Otherwise you'll spend your life going around doing things to make people like you, like some dog. They snap their fingers and you jump, whether it's filling yourself with dope or kissing their ass. Don't do it.'

Danny agreed again. The truth was that he'd already sucked on a hit of grass up in one of the other rooms late at night and he'd been about to tell Gus about it, but now he saw that it wouldn't be a good idea.

His brother still wasn't finished. White people controlled the drugs, he told Danny. They made it, they smuggled it between various countries, and they made huge profits from it. Then they used it as an excuse to harass, imprison and kill black men.

By this time they'd arrived in front of McDonalds.

'If I ever see you using drugs,' Gus said, holding him by the arms, his face only inches away, 'you'll never see me again. If I don't kill you first.'

It wasn't the threat which impressed Danny, because he didn't believe it, but he'd never heard Gus speaking about anything with such anger and intensity. Without hesitation he'd promised, and, in fact, it wasn't a difficult thing to do. Soon after this he'd gone into the sixth form, where he got himself a reputation as a strong-minded individual simply by repeating that he didn't mess with any kind of drug, and after a while he'd begun to enjoy the surprise and confusion he could induce merely by repeating his refusal. When he first made his declaration he'd half expected to be put down as a killjoy, but although, at the beginning, he'd had to struggle through some predictable arguments, most of his friends reacted by looking a bit sheepish and coming back with, 'Yeah, I'm not really into it either.'

By his second year as a student his response had become habitual. By coincidence, Osman was also indifferent to the attractions of dope. He'd been an officer, he once told Danny, in an army where the kicks were to do with life and death, and he'd seen and done things beside which smoking a joint was like drinking weak ginger beer. He liked kif, he said, but the thing about kif was that it fucked your mind up in the long term. Let your men get hooked on kif, and you were going to die.

That was how they were. But in the context, their behaviour provoked rumours all around the university that they had something going for them which was stronger, more devious, and more strange than popping a few tabs of E.

'Everybody knows we don't do drugs,' Osman said. 'That's right. What difference does that make? Think about it. The other night I saw Spin giving a couple of kids a few tabs. I've seen him do it before. You've seen him do it. I've seen his woman buying stuff. What do you think that means?'

Danny thought about it, and the picture which started to come into his head made him shift uneasily in his seat.

'Dave reckons that they'll be raiding places soon,' Osman continued impatiently. 'Spin and Cynthia are passing out names. That's all they have to do. Names of dealers, people who cooperate with dealers. You get me? You're mixed race. I'm Nigerian. We're making money in the clubs. Our names go on the table. Doesn't matter what we've done. They're going to look at us. How'd you like to be dragged down the police station in the middle of the night? Answer questions like who you know, who you don't know. Are you getting a cut out of this shit?'

'All right, all right,' Danny shouted, trying to stop him. He was angry now, because Osman had convinced him, and the more convinced he felt, the angrier he was. 'All right. What the fuck are we supposed to do? We can't stop them now. What do you want to do? Ban them? Why doesn't your mate Dave do something?'

'If he does anything,' Osman said moodily, 'he'll have to let on he's been told, and he can't do that. It's up to us.'

Danny was about to shout at him again, then he realized that what Osman had said implied that he had a solution.

'What are we supposed to do?'

Osman smiled for the first time.

'We go and tell him, very loud, in front of witnesses, preferably the police lady and anyone else who's around, that we've noticed him dishing out dope at the club. Then we say we know that he's a dickhead dopehead, but we don't give a shit as long as he doesn't distribute drugs on premises we're in control of. Then we tell him that if we see him doing it again we're going to shop him to the police.'

Danny laughed. He could see what Osman was getting at, but he also thought there was an obvious snag.

'That would be good if it was credible, man,' he said. 'On any given night there'll be twenty people in there spreading more dope around than Spin ever did.'

'Doesn't matter,' Osman replied immediately, and without any appearance of doubt. 'The important thing is to register that we tried to keep drugs out of our events. If anything comes up, we're clean. You see? If some prat kills himself off in the toilet or the cops raid and find something, all we say is: "Don't know anything, officer. We tried our best to keep the place drug-free. And we've got two police informers to prove it."' He paused. 'I don't know whether we're in any danger, but I reckon this is one way to make sure.'

Danny didn't entirely agree, but, thinking about it, he couldn't see what they had to lose.

'Okay,' he said.

Osman leaned forward and switched on the engine.

'Let's go,' he said. 'I know where he is.'

He said this with an air of supreme confidence, as if he'd been checking on Spin's whereabouts that morning, but that was simply one of his mannerisms. Everyone who knew Spin also knew that he had his breakfast round about noon, or later, in a pizza parlour run by a couple of Bengali brothers. It was close to the university library and Osman, pushing the van through the lunchtime traffic, got them there in a few minutes.

They spotted Doctor Spin immediately through the plate glass at the front. He was sitting with Cynthia at his favourite table near the back, guzzling pizza. Seeing them like that, at a distance, it struck Danny that even though he knew Spin was a dickhead informer and Cynthia was a cop, they looked an impressive couple.

When they first met, Spin had looked like some kind of retro hippy, but recently he'd taken up the *Reservoir Dogs* look, and he was dressed in a black suit over a white T-shirt which said FUCK U 2 on the front. He'd had his hair cut short with a blond patch at the top, and he wore impenetrable wraparound dark glasses. Beside him, Cynthia was wearing a black shirt which barely covered the top of her thighs and made her legs look seven feet long. She was leaning back, drinking coffee and smoking a fag, her face half-concealed behind dark glasses which looked identical to Spin's.

'Let me do the talking,' Osman muttered.

He pushed through the curtain of plastic strips, and strode past the counter. Danny followed, feeling a little ridiculous at the thought that this was all a pretence. At the same time he noticed something about Osman. The moment he'd entered the restaurant he'd somehow grown bigger. Suddenly he was a menacing bulk as he bore down on Spin's table.

Spin had seen them coming, and although he put down the half-eaten slice of pizza and licked his lips, Danny couldn't tell whether or not he was alarmed by Osman's manner and appearance.

'I want to talk to you,' Osman said roughly, leaning with both hands on the table and looming over the couple.

'Man, I'm eating,' Spin replied.

He picked up his piece of pizza and opened his mouth. In his turn Osman reached out and pulled Spin's dark glasses off. Without them the DJ's eyes were an unfocused and watery blue, his expression of surprise crossing over into fear as he took in the grim, angry lines of Osman's face.

'What the fuck's the matter with you?' Cynthia said loudly. 'Whyn't you piss off?'

Osman turned on her in a flash, his hand shooting out, the finger pointing within inches of her nose.

'I'm not talking to you,' he shouted. 'I got something to say to Spin. When I've done, I'll go. You can stay or go if you want, but shut the fuck up.'

Cynthia's lips curled in a sneer. Watching her, it struck Danny that, even with Osman towering over her in a rage, she didn't look alarmed or even mildly worried in the way that a normal girl might have done.

'Hey, hey, hey,' Spin said in a soft, calming tone, before Cynthia could reply. He put his glasses back on, and held up his hands in a pacific gesture. 'What do you want, man? I don't have no problems with you.'

'Yes you do,' Osman said. He moved to the side of the table next to Spin and bent over, speaking close to the DJ's face. 'I have something to tell you.'

Chapter Five

The man on the 2.15 out of King's Cross Station couldn't stop sweating. It wasn't an exceptionally hot day, but the perspiration kept welling up from under the skin of his forehead, and from time to time he took out his handkerchief and mopped it up. When he did that he tucked the briefcase under his arm, clutching it to him as if worried that the woman next to him would make a quick grab for it. When the train pulled in at Finsbury Park, he peered around anxiously, shooting rapid darting glances at the passengers who were entering the coach.

His name was William Potter, he was twenty-eight years old and he had an air of dull ordinariness which went with the name. His hair was a bright red mop of curls, he wore a pair of round, gold-rimmed spectacles, and his face was clean-shaven to reveal a fading tan. He was dressed in sand-coloured trousers, brown shoes with raised stitches and a black cotton blazer. Apart from the frequency with which he wiped his face, there was nothing to distinguish him from a dozen other young white men on the train.

This was precisely the thought which William kept repeating

to himself as he sped deeper into North London, past scruffy back gardens and the half-open windows of curtained rear bedrooms. There was no reason, he told himself, why anyone should imagine that there was anything special about him, or guess that he was carrying a fortune in his briefcase. Thinking about it made him start sweating again, and, in order to focus on something different, he forced himself to replay the events of the morning. As it happened, the whole affair had started a few days earlier, when he'd arrived in the building to find Liz and Bert locked in a cupboard and the Dancing Face gone. This had been Monday, but the curator of the exhibition, Dr Leonard, hadn't received the phone call until a couple of days later. Up to that moment he'd had no news about the mask, and he was still in a state of shock, puffing furiously at his Gauloise, his hands trembling, his bow tie twisted and drooping. Leonard was taller than William, but so thin that he seemed emaciated, skeletal, the sort of man, as William's mother used to say, who a puff of wind could break in half.

His face, too, had the look of a skull, the skin stretched tight over the cheekbones. In normal times it gave him an air of languid, almost enfeebled detachment, and at first William had assumed that the director was suffering from some chronic illness, but after he'd known him for a while he had concluded that Leonard's manner was a pose which had something to do with his image of himself.

They were standing in the second-floor office overlooking Great Portland Street. William's office was a few steps away, but whereas Dr Leonard's windows looked out on the street, the only thing William could see from his own window was a view of the cul de sac at the back. Not that he minded, because this was his first official permanent post, with a title – Assistant to the Curator – and for a few months, as he travelled into the centre of London, he had felt a surge of energy and power which stemmed from the knowledge that he would be in receipt of a reasonable salary for at least two years. When he discovered that their most important exhibit had been stolen, his first thought was to wonder whether this would threaten the existence of the project.

'The police are on their way,' Dr Leonard continued. 'I'm relying on your absolute discretion. They told me that if I called in the police I'd never see it again. So no one except us must know about this.'

At the time, William had been flattered by Dr Leonard's confidence in him. But in retrospect he guessed that the curator must have had precisely this contingency in mind. He couldn't see the good doctor on his way to a rendezvous with a ruthless gang of criminals, and it was reasonable to suppose that it had always been his intention to let William run the gauntlet of any likely dangers. In fact, the thieves had been mercilessly specific. They wanted one of the exhibition staff to carry the loot, which narrowed it down, because the only other permanent employee was the curator's secretary, and Leonard regarded her involvement as being out of the question. To William's surprise, the police hadn't objected either, and he sensed that they were pleased about not having to find one of their own number to do the job.

They were, as it happened, a surprising bunch of cops. They were the same unit of three who had turned up several hours after the robbery to replace the uniformed policemen who had been fiddling around marking time and asking what seemed like point-less questions. This time they'd answered Leonard's desperate call within half an hour, all of them in plainclothes, led by an elegant blonde wearing a short skirt, high heels, and a shiny blouse which highlighted the neat, conical shape of her breasts. She was so unlike what he expected of a police inspector that her presence made William feel distinctly uncomfortable, but she seemed not to notice, taking charge with the cool certainty of a confident hostess setting out to arrange a small dinner party. Her name was Inspector Pritchard. 'Call me Kate,' she'd said in her posh accent when she shook hands with William, but he didn't have the nerve to do so, partly because he had the feeling that her informality was designed to put him off balance. At university and during the two years he'd spent in a variety of temporary jobs round the museums he'd met too many women with her unnerving confidence to be anything but wary. After seeing her at work he was also certain that his cau-tion had been justified, because she ran the operation with a steely authority, arranging for the phone calls to be recorded, summoning up a forensic team with a snap of her fingers, and dispatching her subordinates on mysterious errands. In between she questioned Leonard in exhaustive detail about the phone call and, once again, about the theft. This didn't worry the director, because his reaction to the inspector was the precise opposite of William's. He repeated her name with an almost embarrassing frequency, and when he answered her questions he had an air of zealous and devoted atten-tion, which made William think of a large, balding poodle fawning round Kate's feet. During the hour after she arrived, she made Leonard go through his story two or three times, but William deduced from her persistence that the information she gleaned from the process was more or less useless.

Leonard had received the phone call as soon as he'd come into the office. By now it was Wednesday. They told him that they had the mask and what they wanted in exchange.

The second phone call came on Thursday morning, just as they'd said it would, and this time Leonard was given his instructions on what to do with the ransom. It was shortly after this that William found out he was to be the messenger.

'Ten thousand pounds,' Inspector Pritchard said. Her mouth twisted scornfully, and she crossed and uncrossed her legs, then leaned back in her chair. Dr Leonard bit his lip and squirmed, his little green eyes running up and down her body. 'How much did you say it was worth?'

Leonard hadn't actually put a price on it, largely because he had no idea what the mask would fetch on the open market, and he was accustomed to simply describing it as priceless. But the question put him on his mettle.

'Now there's a question,' he replied. 'It's literally priceless, but if I happened to win the lottery I wouldn't expect to get much change from a million.' He paused for effect. 'Of course, these things don't fetch the prices they used to.'

'That means they don't know what it's worth,' Kate muttered reflectively. 'Or they're just plain wankers. If they were real professionals they'd be trying to raise something closer to the actual value.'

'Not necessarily,' William told her. 'It might be that they know enough to know that it's a dubious piece.'

As soon as he'd spoken William wished that he'd kept his mouth shut. Kate's eyes swivelled round and fixed themselves on his. At the same time, Leonard coughed and gave him a dirty look.

'Dubious?'

She drew the first syllable out as if she enjoyed the sound of it, and Leonard broke in before she'd finished speaking.

'Dubious is hardly the word. There's something of a controversy about its provenance. The argument is more or less academic.'

She frowned, closed her eyes and opened them again. But she didn't look away from William. It was as if she'd seen more than enough of Leonard.

'Why is it dubious?'

William waited for Leonard to say something, but the director simply pressed his lips together and gave him a challenging stare, so he plunged right in.

'It goes back to when they were first discovered. All the heads we have here come from West Africa. Some from Benin. Mostly from the part that's now Nigeria. Those were the days when a British administrator could buy one or pick it up in trade and bring it home, no questions asked. Usually they were seen as curiosities rather than works of art. But at the end of the last century all the museums and collectors were buying these, and there was no real question about whether or not they were authentic – not that anyone cared.'

He smiled, but the inspector's face didn't reflect his amusement. Instead, there was a line of puzzlement between her eyes. William had the feeling that either she wasn't following him, or she was becoming irritable about being lectured. He was accustomed to this reaction, but these were special circumstances, he thought.

'How much do you know about African art?'

The frown on her face deepened, and it struck William that she was irritated by the challenge implicit in his question.

'You tell me,' she said curtly.

William knew then that he'd made a mistake, but there was no way of retrieving the situation except by going on.

'A hundred years ago they'd just fixed the colonial boundaries, and it was a kind of commercial bonanza. West Africa was like a paradise for hustlers going about making deals with the local kings and chiefs to establish territorial rights before the French or the Germans did, and looting the place of anything that looked valuable. The basements of museums and the attics of stately homes are full of figurines and masks and heads that no one knows anything much about – what they were for or who owned them or how they got there in the first place.'

The inspector was looking bored now.

'I understand all that,' she said. 'What I don't understand is what's so special about this one.'

'It's special because it's a mystery,' William told her. 'When they started to find these beautiful naturalistic heads in terracotta and bronze, the government restricted their export. Around that time a German adventurer named Brandt showed up in West Africa. He was a biologist, an ethnographer, a bit of an artist, an explorer, and an occasional soldier of fortune, a real nineteenth-century type. He was also an inveterate collector. He collected everything: cases of rare butterflies, bits of hardwood, strange minerals, leaves and flowers, skeletons and these masks. He got some kind of a hold over one of the local rulers, who sold him or traded him a number of masks including one made of gold. Apparently no one knew of its existence, because the material was practically unique for metalwork in that region. Until the German smuggled it back to Europe. Then all hell broke loose. It was a sacred object. All these masks were sacred anyway, but this one was special. Apparently it had been made for the first great Oba of Benin. They called it his Dancing Face, and it had tremendous ritual importance. The Oni of Ife, who was like the king of kings in those parts, said it couldn't have been legally bought or traded without reference to him, because it was one of his ancestral treasures. The German said it had nothing to do with the Oni because he wasn't in the direct line of descent. Then the diplomats got involved. Eventually they got the mask back to West Africa, or so they thought. Years later a British sculptor was doing a survey of the Oni's art collection and when he examined the dancing mask he found that it had been made by sand-casting. The point being that every other metal object in the region was bronze, made by the lost wax technique, which is how they're still doing it today. The German was dead by then, but the obvious conclusion was that he'd palmed a fake off on the Oni. It seemed that the original had disappeared, but after twenty years a retired colonial governor found something exactly like it propping up a stable door on a farm in Cheshire. He kept it as part of a small collection he'd built up over the years, and he left it to his daughter, who sold it to the museum as a job lot. When they started cataloguing it, one of the local academics twigged what it was and wrote an article about it for a journal. Then the Nigerian government got wind of it and began suing for its return, but by then you can imagine the legal difficulties of sorting out its precise origins and who it belonged to. You couldn't put a price on it, but by the time they decide what to do, millions will have been spent.'

'Maybe someone's trying to save the lawyers trouble,' she said.

Leonard didn't smile.

'In that case they'd hardly be asking for a ransom,' he muttered.

Kate ignored this.

'So you'll know it if you see it,' she said to William.

He shrugged.

'I suppose so.'

He wasn't at all sure of that as he stepped off the train on to the platform of the station at Alexandra Palace. His instructions had been to wait at King's Cross until he was contacted on his mobile phone. It had rung shortly after two o'clock and a voice had told him to get on the two-fifteen train. It also told him that he was under observation and that if he made a false move he'd never see the mask again. William had no idea what would constitute a false move, but he agreed hurriedly and ran for the train. A quarter of an hour later the phone rang again and the voice told him to get off at Alexandra Palace Station.

By this time William wasn't concerned about the mask. The mask, he reckoned, was the least of his troubles. What really worried him now was the prospect of encountering the gangsters, or whatever they were. Frowning, he tried to remember the list of things he should avoid doing. He wouldn't accompany them any-where. He wouldn't get into a car or any other vehicle. He would stay as far as possible from anyone who approached him. The voice on the phone had been high and jerky with a London accent. Almost certainly disguised, he thought, but there was something alarming about the confidence with which the man issued his instructions. Although he tried not to, William couldn't help thinking about the number of fatal assaults and stabbings which had featured in the news during the previous week and which had taken place not far from where he was standing. Kate had told him that her team would be within sight at every stage, but even though he'd made a covert scrutiny of every face in his carriage he couldn't guess which ones were detectives, and, to his alarm, he had been the only passenger to step off on to the platform. As far as he could tell, he was alone and unprotected.

The phone rang again. William had been expecting it, but even so the noise startled him and he fumbled at the instrument as he took it out of his pocket and lifted it to his ear. This time the voice told him to leave the station, turn left and walk over the bridge leading to the palace. Then it went silent before William could protest. He hesitated for a few seconds, then did what he'd been told, walking out into the afternoon sunshine which seemed to be flooding out from behind the facade of the palace and flowing down from the summit of the hill.

Chapter Six

Baz saw the white man come up to the top of the alley and look around. Kind of suspicious, like a mouse sniffing cheese. Only this time, Baz reckoned, he was the one carrying the cheese in that briefcase under his arm. A few short seconds before, Baz had been nervous, the hollow fluttering feeling coming and going in his stomach, but from the moment he saw the man with the briefcase he was cool. Quickly he ran the plan over in his mind. Let him walk past. Don't look at him. Follow him up the path till he gets to where Rodney is sitting on the bench. Then, just as he makes to go past, snatch the case and run up the hill to the bike. Got it.

None of this was a big deal. He'd done it all before. What made the difference was the amount of money Rodney had said would be in the briefcase. Ten grand. It wasn't like winning the lottery, but it would do Baz for a bit. He knew exactly what he was going to do with the money as well, which was trade in his Cortina for a newer model, and install four mega speakers. Standing there, Baz let himself imagine the vicious pounding of the bass, and for a moment he could almost feel the sound vibrating through the frame and rippling in his thighs. The thought steadied him immediately, and as the white man walked closer, he pulled his hat down over his ears and turned away to watch the back of the train as it sped out of sight. He could sense eyes taking him in, but he didn't move until the man was a few yards away.

At the foot of the slope, the man must have sensed that Baz was coming on behind him. He didn't look round, but there was something about the stiff set of his back that signalled he knew something was up. It was as if the same fear which stopped him from looking over his shoulder was driving his footsteps faster and faster away from whatever was following him. Baz guessed what was happening, but he didn't want to scare the guy, not yet, so he slowed down a bit, letting the gap between them stretch. By the time the white man got close to where Rodney was sitting he was still speeding away from Baz. Rodney hadn't made a move yet, and although he was wearing an anorak with its hood drawn down over his face, just like Baz, their quarry didn't seem to have been warned by the similarity. Baz guessed that he was so preoccupied with the threat behind him that he didn't think to be wary of this other guy, seemingly half-asleep in the weak afternoon sun, one leg stretched on the bench, looking over his shoulder at the palace.

Baz almost laughed out loud because he knew what was going to happen, and he was beginning to feel a kind of rage building up in him. It wasn't real anger, because he didn't have anything against the guy, but there was something irritating about the way that he'd started belting away just because Baz was behind him. Disrespect, Baz thought, that's what it was, and, as if stirred by the gleam of the sunlight on the man's bright hair, he began to feel the hot desire of a hunter. In a moment, he knew, he'd be close enough to touch, to hit, to punch him to the ground and kick him till the blood spurted. Without thinking about it he began running. At the sound of his footsteps the man glanced back over his shoulder. In the same moment Rodney came off the bench and tripped the man up with a kick to the back of his knees.

They had talked about this over and over. What Rodney wanted was a smooth handover, like giving the guy a box with something heavy in it, bricks or something like that, then walking away cool. Baz thought this was a stupid idea. For a start the bloke would probably want to look in the box, and then they'd be right in it. The other thing was that he felt messing around with too much trickery was out of order. Rodney always had these funny ideas because he enjoyed talking, kidding people, and laughing at them. Baz was different. What he wanted was straightforward, the kind of stuff he was used to and knew he could do. Check out the guy, take the money away from him, and piss off. If he turned nasty give him a right kicking and all. That was that.

At first it seemed that this was exactly how things would turn out. Baz reached the bench in a few quick strides and by then the red-haired guy was on the ground, his arms up around his head, his knees drawn up to his face.

'Come on,' Rodney shouted. He had the briefcase in his hand.

Baz hesitated, torn between disappointment and elation. He wished the man had resisted, tried to fight, and it didn't seem right to leave him there, completely unhurt, without even dealing out a little slap. At the back of his mind was the thought that if they left the man lying there without giving him some discouragement there was nothing to stop him getting up and chasing after them.

He turned round to say this to Rodney, but Rod was already belting up the hill.

'Come on,' he shouted again, over his shoulder. 'Mek we go.'

Halfway to the top, struggling to keep Rodney's flapping coat within reach, Baz already knew there was something wrong. He had half expected to hear the red-haired guy shouting and screaming behind them, and this was what he was listening out for. Instead, what he heard, springing into his mind with the swift intensity of a dream, was the electronic squeal of a police siren.

There were actually two or three, all of them coming from different directions, the sound going round in a stereophonic circle as all three synchronized, then stopped and started again. Baz kept on running, his thoughts moving fast, revolving around his head faster than the sound of the sirens. Rodney had promised that there would be no trouble, but he hadn't believed that, and right now he didn't have time to worry about it anyway. The big thing was getting out. A picture of the road and the way they would go flashed in his mind. It was a long S-bend, stretching lazily along the shoulder of the mound on top of which the palace sat. On one side was the grassy slope which climbed down to the railway line, on the other was the short steep ascent to the bulk of the palace. On either end the road narrowed to go through an archway which used to be a gate controlling access in and out of the palace grounds. Baz knew how the cops worked, and with a swift surge of panic it hit him that by now they'd have both ends of the road blocked off. With the certainty of doom he knew that they should have been running the other way, down towards the railway lines. He opened his mouth to shout to Rodney, but before he could make a sound he remembered the bike, and he knew that he might as well save his breath. Rodney would never leave it behind.

The next bit was a frenzied jumble which Baz remembered mostly as a sort of addled roaring in his head mixed up with a kaleidoscope of scattered images. A police car was streaking up the hill, blue lights flaring, siren blasting. A couple of cars were pulling over ahead on to the pavement, moving slowly and erratically as if uncertain where they would be safe. A couple of magpies flew across the road, like black-and-white bullets. Rodney, already kicking the Yamaha to life, was shouting. 'Jump on. Jump on.'

The bike was moving by the time Baz straddled the pillion. Rodney had nicked it from outside a house in a backstreet down by the river in Chelsea early that morning, so Baz had only been on it once, and he concentrated on clinging on while Rodney blasted the throttle and swung the bike round towards Wood Green, away from the cops speeding up the hill. The Yamaha picked up, the engine moving through the gears from deep staggering thunder to a vibrating shriek. At the same time Baz saw the snout of the cop car sticking out from behind the bend at the bottom of the hill. He screamed something at Rodney, later on he couldn't remember what it was, and maybe he wasn't using words, but even if Rodney hadn't heard and understood him he must have seen the cops too, because he braked, slewing the bike round hard as it slowed and stopped, then he raced the engine again, and took off across the grass, going up the slope beside the palace and into the clump of trees which climbed over the ridge at the top.

It must have been their lucky day, because the spaces between the trees were fairly wide and Rodney blasted the bike through them, jinking and turning in a zigzag pattern which was meant to bring them back into the open on the other side of the wood. Behind them Baz heard the sirens slow down into a hoarse mutter, fade into silence and start abruptly as the cars raced off. This time, though, they were going away into the distance. He guessed that they were making a run round to the other side of the grounds, but he guessed, also, that they'd have to drive the better part of a mile before they could get to a point where they could cut the bike off. A sudden bubble of elation broke from Baz's heart. He swung his arm and punched the air, shouting to Rodney.

'Gwan, man. Gwan.'

This was the moment that they broke out of the trees and rammed straight into a wooden fence bordering the wood. Rodney had seen it just before, but there was no time to stop, so he'd hit it head on. The fence disintegrated in a flying cloud of splintered wood. Something hit Baz in the face, and next thing he knew he was sprawled on the ground, lying halfway across Rodney. The thought struck him that whatever had happened he was still alive, and he rolled over and looked up at the sky. It was a pale cloudy blue, and as he watched he could see clouds moving slowly towards the bright glare of the sun. Then he remembered; the sound of the Yamaha's engine, still running, bringing back to him the panic of the moment. He was meant to be running, he thought, trying to escape instead of lying around. He raised his head, beginning to feel himself to check whether he'd broken anything. Rodney had got to his hands and knees and, beyond him, Baz could see the bike on its side, the wheels spinning. Suddenly Rodney sprang up and in one stride got to the bike and started lifting it. Baz dragged himself upright and followed, nearly falling over again as the pain throbbing in his leg surged to a sharp peak, then as he hobbled over to the bike he realized that nothing was broken. It was painful, but he could still move well enough to get on behind Rodney.

They were in some kind of children's playground. The middle of the day, but it was empty. Rodney ran the bike, gathering speed, round the swings, past the roundabout, and through the gate into the street facing the huge round window at the back of the palace. In a few seconds they were into a grid of quiet residential streets. Rodney cut the speed, trying to keep the engine-noise down as they zigged and zagged round the corners. In the distance Baz could hear the sirens, but they grew further and further away. In a couple of minutes Rodney stopped by the pavement in a side street. Baz knew where they were. They had come in a big half-circle to Muswell Hill, and he could hear the traffic crashing and grinding, almost drowning out the faint sound of the police sirens.

They walked round the corner and got the first bus they could reach in the little procession going along the Broadway. They sat several seats apart, making out like they didn't know each other, just in case. The only thing was that when they sat down, Rodney turned, grinned at Baz and hugged the briefcase which he hadn't let go of all this time.

They hadn't known where the bus was going, but the first tube station they reached was Bounds Green, and without discussion they clattered off the bus and down into the safe warm gloom of the station. They had to head back towards Tottenham, but the best thing, Rodney said quickly as they queued in front of the ticket machine, was to go up to King's Cross on the Piccadilly, then cut back on the Victoria to Seven Sisters.

Sitting on the tube next to Rodney, Baz relaxed at last. Now he couldn't keep the grin off his face, and, looking round at his friend, he could see the same expression reflecting back at him. Suddenly Rodney's face twisted in a spasm of pain.

'Wha' wrong?' Baz asked him.

'Toilet,' Rodney muttered.

Baz laughed. 'You can wait,' he told Rodney, then he looked at the other boy's expression and laughed again. Then he settled down to ride the journey out, a big smile coming and going on his face.

Chapter Seven

Dr Okigbo's breakfast never varied, no matter where he was in the world. He began with half a pint of orange or grapefruit juice, followed by a soft roll and jam. When he came to the table these would already be arranged, on a spotless white linen tablecloth, in a selection of silver and cut-glass dishes with which he always travelled. His cutlery also was silver, and something about the solid sparkling of the display would invariably lift his spirits and provoke his appetite.

Sometimes he would have two rolls, or a slice of toast, if the jam was particularly tasty. Then he would finish the meal off with a slice of pineapple, melon or pawpaw. These were good for the digestion, and if he missed his fruit he would feel uncomfortable for most of the day. Sometimes, while he ate, the images of where he'd eaten these things before would flit through his mind. On a jet flying low out to Mombasa he had lifted a plastic cup of grapefruit juice to his lips and paused, enthralled by the dust plumes thrown up by a herd of antelope running across the flat expanse of scrubby grassland. As the plane flew over he could see each individual animal, one of them, old or sick, toiling in the rear, the gap between itself and the herd gradually increasing as he watched. He craned his neck, peering through the glass to see what would happen, but in a moment they were gone. Another time, sitting at a table outside a café in Cambridge, Massachusetts, two cars collided as they drove away from the kerb. The drivers, both black, got out, and in the way of the blacks in America, began shouting and cursing at each other. The noise mounted and, as he ate the last piece of pineapple, a police car drew up. One of the policemen emerged and, failing to calm the altercation, pulled his gun and pointed it at their heads.

This stream of images calmed Okigbo after a difficult night and gave him a feeling of being rooted, centred inside himself. This was important, since most of his nights were broken by unpleasant dreams, by anguished thoughts about the future, or by a kind of dull restlessness which he feared and resented yet could not control. Soon after his father died in Lagos he had been told that one of the wives the old man left behind had dreamed a dream in which she saw the death, by fire, of his eldest son, Akinye. He had sent for her, but even though he threatened her with destitution she could not tell him any more. Since then he had seen her many times in his own dreams, her hair wild, her eyes burning. After all his years of travel and business Okigbo had ceased to believe in a world where dreams and spirits had an existence, but there were times, at night, when a kind of uneasiness emerged from his soul and settled in the room. On these occasions he would get up and call for Hadida. Sometimes he would send his chauffeur, Chris, to fetch a woman; sometimes he would merely sit, smoking and drinking, playing through his favourite videos on the television screen.

It was only a few days since he'd last seen Gus, but Okigbo had already succeeded in putting the problem of the mask and its whereabouts out of his mind. This was one of the most important disciplines he practised. There was no real freedom, he believed, for a man who couldn't unhook his mind from the petty anxieties of his daily activities. Sometimes he couldn't stop a picture of the mask from poking through the carapace within which his imagination lived, and, at such times, he was tempted to run through the measures he had undertaken and the arrangements already in train. Instead of doing this, he rehearsed what he knew of Gus, focusing on a mental image of him, and sending a message, as if by this means he could communicate with the real person and control his movements simply by using the power of thought. This was another of his habitual disciplines, and, although he knew that there was no logic behind his belief in the power of his will, he also knew that logic had nothing to do with it.

He was spooning cherries out of the dish in front of him when the telephone rang. Okigbo ignored it. He never answered the telephone or allowed it to be answered unless he was expecting a call and knew who the caller was. Afterwards he would listen to the messages which had been recorded and reply to those which he considered important. His usual habit was to leave the sound control on the machine turned down, so that he wouldn't have to listen to the voices, but on this occasion, as sometimes happened, he had forgotten to adjust the volume.

The voice which emerged was unfamiliar. The accent was the

73

accent of North London, but something about the tone and pitch told Okigbo that this was the voice of a black man.

'Hello, hello,' it said, as if discomfited by the machine. This was a common reaction, and Okigbo allowed himself a slight smile. Then the voice changed, pitching itself lower and acquiring a gravity which Okigbo assumed was intended to be menacing.

'Listen to me carefully.'

Okigbo listened. For a moment he had thought that this was Gus, but after the first word he knew that it wasn't. The first language Okigbo had understood as a child depended for its meaning on the pitch of the syllables, and he had an unfailing ability to distinguish between the values of different sounds.

'I have information,' the voice continued, 'about something that concerns you. Something very valuable. Something old. Something African. I am going to call back at six. If you don't answer I'll know that you are not interested. Then that's your problem.'

After the voice stopped, Okigbo put his spoon down and listened to the tone for a few seconds. Then he got up, wiped his lips with the napkin, and picked up the telephone. He dialled the number of his chauffeur's mobile. When Chris answered he spoke without identifying himself. This telephone number was for his use only.

'Come up here now,' he said calmly. 'I want you to deliver a message.'

Chapter Eight

The message came in an envelope shoved under the door. Justine was the first to notice it. She'd slept at the flat the night before, and that morning she was bustling around making French toast. In the bedroom the smell of burning oil woke Gus out of the doze he'd gone into when she'd got up, and his first conscious thought was that, considering the intensity of her concern with Africa and her assertiveness about her African roots, Justine was remarkably like one of his white foster mothers in most of the things she did. Lucy Big Tits – as he and Danny had christened her, in order to distinguish her from the other Lucys – always made French toast for the kids on Saturdays. They had lived in her house in Leicester for more than a year, and she had been one of the first women he'd really fancied. Thinking about her long legs and generous bosom he sighed involuntarily, wondering where she was at that moment and what she was doing.

When he opened his eyes, he saw Justine leaning against the door, watching him. Seeing her like this was a sort of miracle, he thought. He'd known her a couple of months, but he still hadn't got used to finding himself with a woman who was so beautiful and seemed so right. For a start she was mixed race, like himself, but the resemblance in their backgrounds ended there. Her father was a Nigerian surgeon, while her mother was an English woman he'd met when they'd both been students at Cambridge. She got her green eyes and her light hair from her mother, she said, and her slim, athletic body from her father. In comparison with Gus and Danny, she had lived for most of her life with her parents, more or less pampered and protected in a small town in the Home Counties. When her mother died in an accident she'd gone to Nigeria with her father and then, after secondary school, come back to England to study for her degree. Now she worked for a PR company in Covent Garden. They had met when she sent him an invitation to a party for an African American author. Gus never found out how he'd turned up on her list of guests, and she said she'd forgotten, but he was grateful to his unknown benefactor, because after only a few hours, and even before he'd asked her out, he had realized that he was in love with Justine. It had been one of those unpredictable evenings, when he'd started out not knowing what was going to happen, and he had taken Rodney with him, partly for the company, partly to demonstrate to the boy that he had a presence among the elite of black culture, in the very air where international figures like the American author soared. Justine hadn't minded him bringing a guest. In fact, he suspected that bringing Rodney, with his look of the street and his youthfulness, had earned him a few points.

'Come on, you idle bugger,' Justine said loudly. 'Your breakfast is ready and there's a letter for you. At least I think it's for you. There's no name or anything.'

When she'd gone, Gus sat up and ripped the envelope open. He knew who it would be from. Okigbo always communicated with him like this. A blank envelope with a time and a place printed on a sheet of A4 folded inside it.

After he'd read it, he sat up and thought about the situation for a little while. He guessed the appointment meant that Okigbo was losing patience. In the normal run of things this wouldn't have worried Gus much. He had absolutely no intention of letting the Nigerian get his hands on the mask, or of letting him know where it was. The problem was that if Okigbo got angry enough he might well decide to back down on his promise of coming forward with more money. But this wasn't a prospect which worried Gus too much, because the Nigerian had already financed the most expensive and urgent part of his plan.

Gus hadn't expected so much when they first met. Indeed, the occasion hadn't been particularly auspicious. Gus had been invited to the preview of an exhibition by a black photographer at a gallery in Finsbury Park. He knew the photographer slightly – after he'd become involved in the movement for reparations his presence at such affairs had become a political necessity. At the same time he knew that he would have to brace himself against the sheer predictability of the event. It took no effort at all to imagine the scene. The walls would be lined with dramatic black-and-white close-ups of black faces. In the middle of the room there would be an exotic buffet of oily bhajis, samosas and Bulgarian wine. The room would be full of chancers. All black. Mostly desperate. Unsuccessful photographers, their names and services neatly printed on the cards they handed out to everyone who stood still for long enough. Unemployed graduates, anxiously scanning the faces for anyone who might help them find any kind of job. Occasionally a star, an actor or reporter, a black face from the telly, moving in an eddy of excitement triggered by the aura of success. Among the mob there would be dignitaries from the Jamaican High Commission. And there would be several speeches, grandiose but awkwardly delivered, hailing the exhibition as a milestone in black culture.

As it turned out, Gus's predictions were more or less correct — with one exception. As he'd expected, he'd been trapped in a corner, within half an hour, by a woman who said she knew him by reputation. She had attended a college where he taught classes on African history, and she'd always wanted to meet him because she was devoted to understanding African traditions and exploring her African roots. The problem was that she'd never had the time to follow up these interests properly. Now she was running her own PR firm and her time was even more limited. She laughed and made a rueful face. Being a young black woman running her own business was really tough, she told him, and she hardly had time for a social life.

Gus smiled and nodded in the right places. She was tall, mid twenties, he guessed, her hair cut short, emphasizing the neat oval shape of her head. She was wearing a short black dress with narrow shoulder straps which accentuated her smooth brown shoulders and, when she turned round, exhibited the subtle play of muscles in her back. In other circumstances he would have been seduced by her attention, but there was something about the self-conscious solemnity of her tone which put him right off. This was, Gus found himself thinking, exactly the sort of shallow nonsense which had pointed him in a new direction.

She had just given him her card, producing it from her handbag with a flourish, when he saw Okigbo over her shoulder. At the time he had no idea who the man was, but that first glimpse was enough to pin his attention and stir his curiosity. For a start, Okigbo was taller than anyone else in the room. But it was the confidence of his manner and the elegance of his clothes which set him apart. He was wearing a dark blue suit with a thin chalk stripe, and against the rich bloom of his skin, his shirt collar glowed a brilliant white. He was studying one of the photographs with a faint smile, but when he turned to look at the next in the row, Gus was riveted by his expression. Even at a distance, and, as if by instinct, Gus felt the commanding force of the man. In the same moment, and without reflection, he understood that Okigbo was accustomed to getting what he wanted without question or argument.

Gus studied the card the woman had given him. Her first name was Jean. Although she had told him this at the beginning of their conversation, he'd already forgotten it.

'Jean,' he said, interrupting something she was saying about the cost of the buffet, 'who is that African behind you?'

She glanced round quickly.

'That's Doctor Okigbo.' She moved a shade closer and her voice took on a lower, confiding pitch. 'He's one of the patrons of this gallery. I believe he finances a couple of artists. Usual Nigerian millionaire thing. You know?'

Gus nodded and smiled with her, but now he knew who the

object of his curiosity was, he also knew that the man was very far from the usual run of Nigerian millionaire. In fact he had learned quite a lot about Okigbo during the year that he'd been a member of the committee. Okigbo had been one of their targets, both for his money and his name. But although the chairwoman had treated him to tea at the House of Commons with the committee's parliamentary supporters, and subjected him to a campaign of assiduous flattery, he'd never quite committed himself. He'd never quite said no either, but after a year of courtship the committee still couldn't count on him for anything at all. Surprisingly the committee members showed very little resentment of his indecision. After all, as the chair was apt to point out, Okigbo was a man who lived on the edge. A hereditary chief and former regional governor, he had fallen foul of the government during an election campaign. Charged with embezzlement and systematic corruption, he'd been removed from the management of his construction company and placed under house arrest, while the authorities conducted an investigation. After a year of this he bribed his way out and fled the country, accompanied by a domestic entourage which he subsequently based in Geneva and Toronto. According to some of the cynics Gus had heard talking about the affair, this simply proved that the government wanted to get rid of Okigbo, because he couldn't have got out without the connivance of several highly placed officials. Whatever the truth of the matter, Okigbo was still a very rich man, and, on both sides of the Atlantic, he was endlessly courted and flattered by various groups and organizations, frenzied by the thought of his deep pockets and radical sympathies. On the other hand, the quest to ensnare the Nigerian was a bit like hunting a large and dangerous animal, because Okigbo could be difficult and unpredictable. The chair of the committee, at their first meeting, had addressed him as 'Chief', but to her surprise, he had reacted with extreme displeasure. 'Don't call me "Chief",' he'd said rudely. 'I am a chief, but every village functionary's son in this country calls himself "Chief". My title is Doctor.'

This was the title that Gus was careful to use when Jean, fluttering a little, introduced him to Okigbo. He had looked at her without interest as they approached, and Gus had the feeling that he had no idea who she was, but he'd shaken hands politely enough.

'You are a member of the reparations committee, aren't you?' Okigbo asked immediately.

It took Gus a couple of seconds to recover from the shock of discovering that the Nigerian knew exactly who he was. The other surprise was Okigbo's accent, which made him sound like an upper-middle-class Englishman, a hint of laziness halfway through the sentence. In the moment that Gus heard it he wondered whether Okigbo was mocking him, then he remembered that the Nigerian had attended a public school somewhere in Cornwall, where he'd been a notable rugby player, pursued by county scouts and local newsmen. If he hadn't already been wealthy, the rumour went, he could have played for England.

'I'm not a member any more,' Gus told him, although he suspected that Okigbo already knew this.

Okigbo smiled, without replying. He still looked, Gus thought, like an athlete, the whites of his eyes clear and brilliant, like a young boy's.

'I'm glad to meet you,' Gus said, 'because I want to talk to you about that. I have some plans.'

He hadn't known he was going to say this. In fact, when he asked Jean to introduce him it had only been out of curiosity.

Okigbo smiled again.

'Look around you,' he said softly. 'All these people have plans. Some of them live on the Arts Council. Some of them live on the dole. They join committees, they write letters, they go to meetings. They apply for grants, they make plans and what they get is a few crumbs off the white man's table.' His smile grew broader. 'I hear plans for a new project every day.'

Gus understood that he was being insulted, but he also had the feeling that this was some sort of test.

'This is different.' He met Okigbo's unblinking stare full on. 'I think you'll be interested, but I can't tell you about it here.'

Okigbo didn't reply for several seconds. Instead he kept his eyes fixed on Gus's face.

'All right,' he said, after what seemed like an eternity. He reached into his pocket and gave Gus a card. 'Come and see me.'

Gus had telephoned the following morning and made an appointment to see Okigbo during the afternoon. The bodyguards and the experience of being searched before they ushered him into the Nigerian's presence was a little unsettling, but, on the whole, the process impressed and reassured him.

Okigbo had been abrupt.

'What do you want?' he asked after they shook hands.

Gus started out by telling him about the committee. He had joined when he first heard about it. After completing his doctorate on West African history he'd been overwhelmed by the futility of all he'd done. This was a period of famines in the North, closely followed by massacres in the South. By day Gus studied the ideas and artefacts of African culture in libraries and museums. By night he watched the bodies of Africans laid out in long rows across the TV screen.

'There are times,' Gus said, 'when no African can avoid anger and despair.'

He was speaking from the heart, and if, at that point, the Nigerian had challenged his right to those feelings or commented that he was half-English, Gus would have exploded. But Okigbo was listening intently, only his eyes moved, as if they were scrutinizing and weighing up every shift and shade of expression on Gus's face.

The problem, Gus continued, was that the Committee for Reparations to Africa had been invented by politicians and social workers, and it had become exactly what it was meant to be, part of the circus of minority demands which floated on the outer fringes of British politics. The members lobbied and demonstrated, straining every sinew for a few lines in the press or a letter from a government department, veering between sycophancy and rage according to the circumstances. He had spent over a year arguing for a change in tactics, without success. To these people direct action meant waving a banner in the street, and he had finally left when he worked out that no matter how many official asses they kissed, and no matter how many column inches were lavished on the cause, nothing would change.

Okigbo shifted his posture and leaned forward, still studying Gus's face.

'So why are you here?'

Gus sighed. He had determined to trust Okigbo with his intentions, but for some reason, when it came to the point, the thought of saying what he had in mind made sweat break out on his forehead.

At the peak of his frustration, he told Okigbo, he had thought of bombing the British Museum, and he would have done it too, if he hadn't thought that it would be a pointless exercise, likely to do more harm than good. The Nigerian nodded, and gave a sharp bark of what Gus took to be approval: 'Ah'. Eventually, Gus continued, he had settled on the plan of stealing an important artefact and holding it for ransom against the return of an equivalent sum of money, to be paid to a project in Africa. But the money wasn't the point. The political fallout would be enormous. The issue would be front-page news. Black people would mobilize round it, and once that happened the other nationalities, like the Asians, the Greeks, the Turks and all the others whose culture was locked up in museums and cellars in Britain, would begin uttering demands, either for their return or for some compensation. The issue of reparations would be propelled into the agenda of mainstream politics, and every time the fuss died down, he could do it again. There might even be copycats. No one would know where or how the activists would strike again, and once the door had been opened anything could happen.

Okigbo threw his head back and laughed.

'Terrorism,' he shouted. 'Terrorism.'

'No,' Gus corrected him. 'It's not even theft, because these things are stolen objects themselves. It's justice.'

After that it was relatively plain sailing. Okigbo had handed out the money he needed for the capture of the mask with no trouble, and it hadn't been until their last meeting that Gus had started to worry. Even so, by the time he arrived at Okigbo's apartment, he still hadn't worked out a strategy for fobbing off the Nigerian's inevitable requests to see the Dancing Face. Part of the reason for his inability to manufacture an excuse, he suspected, was the fact that he didn't want to. The bottom line was that he would have to tell Okigbo, sooner or later, to stop hassling and trust him to carry out the plan they had discussed. He didn't know how Okigbo would take this, but he had determined that, whatever happened, he would tough it out.

Okigbo was standing by the window, his back to the door, gazing out. The curtains were partly drawn and the afternoon sun slanting through the fabric gave the room a soft warm glow. For a moment, he didn't speak or turn around and Gus hesitated, not quite sure what to do.

'Sit down,' Okigbo said suddenly. 'I want you to hear something.'

Gus sat down.

'What do you want me to hear?' he asked.

Okigbo didn't reply. Instead he walked over to the phone and fiddled with the machine. Then he straightened up and stood watching Gus intently.

The sound of Rodney's voice filled the room. It was obvious that he had been trying to disguise it, but Gus had a good ear and he knew who it was after a few words. What astonished him even more than the references to a 'valuable' and 'African' item was the fact that Rodney knew about Okigbo.

When the machine clicked into silence, Gus looked up to see Okigbo still staring at him.

'You know who that is.'

It was a statement rather than a question. For a moment Gus thought about lying, then he understood that it made no sense whatsoever. He was clearly the only link between Rodney and Okigbo, but he hadn't told Rodney about Okigbo. He was sure of that.

'Who is it?' Okigbo repeated.

'His name's Rodney,' Gus told him, 'but I swear to you I have no idea how he knows your name, or anything about the mask. It was in a crate when we took it. He never actually saw it properly, and on top of all that it's still in my possession. He's obviously taking a chance you don't know that.'

Okigbo thought this over without taking his eyes off Gus.

'Why should I believe you?' He walked across the room and sat on the sofa with Gus. He didn't smile and although his posture was now relaxed and sociable, the tension in the room seemed to have increased. 'Look at it from my point of view. I help you with this little problem. You say you've hidden the mask. You refuse to show it to me. Then I get a phone call from someone who says he's got it, even though you promised to keep my name out of it, and you don't know how any of this happened. Why should I believe a word you tell me?'

Okigbo said this in such a sad, friendly tone that Gus felt a twinge of guilt which he suppressed immediately because he guessed that this was another one of Okigbo's tricks. At the same time he couldn't resist thinking that what the Nigerian had said was eminently reasonable and just.

'You know the reason I didn't show it to you,' Gus said. 'I didn't want anyone else involved.'

'That sounded more reasonable before your friend started ringing me.'

'It's nothing to do with me,' Gus repeated, suddenly realizing that his voice had risen and he was beginning to sound shrill. He paused, forcing himself to meet Okigbo's eyes. 'This is as much of a surprise to me as it is to you.'

'So who is he?'

For an instant Gus hesitated, but by now he was finding it hard to resist the pressure of Okigbo's unreadable gaze and, in spite of himself, the emotion uppermost in his mind was the desire for exoneration.

'He's one of the guys who helped me.'

Okigbo pursed his lips impatiently.

'I guessed that. Who is he?'

'He used to be a member of the committee too,' Gus said reluctantly. He paused, putting his thoughts together. 'I've known him for years. He was in one of my classes.'

'A student?'

'He was.'

Okigbo frowned, and Gus hurried on to explain. Rodney had supported himself by working in a store on Oxford Street, but after he had lost that job he'd got into debt and dropped out. During the period when Gus tried to move the committee towards direct action, Rodney had been one of his supporters, and he had agreed to help steal the mask without argument.

'You paid him?'

Gus nodded. He had been prepared to take the risk because it was his plan, but he'd felt uneasy about involving Rodney. In any case, the boy Rodney had brought with him wouldn't have done the job without a payoff at the end of it.

Okigbo interrupted Gus with a wave of his hand, as if he'd heard enough.

'Who has it now?'

'I told you,' Gus said, with a touch of impatience. 'It's in my possession. Rodney doesn't even know where it is.'

Okigbo got up abruptly and walked over to the window again. Seen from the back his head seemed massive, and, poised against the flare of the afternoon sun, the way his skull curved out above his neck put Gus in mind of a dome squatting over the top of a pillar.

'Where can I find this Rodney?'

'I don't know,' Gus told him. 'He kind of moves around.'

Okigbo swung round in a movement so fast that it seemed like a blur. In one moment he was standing still as a statue by the window, in the next the light splintered and blazed and Okigbo was a dark shape coming towards Gus, his face contorted with rage. Gus hadn't consciously anticipated this explosion of anger, but his body must have been keyed to the tension in the room, because he found himself on his feet, his fists clenched.

Okigbo came close, his face inches away, the bulk of his body bearing down on Gus like a powerful weight. When he spoke his expression had tightened into a kind of composure, but there were flecks of red in his eyes now, and they burned with the effort of control.

'You must have an address. A phone number. Don't tell me you don't know.'

For a few seconds Gus held the pose, facing Okigbo, their breaths mingling in the space between them. Gus could smell flowers and fruit. Later on he remembered expecting Okigbo's breath to be a hot, feral blast. Instead, to his surprise, the man smelled of fruit, something tropical, like a ripe papaya.

'I can give you an address and a phone number,' Gus said. 'I don't know if it will do you any good.' He moved his feet to the side, away from Okigbo's body and stepped round him, feeling in his pockets for a pen. There was some writing paper on the table and he moved towards it, feeling a sort of triumph at having found a way of escaping the confrontation without backing down. 'The best thing,' he said, bending over to write, speaking without looking at Okigbo, 'is for me to find him and find out what's going on, and sort him out.'

He straightened up and gave Okigbo the paper. He had written an address from which Rodney had moved months ago, and the number of his mobile phone.

Okigbo took the paper, looked at it, and laid it on the table. Gus waited for him to return to the subject of the mask. After hearing the phone call he had been in half a mind to tell the Nigerian what he'd done with it, but Okigbo's show of temper had confirmed his feeling that to do so would be stupid and might even be dangerous.

'No more games,' Okigbo said. His voice was lower and the words came more quickly than before, but he seemed otherwise composed. 'I want the Dancing Face. You don't need it for what you want to do. You can have access to it, photograph it, if you want to prove you have it, do what you like if it helps whatever scheme you have in mind, but I want it in front of me tomorrow. If you don't bring it, or take me to it, I'll come and take it from you. You understand?'

Gus stood still, not quite believing what he'd heard. On the other hand, he had the sense that this was exactly what he'd feared from the moment Okigbo had given him the money. At that moment all he could think of was what a fool he'd been.

'Why?'

He almost stammered the question out, and the moment he opened his mouth he knew that asking was pointless. It didn't matter why.

Unpredictably, Okigbo smiled.

'Get out,' he said quietly.

Gus stood his ground.

'If you want your money back,' he said, 'you can have it with fucking interest, but don't threaten me.'

He half expected another explosion of anger, but Okigbo's expression didn't change. Instead he walked to the door, opened it and motioned with his hand.

'Go.'

Gus walked past him into the hallway. He hadn't seen Okigbo make any kind of signal, but the bodyguard who had searched him when he arrived was standing by the door of the apartment, holding it wide open, his eyes fixed on Gus.

Squaring his shoulders and keeping his head straight, Gus walked towards him. Just before he stepped out into the corridor, he heard the door of Okigbo's sitting room slam shut.

Chapter Nine

Okigbo had picked the restaurant carefully. It had the style and decor to provide a relaxing setting for an agreeable lunch, and it was situated in the West End. Digby's office was on the other side of the river, but it was a short trip by taxi. At the same time, the hotel wasn't particularly fashionable, and it certainly wasn't part of the circuit frequented by celebrities and gossip columnists. He'd had to reassure Digby about that aspect of the place.

Okigbo was precisely on time, but when he was ushered to his table Digby was already seated and perusing the menu. They were on the twentieth floor, and through the wall of glass behind Digby he could see a wide swathe of streets and buildings. The effect was oddly cinematic, as if the view was a moving backdrop in a studio.

'Digger,' Okigbo said, shaking hands with Digby.

'Don't tempt me,' Digby replied, grinning.

He was referring, Okigbo knew, to the nicknames by which they'd been known in their first years at school. Digger and Nigger.

'You wouldn't dare to use that word now,' Okigbo told him.

Digby's grin vanished.

'You're right.'

Okigbo studied him closely. For a moment he had seen the boy with whom he'd shared a large slice of his youth. Then Digby's expression had composed itself into a camouflage of blandness and he was a middle-aged man again, his hair going grey and thinning into a pronounced widow's peak, his face leathery with the remnants of a deep tan. The last time they'd met, Okigbo remembered, had been in Lagos. He'd walked into a nightclub and, on the side of the floor, he had seen Digby at a table near the band. He was with a large party, and Okigbo had recognized three white oil company executives from the North, the company's African spokesman, and a skinny Belgian woman who worked for an international agency and was rumoured to have important connections. The rest of the party were local women, teenage secretaries at the company's headquarters in the city, most of them related to, or protected by, important men. Digby had been climbing rapidly in the hierarchy, and Okigbo understood that the people accompanying him reflected his growing importance. As he paused in the entrance Digby gave him a little wave, prompting the man sitting on the opposite side of the table, with his back to the entrance, to turn round to look. The man was out of uniform, so it took Okigbo a few seconds to register that the face belonged to a soldier he'd seen on television that day, a general who had just returned from the North with a reputation for ruthlessness. Okigbo had met the general years previously, when he was still a colonel, but the man hadn't smiled or given him a look of recognition; instead he turned his back, so deliberately that it seemed a snub. Okigbo hadn't been surprised. At this point various acquaintances had begun to avoid him and, although he would have gone over to greet Digby in normal circumstances, the best option at that moment was to turn on his heel and leave. A few days later he was arrested.

'You're looking well,' Digby told him.

In return Okigbo complimented him on his suit, a light grey pinstripe which was perfectly cut to hide the bulge that Digby had begun to grow around the middle.

They didn't get to the point until the main course had arrived.

'I hear,' Okigbo said, 'that you've lost the Dancing Face.'

To do him credit, Digby didn't pretend surprise. He dropped his eyes to his plate and, with his fork, poked at the skin of his blackened fish for a few seconds before he looked up again.

'You haven't lost your touch,' he said lightly. 'There's been nothing about it in the newspapers.'

Okigbo smiled. 'I collect my own news.'

'So you'll know,' Digby said, 'that our interest in the whole matter is peripheral. We put some money into the exhibition because we support the arts and the culture of the region. The rest of it isn't our problem.'

Okigbo laughed out loud this time.

'That's the official line, I know. But does that mean you don't want to know where it is?'

Digby's face hardened into shrewd lines.

'Have you got it, by any chance?'

Okigbo met his gaze, enjoying the moment.

'No. But I know a man who does.'

Digby frowned, leaned forward, his expression serious and intent.

'All right, Oggy,' he said, 'you know more about this than I do. What do you want to tell me?'

'Don't you want to hear what I'm after?'

Digby sighed heavily.

'I take it that comes later.'

Okigbo smiled at him, confident now that he'd made the right choice.

'I was approached some time ago,' he said, 'by a group. I threw them out, of course, but they told me enough.'

'Who are they?'

'No one you would know. They're not connected with any of the politicians. These are asylum-seekers, exiles, desperate men. They assumed that I shared their feelings. I'd have warned you, of course, but I didn't take it seriously.'

He shrugged and met Digby's eyes with an expression of candid innocence.

'What are they going to do?'

Okigbo shrugged again.

'Embarrass the government. Use the publicity to attack your company in the British media. They know that it's a difficult time. Negotiations over sanctions. Commonwealth conference. Investment in new fields.' He paused. 'But there's never a good moment for bad publicity.'

Digby was frowning now, his eyes sweeping the room as if searching for a concealed threat.

'This is really a matter for the insurance and the police,' he said. 'But as far as I know, and that's not a lot, they haven't submitted any demands.' He stopped and considered Okigbo, as if weighing up how much he could reveal. 'I'm told that there was a ransom demand, but it turned out to be a hoax. Robberies of this kind attract con men, but so far they've kept it out of the news. The ransom demand came from someone who knew.' He tapped lightly on the side of his plate with the fork. 'Unfortunately the police were involved, and they're obsessive about crime and punishment. They concocted some ridiculous trap with a briefcase full of old newspapers, and then, of course, the guys got away. So God knows what will happen now. That is, if their theory is correct. They think that it's just an ordinary gang of thieves, probably working for a collector who wants something exotic. That's the sort of scenario they're familiar with. Seems reasonable. If you're saying this is political, you'll need some proof.'

Okigbo concealed the shock he felt. In a flash he understood that Rodney must have tried blackmailing the exhibition before trying the same act on him. He was certain now that Gus had been telling him the truth. Not that he'd had much doubt about that in the first place. On the other hand, there was always room for doubt. When Rodney telephoned the previous evening, Okigbo had actually been very clear about what to do. Before his caller could do more than announce himself, Okigbo had told him that he knew his identity, quoted his address and telephone number as proof, then pointed out that he didn't have anything to trade and by making stupid demands he was playing with his life. Going by the shocked silence on the other end of the line before he put the phone down, he'd been confident that he'd made the right decision. Now his judgement had been confirmed. Okigbo was experiencing a rising tide of elation at the knowledge that he was in complete control of the situation. He felt like laughing out loud. Instead he gave Digby a sceptical grimace.

'They can't put a blackout on gossip,' he said. 'Everyone connected with the exhibition knows. Everyone at the university. The insurers. The Arts Council. The police. Who the hell doesn't know? You'll probably have half a dozen more ransom demands by the end of the week.'

'All right,' Digby replied. 'They're probably wrong, but that doesn't make you right. You haven't yet shown me any proof of what you're saying.'

'I'm not going to because I can't, and if I could I wouldn't. I know I can get this thing. If you don't believe me you can walk away. Forget it. No one will ever see it again. I can tell you that. But you'll have to take what I'm saying on trust, until I get what I want.'

For a few seconds Digby was silent. Then he pushed his plate aside, and blew his breath out angrily.

'What do you want?'

'I want to go back.'

'That's easy enough,' Digby said. 'Go.'

On the other side of the table Okigbo's right hand curled into a fist, and he tapped lightly on the cloth with it as he spoke. This was the only sign he gave of how much Digby's gibe irritated him.

'I want the charges dropped, and my bank account unfrozen. I want that in writing from the minister. I want a letter from your chairman thanking me for my services, unspecified, to the company, and asking me to return as a consultant.'

'I'm not hearing this,' Digby said. He shook his head, laughing. 'I'm definitely not hearing this. I've got the feeling I fell asleep in my office and I'm dreaming about you, Oggy. I'm not hearing this.'

Okigbo's expression didn't alter.

'You haven't heard what I'm going to do in return,' Okigbo said. 'I'm going to secure the Dancing Face, bring it back to Nigeria and give it to them. Once it's there, they can deny it exists, they can say it's a fake, they can say that they've got no idea how it turned up in the country. They can say what they like when the British come begging, but the one thing they won't do is to give it back.'

Digby stopped laughing as the implications of what Okigbo was proposing struck him.

'That's ingenious,' he said. 'I mean it. That's ingenious. The one problem is that, from your point of view, it's not a big enough inducement. This is a valuable work of art, but not all that valuable. I don't think anyone cares that much. Not enough to get you off the hook, Oggy.'

Okigbo laughed in his turn. He had considered this aspect and he knew the answer.

'You've spent more than ten years in West Africa and you still don't understand. When you poked all those women in Lagos you should have listened to what they had to say.' He held up his hand to stop whatever Digby was going to say. 'Think about it. Before the Europeans, religion was in the centre of all our cultures.

Scratch any one of those self-righteous Anglicans at the cathedral in Lagos, the Catholics in the missions, even the born-again fanatics, and you'll find a little piece of anger about the desecration and theft of sacred things. Every nation has a soul, and ours has never healed.'

As he said this, Okigbo became aware that he had raised his voice. Hearing the passion in it, the waiter, a young white man with blond hair and over precise movements, paused in the act of bending over to refill their glasses from the bottle he'd just lifted out of the ice bucket at Digby's elbow. Okigbo gestured to him, and he filled their glasses deliberately, his face and manner impassive as a stone. Okigbo waited until he'd walked away before starting again.

'Before the Europeans,' he repeated, 'there were many empires in the region. For hundreds of years we've been creating ourselves inside a framework of administration, controllers grappling with our imagination. We're a lot of things, but inside of us there's a magician, a collection of tricksters, subtle and determined, which is how we've survived our history. The magician likes to laugh. You've heard them.'

'I've heard them,' Digby said, 'but I don't know what it's got to do with this.'

'We've been labouring for years under a burden of sanctions and condemnation,' Okigbo said. 'We've been pissed on at every international conference, by every obscure pygmy politician who could persuade the UN to lend him the fare, and the British stand behind all of them, stirring the pot. This is the demonstration of their power that they call morality.' Digby opened his mouth, as if to interrupt again, but Okigbo hurried on. 'First they made a point of forgetting how much they stole from us, and then they pretended it never happened. Now they have the impudence to display the loot, as if it had appeared by magic. Nothing to do with us, old boy.' He spread his hands and winked at Digby. 'All right. The Dancing Face appears in West Africa in exactly the way it appeared in Europe. The British beg, negotiate, threaten, but they get nothing but polite indifference or outright rejection. How do you think the region will react? They'll feel we're reclaiming something that's ours. They'll feel the balance of booty is being restored. They'll laugh. They'll admire the government for making fools of the Europeans, and this time no one gets hurt. There's no pockets of resentment to clean up. In this country they call it the feel-good factor. Better than winning the World Cup. The other side of it is international. If we can get away with grabbing back a piece of our treasure it will make some of the pygmies think again. They'll think the British are losing the grip they've got left, and they'll be laughing too. It's hard to twist a diplomat's arm when he's laughing at you. You can almost guarantee that it will weaken the international consensus.'

Okigbo paused. He leaned back in his chair, looked round the room, and then back at Digby.

'That's going to be worth a lot to them, a lot more than the millions they're paying out to these public relations bandits, and if your company delivers it, you know how grateful these guys can be.'

He smiled happily. Digby was frowning, lost in thought.

'I can talk to people in the company. I don't know what they'll say, but I'll put it to them,' he said slowly. He frowned, put his elbow on the table and rested his chin on his open palm, fixing Okigbo with a look of intense and brooding speculation. 'Tell me one thing though. If I know you, you've got everything a man could want here. Your life is pleasant enough. Even if it's safe for you to go back you'll face any number of problems. It will always be dangerous. Why do you want to do it?'

Okigbo shook his head. He laughed.

'You think I'm like you, don't you? The old school.' He laughed again. 'You're right. My life is pleasant. This is like a beautiful play-ground, but there's nothing here that I want. Don't confuse me with those pathetic immigrants whose greatest desire is to be one of you. I'm a man. Years ago I'd fucked more women than I can remember. I have more clothes than I can ever wear. I eat the best food money can buy whenever I want. But what is that? I'm a man of my nation. Your people are shadows to me. To themselves they're unreal.' He made a gesture circling the room with his hand. 'These men you see around you are nothing without their clothes, without their cars, without their mobile telephones. Strip them of those things and they'd be quaking puddles of flesh, frightened of each other, frightened of women even. In a place like this you can only live with half of yourself. In my own place, when I walk the earth shakes, and I have things to do. Life and death, shaping the world. This is what makes life worth living.' He laughed again at the disapproving look on Digby's face. 'Even you, Digby. You must have noticed how pale and thin your life is here.'

Digby shrugged. 'You were always a lunatic,' he said, smiling, but Okigbo could tell there was something else on his mind.

Almost immediately he leaned forward again and, lowering his voice, added: 'I appreciate how you feel, but this is high risk for you, Oggy. If they're interested you'll have to deliver on what you're promising. If you don't, you know how they'll react. You understand?'

Okigbo nodded, still smiling.

'I know the risk,' he said. 'Just get me what I want.'

Chapter Ten

Gus was already exhausted when he got back home in the afternoon. This was the day after his confrontation with Okigbo, and he'd spent most of the previous twenty-four hours trying to locate Rodney. The first thing he'd done was to ring the number of Rodney's mobile, only to be told by a computerized voice that it was not in use at this time. Then he tried the address he had given Okigbo, where he was greeted by a shaven-headed youth with a gold ring glinting in his ear. For a moment he'd had a leap of hope that this was one of Rodney's friends, who might know his whereabouts, but the boy said he didn't even know who the previous occupant of the room was, much less know where to find him.

After that he had spent the evening touring the South London clubs he'd heard Rodney mention, but although he was out until four in the morning he'd seen no sign of his quarry. At the flat he was greeted by the frantically blinking green light on his answering machine, but he was too tired to listen, and, for the moment, all he wanted to do was go to bed. His sleep had been broken and disturbed, but he'd awoken in the grip of an inspiration.

It was mid morning, and he reached the college where Rodney had been a student just before lunch. It had been years since Gus had last worked there, but his luck was in. The secretary of the faculty was a plump Australian who remembered him, and he persuaded her to look up Rodney's name. He told her the date, and she smiled.

'We're still putting those files into the computer, but I think he'll be there.'

The address Rodney had given on his initial application was in Tottenham. When Gus got there it turned out to be a street he'd driven through several times, a short noisy stretch of road off the High Street, the corner choked with stalls and vehicles. The house itself was in the middle of the cramped terrace. Gus parked, crossed the pavement and rang the bell. Nothing happened for a little while, then he heard a scuffling sound and he pressed the bell again. The door opened a few inches, and a middle-aged woman in an Afro wig was looking at him through the gap. Behind her he could hear children chattering and banging about.

'No. He don't live here again,' the woman said when he asked for Rodney.

Back in the car Gus reflected on what to do. This could go on for days, he thought, and he had no assurance of success at the end of it. If Rodney didn't want to be found it would be impossible. He had set out on this quest in a mixture of anger and panic, trying to assert some kind of grip on events, to put his plan back on the rails. It was time to think again.

On the way home he forced himself towards conclusions. He was finished with Okigbo. He was certain of that, so he had nothing to lose if Rodney made himself a nuisance to the Nigerian. At least that would keep both of them busy and off his back. There was the distant possibility that Rodney might try and collect whatever reward was being offered by going to the police, but without the evidence of the mask he wouldn't get very far. All he'd have against Gus would be his word, because by the time Rodney could get around to doing anything there'd be no trace. Okigbo was a different proposition altogether. He had no idea what Okigbo's plans were for the mask, or what he might do to get it, but remembering the passion on the Nigerian's face and the way he had controlled his fury, Gus had the uneasy feeling that the man was capable of anything. The solution he had in mind was to move out of his flat for a week or two, make himself scarce, because if he couldn't be found Okigbo would be unable to pressure him. He wasn't at all sure that the problem would be solved as easily as all that, but it was a start.

By the time Gus unlocked the outer door and started climbing the stairs to his flat he'd sorted out what to do next and he felt lighter, a kind of relief buoying him up. Halfway up the phone began ringing and, propelled by the new-found decisiveness of his mood, he ran to answer it, fumbling with the keys, and getting there just in time to hear the answering machine switch itself off. The voice had been Eleanor's, and he stood over the phone, indecisive again, wondering why she had called. He hadn't been in touch with her since well before he'd captured the mask, but that was according to plan. Long ago they'd arranged, once he'd done it, to stay out of contact unless there was an emergency. A wave of foreboding swept over Gus. If Eleanor was calling it must mean trouble.

There was a sound behind him and he spun round to see Justine. She was wearing a charcoal suit with a white pinstripe, and a skirt which barely came to halfway down the thighs. He guessed that she had dropped in on her way home from work, because these were her working clothes. On her days off she usually wore jeans. Gus, provoked by their blending of sex and authority, preferred her working clothes, and sometimes, perhaps once or twice during the week, she would arrive like this, unexpected, legs bare, her tights slipped off on the landing in front of the door and already tucked into her handbag. Leaning against the wall, her feet planted wide apart, she would give him a knowing smile. She knew exactly what he liked. This time, though, she wasn't smiling.

'What's going on?' she asked abruptly. 'Where've you been?'

Gus frowned. He'd given Justine a key when they began sleeping together, and he was usually happy when she turned up unannounced, but there was something proprietorial about her tone that grated on his nerves. It crossed his mind that she'd never given him a key to her own flat.

'What are you on about?' he said irritably.

'Look around. You been trashing the place or what?'

Gus looked around. Up to that point he'd been too preoccupied to notice the state of the room. In normal circumstances he was an untidy housekeeper, but he knew he couldn't have left it in this condition. The sofa had been pulled clear of the wall and the cushions were lying on the floor. His bookcase had been overturned, spilling books and papers all round it. In his bedroom the mattress had been removed and the base turned upside down. That was bad enough, but it was the photographs neatly laid out in a row beside the mattress which gave Gus a shock that made his stomach heave. The photographs were glossy publicity snaps of the Dancing Face that Eleanor had sent him. He had hidden them for safety under the mattress, with every intention of burning them after the robbery, but the pressure of the last few days had driven them out of his mind. Now the face stared at him from half a dozen different angles, as if mocking every twist and turn of his frantic brain. Automatically he bent down, gathered them up and laid them face down in a pile. Then he tugged the bed upright and began putting it back together.

'That woman's been ringing for the last hour,' Justine said behind him. 'I didn't know whether to call the police, but I thought I'd better wait for you.' She paused. 'A couple of African men came to the door asking for you. I told them I didn't know when you'd be back.'

Gus dropped the sheet he was holding and spun round.

'African men? What did they want? What kind of African men?'

'Nigerians. I didn't like the look of them much. They looked like the kind of guys you'd see in Nigeria, sometimes they'd be just ordinary gangsters, sometimes they'd be working for the police. Sort of mad eyes. The kind of men you knew had done horrible things.'

There was a note in her voice that Gus recognized, a kind of fear that he'd heard before, when she'd told him stories about some of her father's experiences. One time he'd been treating a patient for gunshot wounds when a gang of men who said they were from the security services appeared and dragged the wounded man out of the ward. When he contacted a police inspector he knew, he'd been told to keep his mouth shut and forget it.

'These things happened all the time,' Justine had said, her eyes clouded and distant.

'These men who came,' Gus asked, 'did they say what they wanted?'

'No. They didn't look like anyone you knew, and they didn't look very friendly.' She walked round Gus, not touching him, and sat on the edge of the bed.

'What's going on?' she asked again.

'I can't tell you,' Gus muttered.

'Right,' Justine said angrily, 'that's it. I'm off.'

She got up and began walking away. Suddenly, Gus felt bereft, as if once she'd gone through the door he would be alone and isolated. Before he had time to think he found himself calling out after her.

'I can't tell you because I don't want you involved.'

She stopped, her hand on the door.

'You don't trust me.'

'It's not a question of trust,' he said. 'It's nothing much and it's better you don't know.'

Justine made a sceptical sound. She moved away from the door, came back towards him, and, before he could stop her, bent down and scooped the photographs up.

'It's something to do with this mask, isn't it? Have you done something?'

He shook his head quickly.

'No.'

'I'm not exactly stupid,' she said. 'You were talking about "direct action", as you called it, when I met you. Then you're always getting these mysterious calls, and now there's all this crazy stuff. I don't notice you rushing to call the police, and somebody took the trouble to lay these photos out like they were sending you a message. It doesn't take a genius.'

Gus shook his head again, not looking at her. She moved round him and sat on the bed.

'We're supposed to be together,' she said. Her voice was tearful, and Gus felt his resistance fading. Perhaps, he thought, she would be more at risk if he left her completely in the dark.

'If I tell you what I can,' he said, 'don't ask me for more. If I get done and you know about it, they can do you, too, for being an accomplice or for conspiracy. Better if you don't know all the details.'

He sat on the bed next to her and told her what he'd done. He left out the names of everyone involved, and he was vague about what he planned to do, but apart from that, he told her everything.

'What did you do with it?' she asked when he was finished.

'It's safe,' he said. 'I sent it out of London.'

Before she could ask him any more the telephone rang. After a few rings the machine clicked on and it stopped. In a few seconds the ringing started again.

'You'd better answer it,' Justine said. 'I'm going anyway.'

By the time he got to the telephone the ringing had stopped and started again. He picked it up expecting to hear Eleanor, and he nearly slammed it down when he realized that the voice on the other end was Okigbo's.

'Look out of your window,' Okigbo said.

'What?'

'Look out of your front window at the street,' Okigbo repeated. 'You'll see a car with a couple of guys in it.'

'What are you talking about?' Gus asked angrily.

'Do it and I'll tell you.'

Gus laid the phone down and went to the window. In front of the block there was a white Cortina with two men sitting in it. They didn't move or look up at him, but even from that distance he recognized the men Justine had been describing. In that instant he felt like pinching himself, or banging his head against the glass to check whether all of this was real or whether he was dreaming.

'So what am I supposed to do?' Gus asked when he picked the phone up. 'This is fucking London,' he said contemptuously, 'not Nigeria. You're not scaring anyone.'

'Those men will be waiting,' Okigbo's voice carried on in the same level tone as if he hadn't heard. 'When you're ready to go and get the Dancing Face, walk across the road and tell them. They'll drive you wherever you want to go.'

'Fuck off,' Gus told him. He slammed the phone down. It began ringing again before he had taken more than a few steps away.

'You've got two hours,' Okigbo's voice said. 'Think about it all you like, but before the next two hours are up I want you to make your decision. If you don't want my men to drive you, telephone me and I'll come with you. I'm a reasonable man. But don't try and run away. That would upset me, and we'll find you anyway. You've got two hours. Two hours.'

When Gus put the phone down he'd already made up his mind. He knew what he had to do. In fact he had planned it months ago. The only problem was that he hadn't envisaged having to set his plan in motion so soon. It was actually Eleanor's plan, hatched during the last weekend they had spent together at her house in Bristol. When she knew that his mind was set on the theft of the Dancing Face, and that she couldn't dissuade him, she had insisted that he worked out an escape route. He could go abroad, initially to the cottage she owned in Brittany, then if it was necessary he could move on to Lisbon, where she had friends at the university who would look after him. As for the mask, once he delivered it to her, she would simply dump it in one of the cupboards in her office at the faculty where she kept boxes of long-forgotten theses, curios from foreign trips, remaindered copies of textbooks and an old raincoat she wore in emergencies. No one opened Eleanor's cupboards any more. Even the cleaners would protest if she gave them that job, and it was the last place anyone would look for the Dancing Face. If she suddenly dropped dead, she said, rolling her eyes at him, they would simply store her belongings and wait for her one remaining relative, a nephew in South Africa, to come and collect them, which might well be never. That was the beauty of living with an antiquated academic code, she told him. Most of the time it made for one of the deepest ruts on God's earth. The other side of the coin was they made a fetish of certain kinds of privacy. The mask would be safe.

The other aspect, she reminded him, was that practically no one else knew about their relationship, even though they'd been so intimate for so long. This was partly because it had all started more than a dozen years ago, when she tutored some of his classes on the history of art. Gus had been one of the few students in those days who had a genuine interest in her speciality, which was African art. But Africa wasn't simply a field of study for her. She had, in fact, been born and partly brought up in Zimbabwe, and although no one could now tell her apart from any other English person, she still felt somewhere in her heart, she told him, that she was an African.

It was as if they shared both an obsession and a secret, and it wasn't long before their mutual attraction found its climax in bed. As it happened, the first time had been in the back of her Volvo Estate rather than in bed. This was on the way back from a trip to the British Museum, and she had parked on a slip road off the A4. While the trees around them sighed in the dark, they kissed and touched, unable to stop, until they scrambled into the back seat and fucked, awkwardly at first, then submerged in a rolling tide of delicious passion.

For as long as they knew each other their relationship kept this same flavour of furtive and irresistible secrecy. Apart from her position as his teacher, she was married. They spent so much time together that there were rumours, of course. But no one could say for certain what went on between them. Some years later she separated from her husband, but by then Gus was sharing a flat in London with the woman he was about marry. It never happened, but by the time he was together again with Eleanor the romance had gone. In any case, they both knew that they would simply do what they had always done over and over again, and that nothing further would happen between them because, for whatever reason, all they had left was the intensity of their sex. That, and a deep-rooted trust which had somehow embedded itself in their relationship during the years when they met to fuck in secret, Eleanor bent over her desk with her skirt up round her waist, or standing against a fence in a nearby alleyway, or kneeling in the front of the Volvo, her hair spread dry and cool over his thighs, her mouth warm and wet on him. 'The things you do to me,' she said once, looking up at him from between his outstretched legs. 'It's like I'm suspended over an abyss, and this is all I have to cling to.'

The truth was that the stealth in which their meetings were cloaked had become entangled with their passion and, even after the necessity had passed, neither of them would surrender lightly to any kind of change. In his absence she hardly ever talked about him, except to her oldest women friends, who called him The Highwayman, because he came and went so mysteriously; and when Gus talked about her to other men, it was his habit to avoid mentioning her name or her circumstances. As Gus moved around the flat packing the big sports bag he used for travelling, he soothed himself with the thought that it would take an extremely thorough investigation for anyone to latch on to his connection with Eleanor.

When he was finished, he scoured the flat for anything that might connect him with the robbery or the mask. There was nothing except for a few scraps of paper with telephone numbers on them, and he burnt those along with the photographs. Then he ripped up the fitted carpet in the hallway, where he'd hidden his passport and some money. There was nearly a thousand pounds there, and he buttoned it securely into his pocket before he went back into the sitting room and rang Eleanor's number. She answered on the first ring, and he said the word they'd arranged between them. 'Parachute.'

After this he opened the door and walked quietly down the stairs. There was still an hour to go before Okigbo's deadline would be up, but there didn't seem to be any point in waiting. Once in the hallway he opened the door to the cellar with his key and, closing it behind him, stood in the dark, waiting.

Several times during the next hour it occurred to him that if Okigbo had been bluffing he would have wasted a couple of hours ducking and diving to no purpose. On the other hand, his instincts told him that he was in danger. He didn't know how far the Nigerian would go, but he was in no position to call in the police or appeal to anyone else for help. To all intents and purposes he was an outlaw with every man's hand against him. Oddly enough the idea gave his spirits a little lift, and in the middle of the slow panic he had begun to feel from the time Okigbo told him to look out of the window, he felt a kind of calm. He would make a good outlaw, he thought, his moves full of the swiftness and stealth he needed to stay ahead of the game. He felt fear, it was true, but he knew now that he could use it, channelling the adrenaline rush in his blood, husbanding it for the right moment.

He had expected the hour to pass slowly, but it seemed no time at all before the glowing numerals told him it was seven o'clock, and, almost at the same time, he heard footsteps mounting the stairs. A herd of elephants, he thought, which meant, as he had hoped, that they were both going up there. Then his stomach gave an unpleasant lurch as it crossed his mind that they were going double-handed because whatever it was they were planning to do to him required two people. The thought left his mind as suddenly as it had arrived when he heard the faint chiming of his doorbell. It was time to go, because, round the angle of the stairs, they'd both be out of sight of the outer door. He picked up his bag and, walking on tiptoe, opened the door and slipped out. His car was parked right in front, opposite the Africans' white Cortina, and he unlocked the door, in that instant proud of the sureness with which his hands manipulated the keys.

He pulled away from the pavement quietly, taking care not to race the engine, and for a few seconds as he rolled towards the High Street he began to believe that he had given them the slip, and he grinned as he imagined them standing in front of the empty flat pressing angrily on the doorbell. But he'd only gone a hundred yards or so when he saw them running across the pavement and over the road. He pressed down the accelerator immediately, but he was still an appreciable distance from the safety of the High Street with its traffic and its myriad of turnings; and as fast as he went the Cortina seemed to be going faster, racing after him with its blazing lights dipping and glaring as it hit the bumps.

Gus pushed his speed up as far as he dared in the narrow street, hoping to catch the traffic signals at the end of the road while they were still green. He was about to let out his breath in relief at having made it, when, just a few yards from the corner the traffic lights blinked amber and then, almost immediately it seemed, went red. In the mirror the headlamps behind him glowed with the intensity of a laser, bathing the inside of his car with reflected light. Gus slowed automatically, then, without thinking about it, stamped again on the accelerator, spinning on through the lights and round the corner into the High Street. As he did so he realized that all his attention had been focused on what was happening to his rear, and he looked round just in time to see a container lorry bearing down on him, the driver pulling frantically at the wheel. Gus had another second of life left, and in this time he understood that there was nothing he could do, so he watched, a sort of fatalistic calm descending, as the lorry slid towards him, like the image of a juggernaut thundering out of a giant cinema screen. In the last moment, though, he understood that this was all too real, and he had just enough time to hope that his brother Danny would be all right without him before the container's massive wheels mounted the roof of his car, trapped him between two plates of grinding steel and, almost in the twinkling of an eye, crushed him to death.

Chapter Eleven

Danny had been trying to collect his package from the Student's Union office all day, but every time he thought about it something turned up to distract him. In the morning he overslept and only just made the start of his first lecture. Later on he'd gone into the computer centre to work on an essay he'd started the previous week and, instead, spent a couple of hours e-mailing with a girl in Leeds who'd begun to send him funny messages which had gradually turned into a rolling screed of soft porn. Then just as he'd begun to be absorbed in the War of the Austrian Succession he remembered that he had to meet Osman in the gym. It was the middle of the evening before he was able to set out to pick up the parcel, but on the way there he saw Simone, just emerging from the library, her bulging rucksack carried awkwardly over one arm. She was wearing a dark red flannel shirt over a tight micro, and watching her long bare thighs striding out ahead of him, Danny felt the evening had suddenly been transformed into a garden of possibilities. After all the hassle of the preceding day, seeing Simone all on her own like this was a stroke of luck he could hardly credit.

'That's the trouble with the library,' he said, coming up behind her. 'You can never get a book, 'cause all the mature students have got them. All work and no play, you spods.'

Close up she had a slightly crooked smile and large, warm brown eyes. She laughed at him, hoisting her bag over her shoulder.

'I've been working on my paper for next week,' she told him. 'Trying to make it at least half as interesting as Karen's. Maybe you'll stay awake this time.'

When he suggested going for a drink her eyes narrowed a little, something speculative about the look, then she turned away, considering.

'Is this a bad time?' Danny asked quickly.

'No. No,' she said. 'Let's go.'

They went to a pub off the campus. The union bar would be full of creeps, Danny told her. If it occurred to her that he wanted to avoid being interrupted, she kept the thought to herself. As it happened, the evening went in exactly the way that Danny was hoping. He was a good listener. Living in half a dozen foster homes and competing for the attention of a succession of mothers had taught him what it took to make himself likeable. Under his sympathetic gaze, and prompted by his questions, hesitant but acute, she relaxed. Being a student was great, she told him, because it was something she'd wanted to do for a very long time, but she felt isolated. Everyone else seemed younger or older or incredibly boring.

'It's this place,' Danny said. 'It's full of nerds, gits, wankers, the lot.'

Simone smiled. She was fascinated by Flegenhauer, she said, because he'd seen and done so much, and she had always wondered what it would be like to be a person like that, in exile from his native country, unable to go back, cut loose from all the moorings that gave most people their feelings of security. It was not as if he'd begun life as some kind of outsider. On the contrary, he'd been a normal person with a normal family. Then it had all been swept away.

Listening to her, Danny felt a sudden flood of anger, unexpected and uncontrollable.

'Don't you understand?' he said suddenly. 'Flegenhauer isn't like that at all. You're talking about some kind of old European peasant or some suburban git whose horizons are closed in by a few acres of land or the neighbour's allotment. My granddad planted potatoes here, they reckon, so I can't move. That's the real rural idiocy, families sat there waiting for the neighbours to come and kill them so they can own the potato field. Little parcels of land, little houses, territory. It's pathetic. It's not even worthy of your ridiculous romanticism. It's nationalistic, xenophobic. You can only think like that because you're locked into a safe narrow-minded existence in a safe narrow-minded country. You can't reduce a man like Flegenhauer to that level however much you try.'

Simone was frowning now. When they sat down she had put her packet of fags on the table next to her drink and now she picked them up and reached for her bag. Seeing the gesture, Danny guessed that she was about to walk out on him.

'Please,' he said hurriedly. 'I didn't intend to offend you. Don't be. It's just that this is about history. The reason why it's worth reading at all. It's the reason why I'm into Flegenhauer too.'

She leaned back, away from his outstretched hand, but she let the rucksack drop to the floor beside her chair.

'I'm not offended,' she said. 'I'm just pissed off at your arrogance. You don't know any more than I do about Flegenhauer. You've got no idea what he thinks about that.'

'Yes I do,' he told her. 'And I've heard that before. Every time a black man expresses a definite opinion somebody says he's arrogant.'

Her face flushed red.

'Oh God,' she said. 'This is ridiculous. I didn't mean that. I'd have said that about anyone.' She pushed her glass away from her. 'I'd better go.'

'Wait a minute,' Danny said. 'I'll take your word for it. Just let me explain what I mean.' She shrugged. He crouched forward over the table, cutting the distance between them, and lowered his voice.

'I don't know much about my dad, but he was born in some hole which he left as soon as he could. So he chose to cut himself off from all the associations, customs, territory, and all the rest of it that you're saying is so important. But that didn't make him less. It made him more than some idiot who sits in the same place his whole life. He exercised a choice to become what he was. Most people don't even know the choice exists.'

'That's different,' she replied.

'Why? You're reducing people to their ancestry or their parentage or the pile of potatoes their granddad planted and saying you can't be an authentic human being without it. That's what happened in Bosnia. Try your home and mother and native country bullshit on that.'

Looking up, he saw that Simone's expression had changed. Now it was almost anguished, and it struck Danny that she was intensely embarrassed, as much by his anger as by what he'd said.

'I'm sorry,' she said. 'I don't know what's going on with you. But I think I'd better go.'

Danny's anger evaporated instantly as he realized that he'd almost lost the plot of the evening.

'Sorry. I don't know why I went off at you. It's nothing to do with you or Flegenhauer. It's just that things are tense at the moment. Don't go. Please.' He struck a pose of supplication. 'Look, I'm apologizing here.'

For a few seconds Simone watched him cautiously as if he might suddenly do something unpredictable or violent.

'So what's your father become?' she asked.

'He got killed before I was born.'

According to Gus, their father had been stabbed in a fight outside a pub in Nottingham.

'I never knew him,' he said, 'so I don't feel much about it.'

This was more or less true, but Simone winced as if she didn't believe it.

'Oh shit,' Danny muttered, 'I really wanted to talk because you're the only person worth talking to in that damn group and I'm getting off on the wrong foot.'

'Oh no,' Simone told him, 'I'm sorry. I didn't understand.'

Danny didn't point out that she had nothing to apologize for.

Instead, he was at his most contrite and persuasive. In the end Simone, relaxing, agreed to go for a Chinese meal so they could talk a bit more, and to give him a chance to make up for having a go at her.

In the restaurant she told him more about herself. It was as if Danny's outburst had broken the barriers between them and she wanted him to know that she too was a person with hidden depths and undercurrents of sorrow and despair. When he asked her why she'd decided to leave a safe job and become a student, she told him that she'd fallen in love with a married man at the age of eighteen and been going with him until it ended a couple of years ago. After that she'd been determined to change the way she was. Resuming her education had seemed the natural first step.

Afterwards, Danny thought of that night as a sort of prelude to the era which was just about to open, as if being with Simone marked some kind of transition in his life.

They went back to the flat which she shared with a postgraduate lawyer. All the way there Danny felt an undercurrent of delighted anticipation. Somehow, he thought, he'd got it right. At the same time her matter-of-fact style confused him a little. Inside the flat they sat on the sofa kissing, but before long she got up, took him by the hand and led him into the bedroom, where, without any further preliminaries, she switched on a reading lamp on the floor, shut the door firmly, took her clothes off and climbed into bed. Light-headed, almost trembling with excitement, Danny stripped, forcing himself not to turn away from her gaze. Then, leaving his clothes scattered on the floor, he climbed in after her. They kissed. Her hand searched, found his penis and stroked it gently.

'You're not circumcised,' she whispered.

'Of course not,' Danny said.

'How old are you?' she asked him. Beside him on the pillow, her eyes shone, drawing him to her.

'Twenty-one,' Danny said. 'Does it matter?'

She shook her head, and, quickly, closing her eyes, joined her open mouth to his. In a moment she shifted her grip to his wrist and moved his hand between her thighs. When she shuddered and gave an audible sigh, the sound vibrated against his lips. Danny's penis rose hard against her belly, and she pulled away suddenly.

'I won't be a minute,' she said.

She rummaged beside the bed, and then she was back facing him, her hands moving skilfully, rolling a condom on him with a couple of swift movements. Then she lay back, one arm round his neck, pulling him down and over her.

Next morning Danny woke up to the sound of Simone bustling about, getting ready for her first lecture. She told him there was coffee in the kitchen and to be sure he locked the door after him when he let himself out. The bedroom door closed behind her, then he heard the outer door slam.

Later, it struck Danny that if he hadn't bumped into Simone that night, and if he hadn't stayed the night at her place, the madness would have started earlier. As it was he had no inkling of what was to come.

The morning was fine and bright, the sun already burning off the last hint of moisture in the air, and Danny strolled comfortably through the city centre, his footsteps weighted down by a kind of languorous, heavy holiday mood, in no great hurry to get anywhere. Even so, he reached the faculty building just in time to get into the lecture room after the mid-morning break. The lecture was about the Treaty of Rome, delivered by a man who cropped up from time to time on the TV news, and the room was crowded. Danny sat at the back, half-asleep. In that state he could hardly hear what the lecturer was saying and, in any case, his head was swimming with dreams and images from the night before. He kept wondering how Simone felt. They'd only had a couple of hours' sleep, so the energy with which she'd banged her way out in the morning had been a surprise. She'd been unexpectedly tender, too, once he was inside her, her arms and legs wound round him, her body moving with his movements with a sweet, slow rhythm he could still feel. Hours later Danny still had an erection and he tugged his jacket over to hide the bulge.

When the lecture was over he sat still for a few minutes, letting the other students file out, while he struggled for control. A hand fell on his shoulder.

'There's a package for you down the union,' a voice said in his ear.

Danny grunted his acknowledgement without looking up. This package, he thought, was beginning to follow him around like some kind of psychic burden. The image took his mind off Simone, and in a moment he was able to get up and start walking over to the union building. This time, he thought, I'm not going to be distracted. I'm going right over there now, and get the damn thing.

He had expected it to be bigger, but it was only a yard long, a rectangle of brown paper, carefully secured with string and sticky tape. Looking at it, he had the strange feeling that, without his noticing, Christmas Day or his birthday had come round. It was on those days that he used to receive parcels like this, tightly wrapped, decorated with red or green labels, marked with broken circles of black ink. There was no name or return address on the outside of it, but somehow he knew it was from Gus. As he carried it awkwardly back to his room, he felt a flush of anticipation at the thought of opening it. When he tore the outer skin of wrapping paper off, however, there was a letter addressed to him strapped to the side of the parcel. There was also a message on the envelope, just below his name, scrawled in big black capitals, as if Gus wanted to be sure he didn't miss it. READ THIS LETTER NOW.

Danny tore the envelope open impatiently. *'Dear Danny,'* he read: *'Please put this package somewhere safe until I collect it. I'm sending it to you because you are the only person I can trust. If anyone asks you what it is you can say that I sent you some books, but it's really important that you keep it a secret. Life and death stuff. Don't open it either, unless something happens to me. I'll try to get up your way in a couple of days and take it off your hands. Thanks a lot. Be in touch. Gus.'*

Danny read the letter a couple of times. He was tempted to open the package and find out what was so important, but then he shrugged his shoulders. Gus must have had a good reason for asking him not to look, and presumably he would reveal the secret when he arrived. For a moment it occurred to him that this might be a present for him which Gus intended to be a surprise. He weighed the parcel in his hands, wondering, but eventually he gave up and put it away in the bottom of the wardrobe, along with his shoes and his sports bag. It would be as safe there as anywhere else, he thought.

He was lying back on the bed, thinking idly about what to do next, when he heard a firm knock at the door. He opened it, expecting to see Osman. Instead, a policeman was standing there, accompanied by another man who he guessed was a plainclothes detective. The panicky thought ran through his mind that Spin and his woman had framed them and this was the result. I'm innocent, he told himself. A phrase popped into his head: They can smell fear.

'What can I do for you?' he asked, with all the coolness he could muster.

'Can we come in?' the uniformed policeman said.

'What's it about?'

If they had come to arrest him, he thought, they would have done so immediately, and they wouldn't have been so polite. This had to be a warning or something like it.

'Are you Danny Dixon?'

Danny thought about denying it, then decided that there was no point. He was a student, he thought, with access to legal help. Besides, he was innocent. The union would support him. He nodded. 'Yes.'

'We'd like a word.'

'What about?'

'It would be better if we came in, sir.'

The cop's polite manner had eventually convinced Danny, and he stepped back to let them in. He left the door ajar, though, and he kept a few paces between them, watching carefully for an aggressive move.

'Do you have a brother by the name of Augustus Dixon?' the policeman who was doing the talking asked.

In a flash Danny knew why they were there. Somewhere inside him he had feared this all along, right from the day when Gus had told him about their dad bleeding to death on the pavement, and then about how their mum had put herself to sleep forever lying upon the bed in the room next to theirs.

'Has something happened to him?'

He could hear his own voice, weak and hoarse, trembling with fear. A sudden pressure was coming and going in his chest. The cops looked at each other. A single quick glance. The policeman closest to him clasped his hands together in front of him, his right hand gripping and squeezing the thumb on his left.

'There's been an accident,' he said.

Chapter Twelve

For the rest of the afternoon Danny sat or lay on the bed staring at the walls. Sometimes he got under the duvet and tried to sleep. After a while he would get up and make himself a cup of coffee. He thought about getting drunk, but there was no alcohol in the room and, in any case, he knew it would make him feel worse. He thought about going out to buy some dope, any kind of dope, but the next thing he thought of was what Gus would say about that. Sometimes he cried. Mostly he tried to think about Gus the way he was in that time years ago when his big brother had been the most important feature of his life. To pull the warm memory of Gus round him would have been a comfort. Instead, his mind kept on returning to the image of the car, crushed and mangled beneath the wheels of a truck, blood leaking from its gaping joints.

The peculiar thing was that he had seen this before. It was a trick his mind practised on him from time to time, and he was never quite sure that this wasn't a game that he played on himself, a legacy of the bad days when grief and loneliness burned in his heart like flashes of red flame. Gus used to say that fear was nothing. It was natural. A man chased by a lion would find that the fear he experienced gave him speed and strength. What was bad, Gus said, was the fear of things you couldn't put your finger on. The fear that kept you awake at night, the fear which came out in dreams and visions inside your head. This was after Danny told him about the dream that kept coming back, the nightmare that he had once killed someone. Sometimes he woke up crying.

Gus had been quiet a long time after he heard this. Then he had told Danny how he'd felt when he found their mum, and knew that she was really dead and gone, and never coming back. Afterwards he had avoided the memory, he told Danny, as if it were an angry dog inside him. Then one day he found himself summoning up her image and confronting his terror. At first, thinking about her like that had given him a shock of pain, a jolt as strong as if he'd stuck his finger in an electric socket. Then the pain began to fade, growing less and less intense until he was able to think about her from the outside, and remember that she'd had a real existence apart from what he felt. That was important, Gus said, to remember that she had been real.

When Danny tried it he found that Gus had been right. Although the things he pictured were terrible, he understood immediately that the way he felt when he had been struggling to fence them off from his imagination was a great deal worse. Eventually something else struck him. This was years later, eating a banana on the bus on the way to school. By then he was in the fourth year, master of his demons, and he was transfixed by the revelation, pausing with half a banana aiming for his mouth, discovering the idea that everything he knew about his parents, and all the feelings he associated with them, had been passed on by Gus. It would have been possible, he thought in that moment, for Gus to have invented it all. He knew that wasn't so, but he also knew it meant that Gus had exerted all the cunning determination he could command in order to fill the void in Danny's heart. It was Gus who was real, and not the mum and dad he imagined so often. It was Gus all the time. It was Gus, too, who had told him that their mother was beautiful and kind and would never have hurt or neglected them, and that she had loved having a new baby, so that what she'd done couldn't be anything to do with him.

'I bet you were lying,' he said aloud.

He laughed, a flood of affection momentarily replacing his misery. His mind went back to Simone and the conversation in the pub. When he talked about his father, he had been thinking about his brother, and his admiration for Flegenhauer was partly to do with an ideal of engagement and intellectual force which he had learned from Gus. One of his constant fantasies had been that Gus would one day write a book about black culture and history which would become essential reading. Somewhere in this future he would stroll into the library with a girlfriend and pick the book up.

'This one's by my brother,' he would remark casually, 'kind of interesting.'

The phone rang in the early evening. It was dark in the room, but Danny hadn't bothered to put the lights on, and he fumbled for the phone, locating it by touch. It was Osman on the other end.

'What's going on? Where've you been? You didn't come down the gym.'

'I've been in all afternoon,' Danny told him. 'Something's happened to my brother. He's had an accident.'

Afterwards he remembered his friend's reaction with a kind of wonder. Osman had gone quiet, and when he spoke there was a tone of shock and concern in his voice.

'I'll come over now.'

It was when he put the phone down that he remembered the parcel Gus had sent. The thought of it lying in the bottom of his wardrobe made him shudder. This must have been his brother's last communication, although he couldn't have known at the time.

He switched the lights on, rummaged for the parcel and dragged it out into the middle of the floor. Somehow it seemed heavier than when he'd brought it back. Danny's fingers trembled as he stripped away the wrapping paper, and as he revealed the contents of the package the light bulb overhead seemed to flicker. He looked up quickly, then realized that it must have been an illusion created by the light glinting off the surface of the mask. He propped it up and looked at it closely, struggling with a sense of disappointment. He had expected something more than one of his brother's African souvenirs. He touched it lightly, but something about it seemed to attract his fingers, forcing them to linger, stroking the warm golden skin. It looked like gold, he thought, and it felt like it too. Then he shook his head. A thing like this made of real gold would be more valuable than he could imagine. It had to be a fake. He turned it round to examine the rectangle of wood on which it was mounted and it was then that he saw the envelope attached by a hinge of Sellotape to the back. Gus had written his name on it in the same big black letters as the letter on the outside.

Danny's hands shook as he detached the envelope and opened it. The letter was handwritten, on several sheets of lined paper, their edges jagged as if Gus had torn them out of a ledger. Danny found himself fighting back the tears, unable to see what Gus had written, and it was a couple of minutes before he could get back enough control to spread the sheets out and begin reading.

'Dear Danny,' Gus had written, 'If you're reading this it means I'm either dead or been nicked, and I just hope that it's not too long after the event. So I'm hoping, for obvious reasons, that you never see this. But I'm writing it because I owe you an explanation, and I want you to know what to do if the shit hits the fan. First things first. You've seen the mask by now, so I'll tell you what it is, in case you haven't guessed. It's called the Dancing Face of the Great Oba and it's a priceless relic that the British stole from West Africa. You don't need to know how I got hold of it. What's important is that once the news breaks that it's gone everyone will be after it. It's meant to be exhibited soon, but they won't be able to, of course, because it's disappeared. My intention is to get as much publicity out of it as I can. There's a Commonwealth conference coming up soon, and I think I can use the mask to put the cat among the pigeons. You'll be wondering why I didn't choose a more conventional way of doing it, I suppose, like writing to the papers or demonstrating or seeing my MP or some other bullshit. I've asked myself that a lot during the last week. The answer being that nobody in this country gives a bugger. Just look at how they treat foreign aid. After all the resources Europe has taken out of Africa, you'd think they'd have some kind of shame. Instead they treat it like the trickle from a tap which they can turn off and on whenever they feel like it, and even that is always used to exploit the people of Africa. So there's no hope of persuading them to take the issue of making reparations to Africa seriously, not even to give back a few of the precious sculptures they robbed, never mind anything more substantial. But you know what we used to say. Don't get mad, get even. The Dancing Face is going back eventually, but not to some bunch of evil dictators. I'm determined about that one. Ideally I'd like the people of South Africa to have it, or someone decent like Jerry Rawlings. I don't know. All that is down the road. What matters is that if you're reading this you're on your own, which I'm sorry about. I don't know what the exact circumstances will be so I can't tell you what to do next. The best thing would be to get in touch with my friend Eleanor and she'll help you sort things out. I want you to bear one thing in mind whatever you decide. Being brought up the way we were, we didn't have a very strong grasp of our background or where we were going. Once I started getting involved with this business I discovered something, though, which is that we're here for a reason. Because of our mum we were born with a kind of ringside seat in the white world. I know we felt like outsiders, but compared with some starving villager in Somalia we were privileged. At the same time, because of our dad we were given a special mission to change things. All right, I know none of us have any obligation to choose the mission. That's European culture, the cult of the individual. It tells you to do what you want and never mind anyone else. If, however, you take the African part of your identity seriously, it means that you have to try and share in some kind of communal destiny. I don't know what it is, but I know that we have a unique opportunity to do something positive that only we can. It's like bringing the two sides of yourself together. But it's not like some meeting of peace and harmony. That's a bullshit fantasy. The two sides are in conflict, *and I think the way to go is to force both of them to recognize that conflict and resolve it. That's what I'm trying to do with the Dancing Face. It's up to you now if you're reading this letter, so I hope you agree with me. I don't know if you do, because we haven't talked for so long and at your age everything changes fast. But I trust you. Whatever you do will be okay. But watch yourself. By now if I'm not around Eleanor will know what's going down. She'll tell you about the sharks. Like I said, I hope you're not reading this, but if you are, one love. Always. Gus.*

When Danny read the last line, he felt tears springing from his eyes. He dropped the sheets of paper on the floor, curled up on the bed and cried for the first time, without trying to hold himself back. It was as if Gus had been speaking to him, and inside his chest Danny's heart felt bruised and broken by the knowledge that he would never see him again.

He was still on the bed, head buried in his arms, when he heard Osman's knock on the door, and he hurried to dry his eyes and splash some water on his face before he opened it. Osman was standing awkwardly, his pose suggesting that he was uncertain about what to do or how to behave.

Inside the room he sat on the floor his back against the bed. Danny told him about the police turning up and how they'd told him about Gus. Osman nodded soberly. He'd never met Gus, but Danny's sorrow was almost tangible, the air of the room thick with its vibrations. When Danny's story came to an end the room went silent.

'Take a look at that,' Danny said eventually.

The mask had been out of the angle of Osman's sight up to that point and Danny turned it round so that it could seen. Osman grunted in surprise.

'What's that? It's not what I think it is. Is it?' He laughed at his gullibility. 'No, it couldn't be.'

'What do you think it is?' Danny asked him.

'It looks like a Yoruba mask,' Osman said slowly. He edged away from it and stood up, then bent over to look at it more closely. 'But if it was it would be one of those they took out of Africa and stuck in a cellar in the British Museum, and that would be impossible.' He looked round at Danny, doubt creasing his face. 'Wouldn't it?'

In reply Danny handed him the letter. As Osman made to take it, Danny hesitated, remembering that Gus had meant it for his eyes alone. Then he dismissed the thought. It was all up with Gus, and if he was going to solve the problem of this legacy he could do with all the help he could get.

Osman read the letter, frowning. When he'd finished he folded it carefully and gave it back to Danny.

'Shit,' he said. 'This is big trouble, man.'

'I don't know,' Danny replied. 'Only if I get involved. I was thinking about dumping it back at the gallery it came from or the British Museum or something.' An idea struck him. 'You could take it in to your High Commission. Say you found it, or just leave it somewhere they'd find it.'

'No way,' Osman said. 'You don't understand. Wars start in West Africa over less than this. It's not just some mask. It's like a sacred thing. It's like Westminster Abbey and the Tate Gallery rolled into one with the bones of your ancestors inside. Own this and you can have as much influence as you want. If I took this to some official I'd probably be killed within the week to shut me up. This is bad news, man.'

'Come on,' Danny said, astonished by Osman's reaction. 'Half of them are Christians. They'll be too sophisticated for that shit. Guys like your father.'

'It's not some bunch of niggers bowing down in front of a fetish, if that's what you mean,' Osman snapped. 'What do you think they keep in Lourdes or Westminster or the Tower of London or Canterbury Cathedral? Sacred objects. Leaders of society go and drop to their knees – no one says they're worshipping fetishes. The difference is that our politics are still tied up with spirituality, animism, call it what you like. It's kind of volatile. Something like this can give you power, it can get you killed, it can start wars. It's trouble. I don't even want to be near it.'

Danny stared at him, dumbstruck. Even after reading the letter he hadn't grasped its implications. Osman looked away from him, something anxious about his expression.

'I know you don't want to hear this,' he said. 'But do you think your brother's accident could be something to do with this?'

'How could it be? The cops said that it was a container coming from Folkestone. They said he jumped the lights and ran straight into it.' Suddenly he was in a rage he couldn't control, and he was shouting at Osman. 'It's not so fucking easy to arrange them things, dickhead!'

Osman held his hands up in a pacifying gesture.

'Sorry, man. Sorry. It's just that this is heavy, you know.'

Danny rested his face in his hands, trying to calm the roaring in his head.

'All right,' he muttered. 'Not your fault.'

'You going down there today?' Osman asked. 'You want me to come?'

The question startled Danny. He'd forgotten, or rather, he'd deliberately put out of his mind the fact that the police had asked him to go down to London and identify Gus. For a moment he was tempted by Osman's offer, and he could feel the warmth of the friendship behind it, but he also knew that he wanted to be alone on this trip. The journey would be like a lone vigil during which he would think about Gus, hoping that, wherever he was, his brother would feel the strength of his love.

'No. I'll go and catch the next train. I'll see you when I get back.'

'What about that?'

Osman nodded cautiously at the mask. Danny shrugged.

'I don't know. I'll leave it here for the moment. I'll talk to my brother's woman and see what was going down. I can't be bothered right now.'

'Take my advice,' Osman said. 'Do what he told you. Keep it quiet. Don't leave it out in the open.'

Danny nodded. He bent down and wrapped it in the original wrapping paper, winding the string round it. Then he lifted it and placed it back in the bottom of the wardrobe. He pulled his dressing gown down and spread it over so that the bump on the floor of the cupboard looked like a bundle of washing, then he closed the door, locked it and put the key in his pocket. Then he looked at Osman, who had made no move to help him, not even offering a hand to carry it across the room.

'I'm going now,' Danny said.

Osman nodded and turned away to go out of the door. He had already opened it when he turned back towards Danny, his forehead creased, his lips pursed tight together.

'Listen, I'm sorry about your brother. Good luck. Hope you're all right.' He paused. 'Just watch yourself.'

Later on, it occurred to Danny that these were almost exactly the same words of warning that Gus had used in his letter. *Watch yourself.*

Chapter Thirteen

When he arrived in London, Danny went straight to his brother's flat because there was nowhere else to go. It was past midnight as he climbed the stairs and in the silence of the building there was an eerie echoing sound about his footsteps. On the landing he fumbled for the keys, then stopped as he noticed that the door was already slightly open. He pushed it, and it swung wide open revealing the dark hallway. He reached in, and flipped the light switch before entering, moving cautiously, one step at a time. After he'd made a tour of the flat, switching all the lights on and making sure that there was no one lurking in any of the rooms, he returned to the door. It had been forced open, and the spring lock was dangling uselessly by one twisted screw. Danny found a screwdriver and fixed it back on. When he finished the door closed tightly enough, but it was obvious that one good push would be enough to open it up again. He turned the key on the second lock and went back to exploring the flat. To judge by the look of it, the place had been burgled. The sofa and the armchairs had been tipped upside down, the lining torn open, springs poking out in every direction like unruly shoots. The carpets had been lifted and rolled back. The bed had been slit open, great handfuls of kapok littering the bedroom floor. There were books and papers scattered everywhere.

Danny set to work in the bedroom, pushing the stuffing back in the mattress and piling the clothes and shoes in the cupboards. Then he took his shoes and his jacket off, lay down, and tried to sleep. He'd left all the lights on, but, even so, there was a kind of expectant silence around him, as if the flat was waiting for something to happen. After a while Gus came in the door and stood by the bed. 'What you doing here?' he asked. 'You've messed everything up.' Danny tried to speak, but all that emerged was a sort of moaning sound. 'You're dead,' he croaked eventually. Gus smiled as if that was funny. 'That's what everybody thinks,' he said.

Danny woke up with a start, fighting to breathe. For a few seconds his only thought was to go back to sleep so that he could bring Gus back and talk to him, ask him the questions which were chasing round inside his head. Then he was awake.

It was already light, a dull morning, the sky covered by dingy grey clouds. Danny went through the flat switching off the lights. Then he made himself a cup of coffee in the kitchen. He opened the fridge and turned his face away, repelled by the smell. It made him think of graveyards, and then, involuntarily, of his brother's body decomposing. Gritting his teeth he foraged in the fridge until he located the source of the stink, a liquefying bundle of spinach and an ancient carton of cream. He felt easier after he'd disposed of them. He drank another cup of coffee, washed himself, shaved, brushed his teeth and put on a clean shirt.

While he got ready for the day, Danny wondered about the wreckage of the flat. In normal circumstances he would have called the police, but the mess the intruders had left behind signalled a careless savagery in which no ordinary burglar would have indulged. It had to be something to do with the mask. His brother's motives had been political, not mercenary, but the police would call it theft, and if he attracted their attention he would have no way of controlling what they found out. At least the burglars must know now that the mask wasn't in the flat, so they wouldn't be back. He was safe enough, and the best thing, he thought, was to do the business, see Gus off, then think about the rest of it. He hadn't yet made a conscious decision about what to do, but, at the back of his mind, he knew that he would keep the package hidden until he understood what Gus would have wanted.

He found the number that the policeman had given him the previous day, telephoned and arranged to make the formal identification at the hospital where Gus had been taken. As he did so his eye fell on the address book Gus kept by the phone. He picked it up and leafed through the pages slowly, trying to remember. Gus had spoken to him a couple of months previously about a new girlfriend. He'd said that he would bring her up to visit Danny as soon as he could manage it. Danny had been curious, but not interested enough for the girl's name to make an impression. Now he was struggling to recall the exact words that Gus had used, and hoping that when he saw her name in the book he would recognize it. Afterwards he was never sure whether he remembered the name in the instant he saw it, or whether it was the way that Gus had underlined it and then circled it. Whichever it was, Danny was certain that he'd located the right one. Justine Oyebanjoh. She answered on the first ring, her voice a little breathless and abstracted.

When Danny said who he was, there were a few seconds of silence.

'Did you say Gus's brother?'

Her voice was pitched higher, the sound of it incredulous.

'That's right,' Danny told her. 'I wasn't sure you knew, so I rang up.'

'I heard.' Her voice wavered a little. 'I thought you were up North.'

'I just came down.'

She didn't reply. Danny imagined her standing at the other end of the line, waiting for him to say something.

'I'd like to talk to you,' he said. 'Can we meet later on?'

'What do you want to talk about?'

Danny felt a twinge of anger. It should have been obvious, he thought, that when your brother was killed suddenly you'd want to talk about him to his friends.

'I don't know,' he said. 'I hadn't seen him for ages. I just want to know what was doing with him. How he was.'

She was silent again, for so long that Danny thought they might have been cut off.

'All right,' she replied eventually. 'But I don't have much to tell you.'

After he put the phone down Danny looked for Eleanor Hutchinson's name in the book. When he rang it he got the university switchboard. The operator put him through to a machine which said that Dr Hutchinson wasn't there but that he could leave a message. Danny opened his mouth to speak when he heard the pips, but suddenly he didn't know what to say and he slammed the phone back on its stand. Immediately he'd done so it occurred to him that Eleanor wouldn't know what had happened to Gus. Reluctantly he dialled the number again, and he listened to the recorded message in a mood of uncertainty, wondering what to say, how to tell her his dreadful news. Somewhere inside him was the desire to hurt her, to say something cruel, something that would make her understand how deep his emotions ran, and the knowledge struck him with the force of a discovery. When he was younger and Gus had gone away, he had wanted to be with him wherever and however he lived, but Gus had always said it was impossible, that he was better off where he was. Later on when Gus talked about Eleanor as his friend, Danny used to nurse a secret fear that she was someone about whom Gus had come to care – more than he cared for his own brother. In his heart he had known that it couldn't be true, but, standing in the empty flat, the telephone in his hand, waiting to tell Eleanor that Gus was dead, the torment of those ancient thoughts filled his mind.

On the way to the hospital his feet dragged as if they'd been encased in lead. The plainclothes policeman who met him was a middle-aged man with a worried expression, a bushy moustache and close-cropped brown hair receding in front. They shook hands and walked down a long curving avenue of gravel which led round to the back of the main building. At the entrance a man in a short white coat led them through a corridor into a long room with a number of tables laid out in a row. Gus was lying on the second table. Danny had been steeling himself for an ugly and shattering sight, but the face was more or less unmarked, except for a slight puffiness along one side. Danny had intended to take a quick look and walk away. Instead he found himself gazing at Gus as if trying to fix his features in his mind. The odd thing was how intensely dead Gus appeared. It was nothing like sleep, Danny found himself thinking. He had seen his brother asleep several times and this had no similarity. This was like death. It was in his extreme stillness. It was in the way his face pointed straight at the ceiling. It was in the shrunken look of him, like a wax model which had come out just a shade too small.

The attendant cleared his throat and Danny turned away at last.

'That's my brother,' he told the policeman.

Outside the hospital gates, Danny began walking without purpose or direction, letting his footsteps take him where they wanted. He had prepared himself for the ordeal, but now it was over he felt empty, as weightless as a dried-up leaf blowing along the pavement.

In front of him a long black car pulled up to the kerb, and a bulky black man wearing a peaked hat got out and gestured to him. Danny looked at him closely, wondering whether this was someone he had met years ago, or whether it was a friend of his brother's. It might have been his mood, but something about the car reminded him of an undertaker.

'Mr Dixon,' the man said. He had a round fat face with a small mouth and protruding lips. 'Doctor Okigbo wants to speak to you.'

'Who's that?' Danny asked him. He'd never heard the name before, but it was clear the man knew who he was.

'In the car.'

Danny heard a faint whining sound. Beside him the smoked glass of the rear window slid down to reveal the face of a middle-aged African, his hair brushed to a glossy sheen and parted in the middle.

'I am Doctor Okigbo,' the man said. 'I was a friend of your brother's. Can I give you a lift?'

Danny hesitated, a long-forgotten memory surfacing in his mind: on the way home from school, holding his big brother's hand tight. 'Never get in a car with someone you don't know,' Gus had said.

The door of the car swung open and Danny got in. On the inside it was as big as it had seemed, with soft leather seats, a lush, heavy carpet underfoot and enough room to stretch his legs out. As Danny settled himself the African watched him without speaking, as if weighing him up. He was wearing a black silk jacket, light-coloured trousers and shoes of the same brilliant white as his shirt. The man's clothes and his pose in the corner of the car's plush interior gave Danny the feeling that he was looking at a glossy photograph in the centre of a celebrity mag. The car moved off.

'Were you his doctor?' Danny asked.

Okigbo shook his head, smiling gently.

'I'm not a medical doctor at all.'

Danny muttered an apology, but Okigbo waved it aside, the same gentle smile curving his lips.

'It's the natural conclusion when you meet a doctor coming out of a hospital. I'm actually an economist, or rather I've got a doctorate in economics, which isn't necessarily the same thing.'

His smile broadened, but Danny didn't respond. It was the sort of poncy self-deprecating remark his personal tutor might have made, and Danny found it boringly pretentious. In ordinary circumstances he might have smiled in order to be sociable, but today wasn't the day. Suddenly he was sorry to have accepted the man's offer of a lift. He wanted to be alone.

'I would have left you alone,' Dr Okigbo said, 'but I have a problem I thought you might be able to help me with.'

'I don't see how.'

'Well, it depends,' Dr Okigbo said. 'This is a bad time, I know. But it is urgent.'

A question struck Danny.

'How did you know I was here?'

'I enquired at the hospital. They said a relative was coming today. It's no mystery.'

Danny didn't know whether or not to believe that. He had the impression that hospitals didn't tell anyone anything they didn't have to. On the other hand, he had no reason to doubt Okigbo's word.

'What can I do for you?'

'You don't trust me.' Okigbo sounded reproachful. 'I can understand that. I suppose Gus never mentioned me.'

'No.'

'Ah,' Dr Okigbo barked. 'Now I understand. I would feel the same in your place. Believe me.' He paused, took a white handkerchief out of his jacket pocket and patted his forehead gently. 'Let me explain. I exaggerated a little when I said I was a friend of your brother's. Our relationship was mainly business. Of course,

I respected your brother. What has happened is a tragedy.' He touched the handkerchief to his face again. 'But this is the problem. I'm a collector of African art. As you know, your brother was very knowledgeable. Sometimes he bought things for me.' He paused. 'I am a very rich man. When people know that I am interested the price goes up. Your brother was very helpful. The problem is that last week he bought a piece for me. A Yoruba mask.'

Danny forced himself not to react, although his heart pounded with the shock of it. He felt at the same moment that Okigbo's gaze had sharpened and was focused, like a single point of heat on his face. Okigbo laughed and tucked his handkerchief away.

'Of course,' he continued, 'it was a fake, concocted by a cousin of mine and sold to a white collector with a story about its age and value. It's easy to fool white collectors about such things. I could tell you some stories.' He laughed again. 'The point is that I asked your brother to buy it, and take it off the market. I wanted it out of sentiment. Also to save the embarrassment of one of my family being charged with fraud. A thing like that could be used against me.' Okigbo touched Danny's knee lightly. 'The problem is that Gus had already bought it when he had his tragic accident, and I don't know where it is. I thought that perhaps you might know.' He put his hand in his pocket and produced a piece of paper, holding it, like a magician, between two extended fingers. 'I thought you might like to see some evidence that what I'm saying is true, so I brought this with me.'

He handed Danny the paper. It was a receipt for two thousand pounds signed with his brother's name at the bottom. Danny looked at it closely. As far as he could tell it was his brother's signature. Okigbo reached out and, with a deft twitch, took the paper back. Deliberately, he tore it in two and tossed it on the floor.

'The money isn't important,' he said. 'That is what I think about the money. I would give more than that to have your brother sitting here with me doing business as usual. But that does not solve the problem. If you have this piece, or you know where it is, or you can help me find it, I will pay you what Gus paid for it. Two thousand pounds.'

Danny's brain raced. Without the letter, he thought, he would have believed Okigbo. Even then, before his conversation with Osman, he might have imagined that Gus had been somehow mistaken. But he knew now that Okigbo was lying. At the same time he had the odd feeling that Okigbo already knew he didn't believe any of it. Behind his performance there was some other purpose.

The idea calmed Danny. If the car, the receipt and the story were merely props in some elaborate game, then Okigbo was just another con man, and he'd met those before.

'Perhaps,' Danny said, turning round to look at him, 'it's in the flat. I could look for it.'

'Perhaps.' Okigbo nodded as if impressed by Danny's willingness to help. 'But I think Gus had other places in which he kept valuable items. You're brothers. Perhaps he told you.'

Danny stared out of the window, pretending to think. Suddenly he was feeling a kind of pleasure at being embroiled in this game. He didn't know the rules, or what the point was, or why it was being played, but the fact was that Okigbo, too, was in the dark, because he couldn't know who held the most important card.

'No,' Danny said. 'The flat is all I can think of. I really don't think I can help you.'

The car stopped. Peering through the window Danny saw that they had come to a halt opposite his brother's flat. Okigbo leaned towards him and offered him a card.

'If you think of anything that might help, please telephone me. Anytime.'

Danny took it without speaking. He noticed that Okigbo's smile had gone, and that something about the atmosphere inside the car had changed during the ride from the hospital. At first Okigbo had seemed relaxed, lolling like a lizard against the soft cushions. Now he was sitting upright, like a cat about to spring, his eyes glaring. Danny fumbled at the door, for the first time feeling a touch of trepidation, and his confusion grew as his fingers slid over the slick lining. The air was heavy with a strange sweet smell. Something like papaya or mangoes, Danny guessed, a corner of his brain clutching at the riddle. Behind him Okigbo grunted. There was a sort of metallic whisper, and the door swung open. Danny got out quickly, and, before the door closed, he looked back just in time to catch a glimpse of Okigbo, sitting bolt upright in the corner, staring straight ahead.

Chapter Fourteen

It had been a big mistake getting in touch with the African, Rodney told Baz for the hundredth time. The problem was that they didn't have the fucking mask, otherwise those university dickheads and the cops would never have dared to give them a briefcase full of paper. Then run them round Ally Pally on top of that. And then on top of that and all, Gus had to go and tell the African everything after all his talk about secrecy and confidentiality. So far everyone had been taking the piss, Rodney said, just because they didn't have the mask. But that was going to change.

Baz didn't reply, but that was his way and Rodney was going to start on again, when Baz suddenly scrunched down in his seat.

'Watch,' he muttered.

Rodney saw the big black car pulling over to the pavement opposite and automatically he reached for his hat, put it on well down over his face and then lay back in his seat. He'd seen the car before and he knew it was the African's. What astonished him, though, was to see Gus's brother get out, look around and walk into the building. Rodney recognized him from the photograph he'd taken out of the flat, and he'd been sitting with Baz in the Escort waiting for the better part of two hours for this Danny to show up, but he had no idea what the guy was doing with the African or how they knew each other.

'So wha go on?' Baz growled as the African's car drove away.

'Me nah know,' Rodney said angrily.

He reached for his mobile and dialled, then listened to the ringing for nearly a minute. No answer. He tapped his fingers on the dashboard, feeling the vibes of Baz waiting for a decision. The plan had been to watch Danny and see what he did, cover his moves in case he led them to the mask, but if the African was involved they could still be sat there while he walked off with the goodies.

'I think we need a new plan,' Rodney said. 'Let's go and talk with this bredda.'

Baz grunted his assent without showing any other emotion. That was the good thing about Baz. He was up for anything, and he didn't argue. In any case, Rodney was confident that he could fool up the boy, or else scare him. He was tall like Gus had been, over six feet, but he had that clean, pretty look you saw on some mixed-race kids – dressed in trainers and an American football sweater like a little kid. Easy.

When Danny heard the banging on the door his first thought was that it might be the African coming back to interrogate him again, or to try and check out the flat for himself. But peering out of the window he could see that the big black car had gone. His next idea was that it might be one of the neighbours, or perhaps a Jehovah's Witness, or some other kind of door-knocker.

Listening to the repeated banging he hesitated, but eventually he gave up, went to the door and opened it.

There were two youths standing there. He'd never seen them before, but something told him immediately that they meant him no good; the stocky light-skinned one glaring as if he owed him money, and the taller black one grinning a kind of crocodile grin.

'You Gus's brother?' The tall one asked.

Danny admitted it cautiously. He guessed that they already knew who he was.

'I want to talk to you,' the tall youth said.

In the same breath he began moving forward, trying to shove past Danny into the flat. Automatically, Danny braced his arm across the doorway, blocking his entrance.

'What do you want to talk about?' he asked.

The eyes flicked sideways and up at him, irritated.

'Confidential.'

'Shit,' Danny said. 'I've never seen you before, man. How confidential can it be? Just tell me.'

The youth moved back a step, considering Danny.

'It's about Gus.'

Danny felt he knew what was coming. This had to be about the mask. Again.

'What about Gus?' he asked.

'Don't want to talk out here,' the youth said stubbornly.

'Who are you?'

At least, he thought, Dr Okigbo had told him who he was before he started his pitch. The youth looked round and down the stairs as if checking that there was no one to hear him.

'I'm Rodney.' He jerked his thumb back at his companion. 'Call him Baz.'

Danny made up his mind. Perhaps this pair could tell him what was going on. He stepped back and retreated into the sitting room, not turning his back on them as they prowled forward. In the room the two youths looked around with open curiosity.

'Somebody really mess this place up,' Rodney said, grinning widely.

Suddenly Danny felt he'd had enough of the cat and mouse game they seemed to be playing.

'What do you want?'

Rodney's grin grew wider.

'I want to know where it is.'

As he said this Danny noted that he'd dropped his street accent, and he had a hunch that Rodney had planned the question so as to give him a shock. He forced himself to keep a straight face.

'I don't know what you're on about,' he said.

'Yes you do,' Rodney said. 'You're taking the piss.'

Danny shook his head slowly, letting them see how cool he was.

'No. I really don't know what you're on about.'

Rodney stared at him for a few seconds, sizing him up.

'It's an African mask,' he said. 'About this big.' He held his hands apart in front of him, measuring the size. 'We were partners with Gus. We were with him when he nicked it. Only he didn't have a chance to tell us where he left it.'

That was it. The thing that had been puzzling Danny was how these youths had been connected with Gus. Now he could see that it made sense.

'I still don't know what you're on about,' he said.

Rodney kept on staring, as if trying to read his sincerity, and Danny returned his gaze, wide-eyed and innocent.

'Listen to this,' he said eventually. 'It's all right. You're Gus's brother. You're entitled to what he was entitled to. Share and share alike. You understand me? You're dealing with serious money here, man. We're not greedy. We just want what's right-eously ours.'

'It's no good asking me,' Danny told him. 'I don't know any-thing about it.'

Rodney stuck out his index finger and pointed it in Danny's face.

'So why you were driving with the African? Just dropped you off in his car. Think we're stupid? You taking the piss.'

His street accent and manner were back, and in response Danny felt the stirring of a rage which had been building inside him since he'd been told about Gus.

'Why don't you fuck off,' he said, his voice barely under control.

Rodney didn't flinch.

'Mek I tell you something,' he said. 'Gus rob I and I, so don't fuck with me. I want that thing, and if you don't want to give it I feel to cut your ass up.'

By some instinct Danny caught a flicker of movement, in the margin of his vision, as swift as a bird flying. For an instant he couldn't make sense of it, then he realized that what he'd seen was Baz's hand emerging from his pocket with a knife from which the long blade protruded as he held it down by the side of his leg.

Danny didn't hesitate now. He had already measured with his eye the gap between himself and the door of the kitchen and almost by reflex he whirled and ran for it, throwing himself through the open door and then slamming and locking it behind him. As he stood panting on the other side the door knob rattled and then the wood shook from a heavy blow.

'Bwoy,' Rodney's voice called. 'You have to come out sometime.'

Danny pushed the little kitchen table up against the door, blocking the way. Then he opened the drawer next to the sink and took out the big carving knife and the meat cleaver.

'Bwoy,' Rodney called. 'Don't mek I have to come in there.'

Danny leaned over the table, turned the key, and threw the door open. It crashed into Rodney, making him stumble backwards into Baz, and as they disentangled themselves from each other and looked up they saw Danny, braced on the other side of the narrow doorway, beyond the table, brandishing a blade in each fist.

'Fucking come on then,' Danny said. 'Come on.'

For a moment he thought that Baz was going to spring at him, but Rodney retreated, the crocodile grin back on his face.

'Let's go,' he told Baz, who was still holding his knife by his side, standing staring head on at Danny. Rodney tugged at his sleeve. 'Let's go.'

They walked away, backs to Danny, the pose telling him that he was no threat. Just inside the hallway, Rodney turned to look at Danny.

'Hey bwoy,' he said. 'Don't go nowhere. Next time I coming back with a gun.'

Danny waited till he heard the front door slam. Then he came out and double locked it. Through the sitting-room window he saw Rodney and Baz cross the road and get into a shiny customized Escort. After a few minutes, when the car didn't move, it was obvious that they were waiting, like cats over a mouse hole, for him to come out.

Now it was all over, Danny's legs trembled so that he could hardly stand. He lay on the floor, staring at the ceiling. Gus had made a point of telling him what a big secret the mask was, but everyone in London seemed to know about it. Remembering how Osman had reacted, he had the feeling that the thing had marked him, so that everyone he encountered knew that he had looked at it and touched it, as if there was trail of golden dust which led right back to where it sat, crouching in the dark. Osman's manner had seemed superstitious, almost ridiculous at the time, but perhaps the thing was bad luck.

He sat up, crawled to the window and peered out at the street. The Escort was still sitting opposite, and it struck Danny that perhaps they were waiting for nightfall. He looked at his watch. It was close to the time that he'd arranged to meet Justine. He had to leave, but he couldn't risk simply walking past them. What he needed was a bodyguard, or, at least, a diversion.

He located his mobile in the debris and got the number of the local police station from the directory. As he pressed the buttons he imagined himself addressing a gruff and sceptical sergeant, but instead a woman's voice answered, asking which service he wanted. By the time he reached what she told him was the correct department, his confidence was beginning to ebb.

'I'm in the Neighbourhood Watch,' Danny told the policeman who eventually picked up the phone. He pitched his voice higher, trying to give it the merest hint of a quiver. 'I don't want to trouble you, but there's two black men sat in an Escort in my road all afternoon. They're sat there shouting the odds and watching the schoolkids coming home. I'm not prejudiced, but they told us to watch out for things like that. I don't like the look of them. It's bad enough women and children won't walk down here for fear of getting mugged, without all that.'

When the policeman asked, in a bored tone, for his name and address, Danny gave him the number of one of the houses opposite and gave his name as G. Washington.

'You going to send a car round or what?'

The policeman promised that a patrol car would pass by, and Danny settled down to wait. While he did so he thought about Gus and his involvement with people like Okigbo and Rodney. He knew from the letter that Gus had no doubt about whether what he had done was right. But Gus had always believed that he was right, and the sheer passion and certainty with which he held his beliefs had been one of the qualities Danny had admired in his brother. Sometimes those same qualities had driven a wedge between them. For a long and difficult period Danny had hated it when Gus lectured him about their African heritage and his duty to the race. All he could feel when Gus talked like that was rebellion and resentment about the way that Gus burdened him with his anger and desire for retribution, the way that he'd assumed the inevitability of his younger brother becoming a sort of soldier in the struggle for equality and justice for Africa. 'I thought you said our dad was from the West Indies,' he murmured slyly one time, but he soon learned that trying to contradict Gus was a mug's game, because he'd only go on and on, getting more and more irritable if Danny didn't agree. Gus had been too stubborn, Danny reflected, to admit the possibility that he might be conned by a character like Okigbo, as long as the guy fed him with enough bullshit about Africa. Perhaps Gus would still be alive if he'd been more suspicious, less wrapped up in his ideals.

The sheer disloyalty of the thought stung Danny, like a spike in the brain, opening up a gateway into another world where he was alone, a solitary drifter in a cosmos of uncertainty. He sat up straight, unnerved by the prospect, and suddenly conscious that he'd been on the verge of sleep. On the street outside the light was fading, and the scene was unchanged, the Escort conspicuous in the line of cars opposite. But as Danny watched, the streetlights switched themselves on, and simultaneously, as if by magic, a police car cruised round the corner and stopped next to the Escort.

Danny ran for it. He shouldered his bag, slammed out of the door and leaped down the stairs. In seconds he was striding up the street. Out of the corner of his eye he saw one of the policemen prowling round the Escort, peering at the tyres, and for a moment he entertained the vicious hope that they'd find something wrong. Anything.

Justine was waiting at the entrance to Covent Garden tube, and even though his memory of Gus's description was vague, he recognized her at once. She was wearing a dark grey woollen dress, the hemline coming to about an inch below her black jacket. In one hand she carried a briefcase, and the combination immediately put Danny in mind of what Gus had said when he first met her — 'a mixture of sex and bossiness, irresistible.'

Danny didn't think she was irresistible. In fact, his instinct was to dislike and distrust, if only because she was part of the sphere in which Gus had moved, and which had turned out to be so deadly.

'I booked a table at a restaurant near here,' she said. 'Have you eaten?'

The question reminded Danny that he hadn't eaten anything all day. At the same time, he felt like telling her what a stupid question it was. Of course he hadn't eaten, because they'd arranged to go out to dinner, and if he had, what difference would it make?

They went to a little restaurant near the station. There were only about a dozen tables, dark wood giving off a dull glitter in the candlelight. The walls were painted in a drab, institutional brown and yellow, and lined with posters of old movies, but Danny knew enough to guess that it was probably a fashionable and expensive restaurant. At that time in the evening, halfway between the office workers going home and the ravers coming out, only four of the tables were occupied, and Justine headed for one which was hidden round the corner of the bar.

During the next half an hour they talked uneasily about nothing very much. Justine asked him about his studies. He asked her what kind of work she did. Danny had the feeling that they were sparring like a couple of boxers at the beginning of a fight, neither of them willing to throw the punch which would start the real contest. Swelling below his hesitancy he could sense a reluctant attraction. It was something about her skin that he noticed first. It was almost the same shade of light brown as his own, but it had a smooth, soft look that made him think of honey. Below her eyes two patches of dark rose came and went as the blood pulsed. In the gloom of the restaurant the candlelight glittered green in her eyes, giving them a strange, fey sheen, as if she were looking at him through a gap in some other world. Surrounded by the warm, luscious smell of food, the glow of the wine creeping through his blood, Danny felt his resolve ebbing away, as if she were, little by little, draining the willpower out of him.

'How did you come to meet Gus?' he asked her abruptly.

'At some reception.' She shrugged. 'But that's not important. What do you really want to ask me?'

'I don't know.' He gestured. 'Seems like Gus was mixed up with some real weirdos. I met this guy coming out of the hospital today. A Nigerian named Doctor Okigbo. You know him?'

She frowned, watching him intently. 'At the hospital?'

Suddenly he sensed that she knew what he was talking about and that her question was playing for time. Rage bloomed in his head.

'Do you know him? He said he did business with Gus.'

She screwed up her mouth and shook her head slowly.

'What about Rodney? And Baz?'

She shook her head again.

'I don't know these people.'

'Why are you saying that?'

She flinched as if he'd raised a threatening hand. He leaned over the table towards her, keeping his voice low, trying to restrain the heat rising inside him.

'What do you mean you don't know these people? You hung out with Gus. I'm in London a few hours and all these guys find me and start pressuring me, and yet you never heard about them even though they know all about Gus. Somehow they never came and talked to you or anything. Did you all think that Gus was so stupid that his brother must be an idiot? I mean, I'm beginning to wonder what really happened to him. With friends like you, he must have been in real trouble.'

Justine was leaning away from him, her pose stiff and frozen, as if the words had immobilized her limbs. Abruptly she moved, standing up and bumping against the table.

'Excuse me,' she said.

She turned and walked quickly, threading her way between the tables, towards the back of the room, pushed a door open and disappeared. Danny sat back, hoping that the unmarked door led to the toilets. He pushed his plate aside. He had ordered the shank of lamb, a dish for which Justine said the restaurant was renowned, but he hadn't been able to eat more than a mouthful. The meat had tasted like rubber in his mouth and when he remembered Gus his stomach heaved in revulsion at the thought of eating burnt and broken flesh.

As it happened, his sense of disappointment was now so intense that he would have found it impossible to enjoy the meal. He had been hoping that Justine would confide in him, tell him what had been happening to Gus, and somehow help him to resolve the question of what to do with the mask. Instead, her refusal to be open with him seemed to indicate that she was part of the conspiracy he had stumbled into. He had been wary of Okigbo and Rodney, and he felt that whatever happened he could handle them, but during his conversation with Justine he had experienced a sense of betrayal which filled him with fury, and which was something to do with his sense that she should have been on his side, against the world.

Thinking about her made him remember that she'd been gone for a long time, and he was just about to get up and check whether there was another way out at the back when she pushed the door open.

'We can't talk here,' she said as soon as she sat down. 'Come back with me.'

They took a taxi to Shepherds Bush. Justine hardly spoke during the journey, and Danny, resisting the temptation to stare at her long straight legs, looked out of the window, recognizing bits of London he had travelled through with Gus, trying to remember the things his brother had talked about.

'Take a good look,' Gus had said once as they went past Marble Arch. 'All these monuments are about triumphing over some bunch of poor bastards somewhere else in the world, or they're displaying the loot they stole. Look at us, they're saying. We're so powerful we can take whatever we want and you can't do shit about it.'

Justine lived on the ground floor of a terraced house in a quiet turning off the main road. She led him into a sitting room which looked out on to a small garden lit by a couple of lights that gave the bushes a translucent look.

'You said pressure. What's the pressure about?'

During the taxi ride Danny had made up his mind to tell her everything that had happened with Okigbo and Rodney. His most urgent problem was working out what Gus had intended to do with the mask. Even if Justine didn't know the details of his brother's plans, he was sure now that she could tell him more. At least, he could make a guess about which side she was on.

'They think I've got some mask that Gus had, and they were offering me a share of the profits.'

Rapidly he told her about being accosted by Okigbo and about his confrontation with Rodney and his friend Baz. She listened, frowning, her hands twisting together in front of her.

'What are you going to do?' she asked when he stopped.

'I'm going to find out what it's all about,' he told her. 'For a start, I'd like to know how Gus got mixed up with those people and what he was doing.' He tried to meet her eyes, but, instead of turning towards him, she sat back and gazed out of the window. 'I can't believe you didn't know something, at least about what he was thinking.' He gestured, feeling now that he had to try and get over his bewilderment about what had happened to Gus. 'I mean, Gus was a college lecturer. That's what he wanted to do. When we were kids he used to have a go at me about nicking sweeties out of shops. He was too proud to do things like that. Now these guys are telling me he was a big-time thief. I don't understand.'

She was silent for a long time and he waited, choking down the urge to shout at her.

'It's all politics,' she said eventually. Her voice was low and hesitant, almost as if she were talking to herself, working out what she thought as she went along. 'He used to sit and watch the TV, getting mad at the way they ignored all the things he thought were important. Lately when they talked about compensation for victims of the war, like Japanese POWs and all the rest of it, he used to shout and throw things. "Who's ever paid compensation for slavery and colonialism, you bastards?" he used to go. He wanted to make a big gesture. Something they couldn't ignore.'

'Nicking an old mask out of a gallery isn't exactly big news.'

'He was going to make it news.' She shrugged. 'I don't know. He thought they'd keep it quiet for a while, to see whether they could pay a ransom, get it back without a fuss. That's how they do things. Then he'd start making demands, get diplomats excited about it. If people in government circles in Africa knew that Britain had lost it, he said, it would cause a lot of official embarrassment. Rumours would start about terrorism and all the rest of it. The longer it went on, he reckoned, the more attention it would get. He thought it could be some kind of catalyst.'

'I think that was dumb,' Danny said. Saying it hurt, because he understood now exactly why Gus had done it, and instead of making him feel closer, the knowledge was forcing him away, as if the image of his brother which had stayed in his mind all these years was fading and growing smaller as it receded into the distance.

'Not so dumb,' Justine's voice was stronger, with an edge to it, as if he had upset her. 'You don't understand. This isn't just some old mask. It's a religious relic and a political symbol. It could spark off a lot of interest. I don't think he was wrong about that.'

'I don't mean that,' Danny told her. 'Maybe all that is true, but

I was thinking about him. What he was feeling. I could understand it better if we were African. Or if our dad had been.' Even as he said this he remembered that Gus would have disagreed passionately.

'Gus would have said that all black people were African.'

'I know.' Something Danny had been thinking for the last two days began to coalesce. 'But that's abstract. You choose to believe in it, like saying all people in the world named Mac-something are really Scottish. Well, some of them are Argentinian and some of them are West Indians and some of them are even Africans. But it all comes down to race. Right? And God knows what that means when you've got all kinds of blood in you like we do.' He leaned across towards her, pressing closer, the words pouring out of him without deliberation. 'That's what makes me mad. Gus used to tell me that we were free to make ourselves and our own history. That the privilege of being all these ambiguous things, of not being part of anybody's club, was freedom from the past. He said it was crazy to try and buy acceptance from white people because we were ahead of the game, and anyway it killed your soul to bribe your way into a sense of belonging. Now what he's done is just like trying to buy his way in, to prove that somehow he's just as African as a real black man. So he goes further and does it while they're only talking. But it's the same thing. He said that was a strategy that never worked, couldn't work. Then he goes and does it, and it's supposed to be all right because he's doing it for Africa.'

Danny's voice had risen, and he felt the control he'd exerted over his feelings slipping away. In that instant he was overwhelmed with anger at Gus. He wanted to shout, to scream, to get up and throw something. Justine had turned her body so she could look at him, the frown etching deeper into her face.

'So why don't you just give the mask back to the university and forget about it?' she asked suddenly.

Danny opened his mouth to answer, then realized that he'd been trapped. He cleared his throat.

'I didn't say I had it.'

'Of course you've got it,' she said calmly. 'Gus only trusted a couple of people. He wouldn't have left it anywhere, or buried it in the back garden. He might have sent it to that woman in Bristol, but she was ringing up all the time as if she hadn't heard from him. You're the only one left. If you didn't have something to hide, you'd have gone to the police or something when those guys attacked you. Of course you've got it.'

For a few seconds they stared at each other. Danny's brain raced. What to say? Her eyes seemed more intense, as wide open and unblinking as a child's.

'So what do you think I should do?' he asked her eventually.

She shrugged. She turned away, her gaze focused on the garden, her eyes shining with the tiny gleams of reflected light.

'I don't know,' she said. 'It's up to you.'

'I'm asking you,' Danny told her. 'If it was you, what would you do?'

She shrugged again.

'I really don't know. Maybe I'd do what Gus set out to do. But I'm different to you. My dad was African, and I lived there for a bit. When I'm in Africa I feel African. When I'm here I feel English, but I can't line myself up with the English. I can't just forget about history the way you can. Maybe if being English allowed you to admit the way things were and do something about it. But it doesn't. That's why what Gus did doesn't surprise me.'

Danny struggled for an answer. He had the feeling she was accusing him in some way, but of what he wasn't sure. Instead of waiting for a reply she got up.

'What are you going to do now? I wouldn't fancy going back to Gus's place if I were you.'

He'd already decided on that.

'I thought I'd catch the midnight train back.'

'You're too late.'

He looked at his watch. More time had passed than he'd thought. It wasn't quite twelve, but by the time he got to the station the train would be long gone.

'You can sleep on the sofa,' she said.

Gus came back that night. They sat in McDonald's drinking milkshakes, but Danny's throat was so dry that he couldn't speak, even though he sucked desperately at the milkshake and could feel it going down.

'You think it's easy being a black man,' Gus said. 'You should try it some time.'

When Danny woke up he looked automatically for the familiar outlines of his room, and felt a moment of near panic when he discovered that they were gone. Dimly, he sensed a presence next to the sofa, and he whipped round to defend himself from whatever it was. His memory flooded back the moment he saw her, wrapped in a short white towelling robe, her arms folded round the front of her body, her expression troubled. He looked at his watch. It was only two hours since he'd gone to sleep.

'You were muttering and groaning in your sleep,' she said.

'What did I say?'

'Don't know. I couldn't make it out. I made some tea.'

She sat on the sofa next to his feet, her legs stretched out and resting on a coffee table. They could have been friends, he thought, after a night out back at the college, but his life there seemed to exist on the other side of a gulf.

'There's one thing you have to understand,' she said. 'I loved your brother. I really didn't know that I did till he was gone.'

Suddenly she was crying, huddling into the fabric of the robe, her body heaving with great gulping sobs. Slowly, Danny leaned over and embraced her. She nestled against him, her body shaking. Feeling her trembling against him was like a switch that opened up a memory of himself as a small boy clinging to a woman he couldn't remember. 'Shush,' he kept saying stupidly, patting Justine on the back. 'Shush, baby.'

The storm was over quickly. In a minute Justine pushed away from him and got to her feet. She kept her back turned towards him.

'I'm going back to bed,' she said. 'You can come if you like. I could do with some company.' She turned and gave him a quick glance before looking away again. 'I don't want to have sex, if that's okay.'

In the darkened bedroom she put her arms round him again. She hadn't taken off her robe and he buried his face in the soft pile of the cloth, feeling her flesh pulsing below it. She didn't speak. After a while he began to drift off, then, little by little, like a distant sound stealing into the ear, he felt his penis gradually rising against her naked thighs. Her legs moved, away and back again, but her grip round his neck didn't slacken. He pushed gently, trying to put a space between them. He hadn't intended it, but somehow his hands were moving on her breasts.

'Sorry,' he whispered.

'It's all right,' she whispered back. 'You can do it if you want to.'

Chapter Fifteen

When he ran out of Gus's flat on the previous night Danny had intended to get out of London and back to his room as soon as possible, but by the morning his mood had changed. His night with Justine had calmed some of the turmoil inside him, and when he woke up he found himself looking back at the previous twenty-four hours as a period when he had been more or less out of his mind. At the hospital, for instance, the policeman had told him about the inquest and what he ought to do about making arrangements for the funeral, but he had been too agitated to listen. Opening his eyes to find himself in Justine's bed, this was the first thing he remembered.

Similar thoughts seemed to be occupying her.

'What are you going to do today?' she asked him. She was sitting at the foot of the bed fully dressed. 'I have to go.'

Danny couldn't tell whether or not this was a signal for him to get up and leave, but he scrambled out of bed and began picking up his clothes, which she'd left in a neat pile next to the bed. She handed him a cup of coffee.

'If Gus left a will or anything like that, you ought to find it,' she said.

Danny agreed. He knew that Gus had made a will and he would have liked to ask her what to do with it when he found it, but this morning she seemed distant, unapproachable, as if she wanted to forget lying in bed wrapped round him, or to pretend that it had never happened.

'You should get some advice,' she said. 'Do you know what to do?'

'Of course,' Danny told her, although at that moment he hadn't the slightest idea. 'I'll sort things out and let you know.'

In the street she gave him a brief peck on the cheek, got into her car, and drove away, leaving him to make his own way to the station. He trudged down towards the tube station feeling deflated. He had told Justine everything, but what he'd learned from her wasn't much more than he already knew. Now he felt just as incapable of making a decision as he'd been in the first place, and, to make matters worse, he didn't have a clue about how to deal with Okigbo or Rodney or anyone else who might turn up.

He approached the flat cautiously, walking up and down the street, peering round the nearest corners for Rodney's Escort. After he'd determined that the coast was clear he crossed the road and let himself in.

The will and an insurance policy were in a big brown envelope in the kitchen drawer where Gus kept his documents. Danny stuffed them into his bag and walked away without bothering to shut the drawer. Back at the front door he stood looking around.

When he left it would be as if he was parting from Gus for the last time, and for a moment he had the mad notion that he would stay, clean the place up, put on his brother's life like a new skin. His legs trembled and he leaned against the wall, his body limp, incapable of moving in one direction or the other.

That was the worst moment since he'd heard the news about Gus. Afterwards Danny remembered it as an experience in which he found himself struggling with some monstrous task, an insect climbing the sheer sides of a fathomless pit. The memory stained the day with a wash of pain and despair, but from the time he dragged himself out of the flat and shut the door on the wreckage, he felt that a barrier had gone up inside him, a protective act of will against the tide of misery which, minute by minute, threatened to engulf his soul.

For the rest of the day he pushed his body, as if directing a zombie, through the tasks he'd set himself. He went to the solicitor's office in the High Street, where Gus had drawn up the will. He went to a nearby undertaker's. He went to the bank and back to the solicitor.

During all this time the people he met treated him almost as if he were an invalid, or desperately ill, lowering their voices, speaking softly and giving him a special smile of sympathy. Oddly, he found this comforting rather than irritating, and it fitted the way he felt, like a man tiptoeing on the edge of disaster, his route lined with anxious and supportive spectators.

Late in the afternoon he telephoned Justine's office. Throughout the day he'd kept recalling, in vivid flashes which lit up his brain and electrified his body, the soft touch of her hands as she guided him inside her. After a while he had realized that she was crying, tears flowing down her cheeks and soaking the pillow below her. He had stopped moving and begun to pull away, but she held him tight, pressing him deeper into her. 'No. No,' she gasped. 'I'm all right. Don't stop. I'm all right.'

In the back of his mind, Danny was nursing the hope that she would suggest seeing him again that night, but the woman who answered the phone said Justine was in a meeting and she would telephone if he left a number. He hung up, frustrated and angry with himself. Perhaps, he thought, her moment of vulnerability over, all she would remember was his youth and inexperience. Perhaps she regretted it, looking back on his eagerness with anger and contempt.

The thought made him squirm on his way to the station, but once he was on the train he found himself relaxing and forgetting, as if the act of leaving London cleared him of the burdens he'd acquired there. Soon he was asleep, lulled as usual by the rocking movement and the rhythmic sounds under him.

By the time he got back to his room it was nearly closing time. He had walked through the centre of town, and if things had been normal he would have dropped into one of the clubs looking for Osman or another of his friends, but he wasn't in the mood for company. The other thing driving him on was the desire to see and touch the mask. From the moment he stepped off the train he'd felt like running down the platform. All of a sudden the memory of its warm, smooth surface filled his mind.

The house was quiet. The rooms were all rented to students and most of them wouldn't be back until later. There were lights in the windows of the flat on the top floor, but that was because it was occupied by three students from the Middle East. They were nice enough guys who said hello when they saw him, but as far as he could make out, they did nothing except study and pray. By this time of night they were always in, doing whatever they did, quiet as mice.

He knew something was wrong the minute the door opened. For a start the key stuck and he had to twist it round and round before it worked and, when he pushed, it only opened a couple of inches before being blocked by something behind it. He pushed harder and there was a noise as if something had fallen over, then the door grated open by another foot. He squeezed through. The object behind the door was the armchair in which he sat reading and watching telly. It had been moved and when he pushed the door it had gone over on its side. Automatically he picked it up and moved it back to where it had been. The room was a mess. The neat piles of stacked books and folders for which there was no room on the shelves had been kicked over. There was paper strewn everywhere. The doors of the wardrobe were wide open, the shirts and trousers flopping out like a collection of rags, and he knew without looking that the mask had gone.

He went to the door and looked out, then he peered through the windows. Nothing. Everything was quiet and still, as if nothing had happened. For a moment he thought of going up to ask the Iranians whether they'd seen or heard anything, then he rejected the idea. Whoever had broken into his room had done it without being interrupted or noticed. That would have been easy enough, because the house was a tolerant place to live. The landlord, a taciturn Indian who owned a kebab and chip shop a few streets away, hardly ever visited. When he did, he was in and out fast enough to avoid any questions about the plumbing or about clearing up the rubbish in the back garden. Unless one of Danny's friends had been on the spot, no one would have paid any attention to a bit of banging about, or worried about strange faces on the stairs.

In any case, the mask was gone and there was nothing he could do about it. Before going to London, he reflected, he would have felt relief at getting rid of the problem. Now he felt an anger and an overwhelming sense of loss. Gus had left it to him, and left him the task of finishing what he'd set out to accomplish. Danny hadn't known what to do with it, but he had begun to see the mask as being tied up with the kind of person he was. For Osman, the mask had been some kind of national icon; while he could understand that, he couldn't feel it in his bones in the way his friend did. But when he thought about Gus, and about why the mask had been so important to him, he'd begun to feel a trickling of new emotions. Dim at first, they started to become stronger and sharper the more they filled his mind. For Gus the mask hadn't just been about politics, and he hadn't been trying to prove how African he was. It was something to do with history, with taking possession of it for himself. That's why, he thought, there was something so alive, so familiar and urgent about the touch of it. Gus said that their mum used to call them 'My golden boys'. He had remembered that phrase when he first saw the mask, and at the back of his mind he'd been sure that when his brother touched the golden skin of the face he had remembered it too. When Gus took the mask he was claiming it for himself and Danny. That was why he had no plans about returning it, and why he was so vague about what to do with it, because once he had touched the thing it belonged to him. It was the same impulse that had driven Danny when he sat reading late at night, his head weighted with the drag of history. Possession. What he knew had become his private property, and he guarded it with the same passionate secrecy.

The telephone rang. It was Osman.

'You're back then.'

For an instant it crossed his mind that Osman had been the only person he'd told about the mask. Then he put the thought out of his mind. Osman hadn't even wanted to touch it.

'Some asshole broke in and stole the fucking mask,' he said. 'Bad news.'

'Shit. I knew that was trouble. What are you going to do?'

'Don't know. I'll think about it for a bit.'

He broke the connection without telling Osman anything about London or about what had happened. He wanted to be alone with the thoughts whirling around inside his head. The feeling of weariness and lassitude he had experienced in London had come back and his bones seemed limp and rubbery, too feeble to bear the burdens he had to carry around.

The sound of knocking broke through his mood. At first he ignored it. It would only be one of the other students, he thought, coming to tell him that someone had broken in. He had no idea how long he'd been sitting there staring into space. Perhaps it would be Osman. He went to the door and opened it.

The two men standing outside were complete strangers.

African, Danny thought. They were wearing identical dark grey suits, and both of them were scarred on the left cheek, the hair piled on top of their heads in a bushy, unkempt mass. For one moment Danny had the impression that he was seeing double.

'You are Danny?' one of the Africans asked.

Danny was slow to answer. Something about the men puzzled him, then he noticed that their suits were actually the same size, but while it fitted the smaller African perfectly, on the bigger man, who towered above Danny by inches, the jacket was stretched tight across the chest, giving him an awkward, clownish air.

He was about to ask who they were, but he never got the words out because the big African pushed at the door, forcing him backwards into the room. For a few seconds Danny teetered on the edge of tumbling over on his back, and by the time he'd recovered his balance, he was standing in the middle of the room, facing the big African, while the other one prowled the room peering under the bed and opening the doors of the cupboard.

'Where is it?' the African asked.

Something about his size and the shape of his face reminded Danny of Okigbo, but unlike Okigbo he had a strong accent.

'I don't know what you're looking for,' Danny said, 'but I want you to fuck off out of my room.'

From behind him there was a brief cackling of laughter, and then a burst of speech which confused Danny for a moment, until he sussed that it was in an African language.

'Where is it?' the big man repeated stubbornly, as if he hadn't heard Danny.

Danny had been rehearsing the options in his head. He was

surrounded, and while there were a number of objects in the room he could use as weapons, he was sure he couldn't reach any of them without being grabbed. He suspected that the men had been sent by Okigbo, but whoever they were they wanted the mask, and he guessed that there was no point now in telling them that he knew nothing. They didn't look like men who would be interested in his denials.

The big African said something in his own language and Danny felt a movement behind him, but before he could move something snapped around his neck and tightened. Automatically Danny tried hitting out with his elbows, then when that had no effect he tried kicking backwards and stamping, but that didn't work either. Nothing worked, and the pressure round his neck kept squeezing tighter and tighter until he was standing on tiptoe, choking and clawing at his throat. This was how it ended, he thought, and he would never get to do any of the things he had planned. In front of him the face of the African blurred and danced. Inside his ears the blood roared and sang. Suddenly the pressure relaxed, and Danny sank to his knees gasping for breath.

'Where is it?' the African said.

'I left it with a friend,' Danny croaked. He took a deep breath and said it again. 'I gave it to a friend to keep for me.'

His plan was complete. Even while the wire round his neck was blotting the world out, he had been working on it, desperation making his brain click smooth and fast below the agony.

'Who?'

'Osman. His name is Osman.'

'Where is he?'

'I don't know.' He sensed a movement behind him, and he gestured quickly, hurrying to explain. 'He moves around. He lives in a van. It could be parked anywhere, but I know where to find him. I have to telephone.'

Another conversation in the guttural language, longer this time. Then someone thrust the telephone into his hand.

'Telephone.'

He tapped out Osman's number rapidly. He noticed that the big African was watching the electronic display as he did it. He sent up a silent prayer that Osman's phone was switched on.

'The Cool One,' Osman said abruptly.

'Ozzie, Ozzie,' Danny gabbled. 'This is Danny.'

'I know that,' Osman said. 'What's up?'

'I need to pick up the mask. I've got some friends here I have to give it to. They insist. You understand? I'm going to bring them to the club after it closes. Can you wait till I arrive? After two o'clock. Okay? Just help me out here.'

There was a long silence on the other end. Danny could hear music in the background. The African reached for Danny's hand and brought the phone closer to his own ear. In close-up he was scowling in concentration, his eyes, dirty yellow and shot through with red veins, seemed to burn with rage.

'Okay,' Osman said. 'I'll see you later.'

The line went dead.

'Let us go,' the African said.

'We can't do that,' Danny told him. He explained that the club where Osman had hidden the mask would be full of people until about two, and they would attract too much attention. Later on, he said, it would all be simple. They could just walk in, pick up the mask and walk out again.

The African nodded, his eyes burning at Danny. 'We will wait,' he said.

He unbuttoned his jacket and drew a gun from a holster clipped to his belt. It was the mass of this gun which had given his clothes such a stretched and bulbous look, but Danny hadn't noticed it until then. The African held it casually by his side, and with the other hand pointed Danny towards the bed.

'Sit down,' he said. He gestured briefly with the gun, still staring fixedly at Danny. 'I'll tell you one thing. If you lie you die.'

During the next hour the Africans spoke very little, and then only to each other and in their own language. Danny tried asking a few questions, hoping to make some kind of contact with them, but when he did so they simply ignored him. When he asked point blank whether they'd come from Okigbo, the big one seemed about to react, but then his companion barked out a few words and he looked away. Danny was certain now that they were Nigerians. He knew that Nigerians came in a variety of shapes and sizes, but he could usually tell them apart from any other kind of African. For instance, neither of them had the slim build and sarky smile of an Ibo. Beyond that he couldn't put his finger on what tribe they came from, but the way they spoke and moved had so much in common with Nigerians he'd known that there was no doubt in his mind.

They travelled to the city centre in the Africans' white Cortina, with Danny giving the driver careful directions. Levitation, the club where Osman was working that night, was situated on the fringes of the biggest shopping mall in town, and since it was a week night they'd be closing early, about two. He explained this again to his silent warders, turning to look at the big Nigerian who was sitting in the back. He had stowed his gun away under his jacket, but although Danny thought from time to time about leaping out at a traffic light, it also struck him that this might be the quickest way of committing suicide. Going past some of the pubs he often visited with Osman or some other friend, he kept thinking that only a couple of days earlier he'd been a carefree student with nothing more serious on his mind than getting off with Simone. Now he wasn't certain whether he'd survive the night.

From the street outside the club was dark and silent. Earlier on or during the weekend there would have been groups of kids hanging around outside or walking past on their way to one spot or another, but tonight there were only a few stragglers outside the Texas Pizza Parlour lower down the road. Two battered blondes and a tall, crazy-looking man; the usual city-centre dross.

Danny banged on the door, and there was the sound of chains rattling before the handle turned and it opened.

'Hey. You're late, man,' Osman said.

He was standing silhouetted against the gleam of light from the bottom of the stairs. In the rush of relief Danny felt he could have hugged and kissed him.

'I had to wait till everything was quiet.' He made a half-turn towards the Nigerians. 'These are the guys.'

He'd hardly got the words out before the big Nigerian pressed closer and pushed him through the door. Osman backed off quickly as Danny barged towards him, but instead of speaking he turned and began walking down the stairs. The Nigerians hesitated for half a second, then the big one plunged after Osman, the gun dangling by his side. Halfway down the stairs made a ninety-degree turn, forming an acute angle, and when the Nigerian got to it he paused, cautiously peering round the corner before pressing after Osman.

It was a long narrow room. Beyond the deserted dance floor, the far wall was a sheet of mirrored glass, giving the illusion that the place was twice its actual size. At this late hour the room was illuminated only by the lights above the bar. In the gloom below the DJ's station, opposite the stairs, a couple were stacking chairs and sweeping up. They looked up at the clatter on the stairs, and Danny recognized Doctor Spin and Cynthia.

Osman sat on one of the high stools by the bar, and picked up the half-drunk pint he'd left sitting there.

'So what's going on then?' he asked, looking at Danny. If he saw the gun in the Nigerian's hand he paid no attention.

Danny sat beside him and rested his elbows on the bar. Now he was with Osman he felt as if he was on his own territory. Nothing could happen to him here, and if it did he was in good company.

'Where is it?' the Nigerian said.

Danny laughed, feeling on the verge of giggling hysteria.

'Look at my fucking neck, man,' he said to Osman. 'These guys choked me half to death. They're kind of serious.'

The Nigerian took a step backwards. He raised the gun and pointed it at Doctor Spin and Cynthia.

'You,' he shouted.

Spin did his startled, innocent look, pointing his fingers at his chest.

'What, me?'

'You,' the Nigerian shouted again. 'Come.'

Spin and Cynthia walked slowly towards the bar.

'This is too heavy,' Osman said. 'What you're looking for is over there, in the office through that door. I'll get it.'

He began levering himself off the stool, but the big Nigerian gave a sharp bark of warning. 'Ah.'

Osman raised his hands in a gesture of surrender and sat down again. The smaller of the pair said something and walked quickly over to the door in the far corner where Osman had pointed. He threw it open and looked warily down the corridor beyond it.

'Second on the left,' Osman said helpfully. 'The ones on the right are the toilets.'

Danny had no idea what Osman had planned, and he was ready for anything, but what happened next was the biggest surprise of the night.

'I want to show you something,' Cynthia said to the Nigerian.

He frowned, and glanced over at the door his friend had gone through. Cynthia reached up and dipped her fingers slowly into her shirt pocket. The Nigerian lifted the gun and moved back another pace, but her hand didn't stop moving. It came out of the pocket with a card in it. She held it up high so he could see it.

'See my picture?' she said. 'I am Detective Cynthia Bracegirdle, West Midlands Police, and I'm placing you under arrest.'

The Nigerian's jaw sagged in disbelief. Looking at Cynthia

with her spiky black hair and her ripped jeans, Danny found it hard to believe as well.

'Bracegirdle?' Osman said, laughing. 'Bracegirdle?'

'Shut your mouth,' the Nigerian shouted. 'I don't care if you are fucking Inspector Morse,' he said to Cynthia. 'If you move I'm going to shoot you.'

'Put the gun down. Give it to me,' Cynthia said. 'Be sensible. You haven't committed any offence yet.'

The Nigerian ignored her. Instead he shouted something in his own language. By now Danny was getting used to the sound of it, and he thought he made out the word 'Ola', so he waited for an answering shout, or the sight of his other captor piling out of the office door. Nothing happened, and the Nigerian shouted again, a note of desperation in his voice.

There was a shuffling sound and the half-open door swung out wide. Ola came through it, followed by City Centre Dave, his left hand gripping the back of the Nigerian's neck, his other hand holding a gun against the man's bushy skull.

'What you gonna do now?' Dave said, his voice rumbling in the silent room. 'Give her the fucking gun.'

The Nigerian hesitated for a split second, then he lowered the gun. Cynthia made a quick step forward and grabbed it out of his hand. Dave let his friend go and pushed him hard, so that he skittered across the room, trying to keep his balance.

'All right now,' Dave thundered. 'Piss off out of my club.'

'Wait a minute,' Cynthia said. 'I'm going to nick these bastards.'

'No. You're not,' Dave told her. 'My job is stopping trouble in my club. I've stopped it. I'm not messing about with bullshit, and you're supposed to be undercover. These guys are from London and after tonight they'll be off your patch. Know what I mean?'

'I'm keeping this anyway,' Cynthia said snappishly.

She hoisted the gun and laid it on the polished surface of the bar. It made a clunking sound, and the Nigerian's eyes followed it wistfully. His companion pulled at his arm, said a few words, and they turned away back up the steps.

Abruptly, just as they were about to disappear round the angle of the stairs, Osman stood up and shouted in the same language they'd been using. Dumbstruck, both of the men spun round, coming to attention automatically, their arms stiff by their sides. Osman shouted again, and the smaller man answered, his tone suddenly humble, almost apologetic. In reply Osman delivered a long stream of words in a quieter, more even tone. When he was finished he made a gesture of dismissal, waving them away.

'Now you're going to tell me,' Cynthia said, as the outer door slammed shut, 'what all that was about.'

Osman sat back and propped himself up against the bar. He grinned.

'Cynthia,' he said. 'You were beautiful, but I don't know bugger all about this. All I know is the phone call I got. Ask Danny.'

Chapter Sixteen

Danny didn't get away from Cynthia until five in the morning. They went to the all-night pizza joint down the road from the club and sat round one of the tables. Osman and Danny on one side, Cynthia and Spin facing them on the other.

At first Danny tried to joke his way out of it, but it was as if Cynthia had undergone some magical transformation and the pasty-faced hippy had been replaced by a stiff-bosomed Amazon with stony eyes and a firm chin.

The only bright spot about the situation was that Osman hadn't let out anything about the mask.

'You had that much sense,' Danny told him later on.

Osman shrugged.

'I didn't know what was going on when you rang, so I told Dave some heavy assholes were leaning on you. He told Cynthia and it went on from there. She didn't like us knowing who she was, but Dave said we'd already sussed her and we'd keep our mouths shut.' He did a dramatic pause, and then slapped his forehead with his hand. 'Oh, and I almost forgot. She said she'd nick us if we didn't keep our mouths shut. She's cool.'

Cynthia's coolness seemed to have deserted her for the moment, as she stared at Danny over the table.

'So who were those guys?'

'I don't know,' Danny told her. On the way from the club he had been trying to manufacture convincing lies, but he was so tired now that it seemed like an almighty effort of the imagination to think of anything. 'Yardies?'

Cynthia's eyes narrowed, and her chin jutted at him. 'Those were never Yardies.'

'You're right,' he said. 'What it is, I reckon, they're trying to set themselves up, but Yardies rule the black clubs, so they're looking for new places to sell.' Cynthia frowned, unconvinced, and Danny ploughed on. 'A man came to see me a couple of weeks ago. He wanted me to help them get into the clubs here. I told him to piss off. Then tonight these guys turned up, threatening me.'

'Wait a minute,' Cynthia said. 'They were looking for something. What was it?'

'I wasn't going to sit there and let them pull my toenails out. I told them I'd go in with them and that I had a load of rock stashed down the club. They believed me, and I rang Osman making out like I was arranging to pick it up.'

As soon as Danny said this he could see she was beginning to find his story credible. Like all specialists, her imagination focused on the raw materials of her trade, and what he was telling her was what she wanted to hear. Even so, she kept on at him for the better part of the next hour, going over the details. In the end he told her that he'd had enough and he was going home.

Back in the van he asked Osman the question which had been burning in his brain for the past hour.

'What did you say to those guys?'

Osman laughed.

'Remember I was an officer? That was my parade ground act. I told them to stand still, give me their names and answer me truthfully.'

'Who were they?'

'Nobody. They said they used to be policemen, which might be true. They were definitely soldiers at some point. My guess is they're the sort of messenger boys the police or the army used for anonymous jobs, like burning out villagers, getting rid of small nuisances. You were lucky. These are bad men.'

'Shit,' Danny breathed. 'I wonder who sent them?'

'I asked them that. They said a big man sent them to fetch a thing you had stolen, but they couldn't give me his name. A big Yoruba chief. You know any big Yoruba chiefs?'

'Yes, I do.'

Osman went quiet at that. He looked sideways at Danny.

'I'll park in St Osric's and we can talk.'

Danny was too tired to argue. In any case, after all that had happened, his head was buzzing with unanswered questions and riddles. Thinking of the wardrobe gaping open he knew that he wasn't ready to go back to his room.

St Osric's was still wrapped in silence. Across the park the trees were a black soft mass against the grey streaks on the horizon. As

Danny watched, the dark landscape blurred, and he closed his eyes then opened them again to clear his vision.

'I don't think those guys will be back,' Osman said. 'I told them you had police protection, and if they didn't get out of town they'd be arrested. I figured they were illegal. They won't be back.'

'That's not what worries me,' Danny told him.

This was only half true, but the thought uppermost in his mind was that the big man who sent them had to be Okigbo, and if that was true someone else must have taken the mask. Apart from Osman, Justine was the only person who knew for certain that he had it, and he couldn't believe that either of them had betrayed him.

'Did you take it, Oz?' he asked.

He didn't know why he was asking the question because he found it inconceivable that it could be Osman. Later on he knew that he had asked because he wanted to hear his friend say it, as if the denial would give him a point of certainty on which he could stand. In the darkness he felt Osman shift and turn to look at him.

'Take what?'

'The mask. It's gone.'

'No.' A short pause. He could feel the energy gathering round Osman. 'If that's what you think, you don't know me, man.'

'I'm sorry,' Danny said quickly. 'I had to ask, because Justine is the only other person I told. I just wanted to be sure.'

'Who the fuck is Justine?'

Danny started telling him then, using the confidence to soothe Osman's anger at being accused. When he finished, Osman was silent, taking it all in.

'I heard of Okigbo,' he said eventually. 'He was one of the big boys back in the days when those guys were doubling their money every week with government contracts.' He laughed. 'That was before the army came back. They used to be shameless. Everybody was building or digging holes in the ground, taking millions out of the oil revenues to pay for it. If you were related to a government minister or some official you could do wonders.' He laughed again, shifting round to face Danny. 'There was this contractor who was building a college. He was billing the ministry for materials, labour, everything, lorries cranking about the place. They knew he was stealing them blind but nobody cared. That wasn't the point. It was like the trickle-down effect, everyone was getting a share. So that was okay and it went on for a couple of years until the day that the building was due to be unveiled. They had this procession of ministerial cars, a hundred and twenty-three headmen and all the rest of it lined up for the opening ceremony, and when they got there, there was nothing. Not so much as a building site, man. The guy hadn't even cut a few trees down to make it look good.'

'Was that Okigbo?'

'No. That's not the point. The point is that this is how these guys work. They don't put their hands in the cookie jar. Show them a cookie jar and they'll pick it up and walk away.'

The sound of Osman's voice rang and jangled in Danny's ears. It didn't seem to make any sense. He closed his eyes and felt a dark stain creeping over his brain.

'What's that got to do with it?' he murmured.

'I don't know,' Osman said. 'It's just that whatever's happening I'd bet you anything that Okigbo is doing it. Forget about Justine or whoever you think it is. It will be him.'

Danny considered this for what seemed like a long while, working it out. He thought Osman was nuts.

'I've got to get it back. I've got to go and see Eleanor,' he found himself saying abruptly. He'd never met her, he told Osman, but he'd spoken to her on the phone in the past and she would know who he was.

'How will that help?'

The sky was lighter now, the dark retreating out of the air around them. When he opened his eyes and looked down, he could see the grass beginning to turn green.

'I don't know what else to do,' he told Osman.

Chapter Seventeen

Dr Okigbo spent the night at his house in Ladbroke Grove. He didn't do this often, but it was the place he went to when he was especially anxious or bored. He thought of it as his safe house, where he could retreat from the routine of his normal life and find the privacy to indulge in some of his less decorous tastes.

He had actually bought the house for the periods when his children would be on vacation from the private schools they attended; the three boys in Surrey, the two big girls in Geneva. At these times the house would be full of life, with Okigbo revelling in the role of the almighty and forbearing father. Occasionally, when his patience was strained, he dispatched them all back to his first wife's house in Geneva, but in the general run of things the house was a warm and happy place.

The caretakers lived in the basement flat, which was completely isolated from the rest of the house and had a separate entrance. Okigbo called them caretakers because they guarded the house and did whatever little jobs he wanted. On the other hand, they weren't conventional servants, even by West African standards. Their names were Ola and Ogu. Okigbo had been their patron ever since the days when he'd been a politician, a big man in the regional government. He'd hired them, the first time, to do a trifling job; a little stone-throwing, no more. They'd been transients then, orphaned for a second time when the army they'd joined as teenagers reduced its numbers by half, and like thousands of their former comrades they were at a loss, with no family or prospects to which they could return. Even the village in the North that they called home had been blasted out of existence years before. Okigbo became their father, Babatunde, and while his star shone they were something more than small men. Later, when it was time for Okigbo to leave, it was Ola who drove him to the coast, with Ogu perched in the passenger seat, nursing a Kalashnikov. Their loyalty turned out not to be misplaced, because with Okigbo gone, his protégés realized that their impunity had vanished, and that it would only be a matter of time before they were arrested. Even so, it took them almost two years to make their way through North Africa into Europe, and they finally arrived in England locked in a container with eleven Bangladeshis and three half-crazed Romanian women.

When they contacted Okigbo he greeted them with amusement and the admiration a dog lover might display for a pet who had tracked him down over an impossible distance. There was also a measure of relief for him in seeing them again, partly because he was uncomfortable about relying exclusively on the mercenary services of the bodyguards he hired from an agency in London. On one occasion they had tried his patience by actually sending him a female guard. After the first day he had got her removed, but even so, it was a symptom of their priorities which made him feel insecure. With Ola and Ogu he felt safe, and he moved them into the basement at Ladbroke Grove without delay. The only problem, as he told them, was that in this country you had to have a sort of parallel identity, written down on paper and kept in various files, which proved your existence and justified your right to be alive in that time and place. Until he could arrange that, they had to live quietly, avoid calling attention to themselves and obey his instructions to the letter.

So far the pair had not disappointed him, but throughout the long night in which he waited for them to return with the Dancing Face, Okigbo was haunted by the knowledge that, even though they'd been in the country for over a year, their unfamiliarity with England and the English made them, at best, vulnerable and, at worst, dangerously unpredictable.

To keep these worries at bay, Okigbo prepared for a rare evening of domesticity, alone with Hadida. These occasions were unusual, partly because they were so precious to both of them. It had been only a few years earlier, at the time when he was contemplating the prospect of permanent exile, that Okigbo had understood how important Hadida was to him. It was then, while considering what arrangements he had to make, it struck him that it would be possible to leave everything behind except for her. He had bought her at the age of seven or eight, she wasn't certain which, on the Spice Coast near Mombasa. At the time she was actually a refugee, a stranger to the region. According to the fisherman who had taken her to live with his family, she seemed to be a Derode from Somalia. Her entire family had been killed by a mine or a bomb blast, and she had walked, quietly, attracting no attention, until she reached the sea, where she had sat on the sand, a little scrap of skin and bone, waiting. What she was waiting for, she didn't know and no one could guess. The fisherman, a pious Muslim, had obeyed the precepts of the Prophet and taken the little stranger in, but a few months later, helping to pull in the nets, she had caught the eye of an Arab trader who had come dipping over the ocean in a pink-sailed dhow full of carpets from Boukhara. Okigbo, who was then working for the World Bank's Eastern Africa Fund, arrived on the dock in time to see the beginning of the transaction. On a whim he interrupted the Arab and offered to take the child of Allah off the fisherman's hands.

Okigbo hadn't known exactly what he intended to do with the child. She worked in the house and lived with the other servants while he stayed on the coast, and he had her educated in a haphazard fashion because he had some idea that it would be useful if she could read and write and speak English. When she was fifteen he noticed that she was becoming a beauty, tall and graceful as a gliding snake alongside the swaggering buttocks of his native region's women. He married her in a Muslim ceremony. She was his fourth wife. Unlike the others she failed to conceive, but this meant that she had nothing to distract her from focusing all her interest and affection on Okigbo, the man who had appeared from nowhere to give her new life.

In his turn, Okigbo had come to regard her as a treasure, a pearl plucked from the Indian Ocean, which he had discovered and reared and moulded until she was almost a part of him. What he had not expected, at the beginning, was the extent to which

Hadida would mould his own tastes. Years ago, while they were still on the coast, she had revealed an unexpected gift for languages, which had been nurtured in the Islamic school where she first learned to read. At the same time he discovered that the paper-covered books she was reading at the end of the veranda were Nyerere's Swahili translations of Shakespeare, and that night he made her begin reading aloud to him from the pile of books beside her bed. During the long, soft nights she had read him Shabaan's stories and the *mashairi*, epic verses, of al Ghassaniy and Ahmad Nassir. On such nights he would lie sprawled on a bed strewn with rose petals, every shift of his bulk bruising a tiny fragile skin, while Hadida's voice lulled him into sleep. He was sleeping like this when Ola and Ogu returned. Hadida woke him at once, because it was already late. Ola had got lost on the way back to London, and the journey had taken twice the time that it should have. When the two men finished their story, Okigbo questioned them about the details: how they had been lured to the club, the sudden appearance of the policewoman, whether they had mentioned his name. Afterwards he dismissed them calmly enough, but below his assumed composure he was raging with anger and frustration.

He didn't receive the letter until he returned to his flat. He had left Hadida at the house and stepped into the waiting car without a word to Chris, but the chauffeur, who knew his employer's moods and habits, simply drove him back to Kensington without asking for instructions. On the way Okigbo tried to concentrate on the problem. Part of his anger was directed at himself for being so naive as to think that the mask could be secured simply by intimidating the boy. Reflecting on his own actions in the matter he understood that he had underestimated the brothers because of what they were, and he had assumed that they could be handled by Ola and Ogu, men who were also rootless and desperate orphans. So his contempt had overtaken and swamped his good sense. He closed his eyes to blot out the sight of the slate grey of the wet pavements and the puffs of blue smoke circulating in the traffic haze. Flickering in his mind were other mornings into which he had floated on the perfume of fresh green kif. On the horizon a slice of red sun rising out of the sea, the feathery whirring of parrots' wings mingling in his memory with the murmuring of Hadida's voice.

The letter was waiting for him in the hallway of his flat. Enclosed was a picture of the Dancing Face propped against a blank wall. In front of it, partly covering its lower half, was a newspaper, carefully folded to show the date. There was no message.

Okigbo studied the picture with a feeling of relief. His spirits lifted. For the last hour he had faced the prospect that the mask had been destroyed or permanently lost, or that locating it would require an exhaustive and unpleasant investigation. Instead, the problem had resolved itself into a simple one of negotiation. He didn't know who his opponent was, but that didn't matter. He had negotiated with some of the most unreasonable people in the world in circumstances which were very much less promising.

The telephone rang. The tape clicked on, and Okigbo recognized the voice immediately.

'If you got my letter,' she said. 'You'll know that I've got it.'

'I'm glad to hear it,' Okigbo said, 'but we have to meet and talk about this.'

'There's nothing to say. You've got a lot out of me already. I've done exactly what you asked so far, and I've got nothing to show for it. Now it's my turn, and I'm not messing around with you. You know exactly what I want.'

'I know what you want,' Okigbo told her patiently, 'but all I have here is a picture. You could have got it from someone else. If I have to negotiate with other people, it will be difficult enough. What you're asking is not easy. I have to say that I've seen it. I have to be confident in what I'm doing. We have to trust each other.'

'I wouldn't trust you as far as I can throw you,' she said.

Chapter Eighteen

They made an early start for Bristol. Danny had spent most of the previous day wandering through the library and the canteen. In the afternoon he went to another lecture on European institutions, found he couldn't focus on what was being said, and skipped down to the computers where he sat reading the latest messages on his e-mail. Later on he was too exhausted to worry about whether the Nigerians would come back, and his memory of the wire round his neck had begun to fade, so he went back to his room and slept. Sometime during the evening he had been awoken by a pounding on the door and Osman's voice shouting.

'So what?' Osman said, following him back into the room. 'You going to spend the rest of your life lying around here like a mug?'

In the end he had telephoned Eleanor and got her answering machine. He told it who he was and that he was coming to see Eleanor the next day.

'Me too,' Osman said.

'I thought you didn't want anything to do with it.'

Osman shrugged.

'It's something to do.'

Danny was too tired to argue and, in any case, he was relieved that he would have Osman's company. He had the feeling, also, that underneath his casual air Osman's imagination had been gripped by the Dancing Face. In some corner of his mind he felt a claim on the mask.

'Come early,' Danny told him.

When they got to Bristol it was already the middle of the morning. The lobby of Dr Hutchinson's building was so familiar that Danny had the sudden impression that they had travelled in a circle and ended up back in their own college. There were what seemed like the same noticeboards, crammed full and spilling over with notices and posters, the same air of busy aimlessness, and the same students loitering or wandering back and forth. There was also a black security man sitting behind a sliding glass panel labelled RECEPTION. He wore his uniform with the ostentatious elegance of someone who knew that his suit had been chosen and made to measure just for him, and when Danny asked for Dr Hutchinson's office, he directed them to the fourth floor with a supercilious lift of an eyebrow, as if the triviality of their request had been a disappointment.

They got into the lift behind two tall boys wearing rucksacks, a white-haired man who Danny suspected was a professor, and a red-haired girl in a black boiler suit with the top buttons undone to display a round and rising cleavage.

'Funny thing,' Osman said, as the lift started. 'Half the security men you see around are black.' The lift was silent, but Danny could feel the attention of their fellow passengers focusing on them. He mumbled something, hoping to deflect Osman's remarks. Instead, Osman gave him a 'don't give a shit' look and carried on, speaking louder this time. 'Great irony that is. Everyone reckons we're all criminals, and half the property in the country is guarded by little black men. Even fucking John Major gets driven around by some black man, holds open the door every time he gets out of his car.'

The professor coughed. Danny would have loved to turn around and get a look at his expression, but he decided against it. At the same time the lift doors opened and they strolled out on to the fourth floor.

Eleanor's office was at the end of the corridor. Danny knocked on the door but there was no answer. He looked around and shrugged at Osman, but before he could speak, a short, fat girl, who they'd just passed loitering in front of a noticeboard along the corridor, walked a few paces towards them and called out that Dr Hutchinson hadn't come in yet, but that when she did, she was first in the queue to see her. Danny nodded his assent, then he leaned back on the wall next to Osman, preparing for a long wait.

After about half an hour the fat girl disappeared into one of the offices along the corridor. In a short while she emerged, started towards the lifts, then changed her mind, came back, and told Danny that Dr Hutchinson had cancelled her tutorials, no one knew why, but the word was that she might be in sometime during the afternoon.

'I'd call in later, if I were you,' she said.

Danny thanked her.

'Let's go eat something,' Osman said.

They drove along Whiteladies Road towards St Paul's. On the other side of the pavement the glitter of the stores seemed like a counterpoint to the classical calm of the public buildings behind. It was as if the city was flaunting the fact that no matter how many layers of change it had to embrace, the residents had always managed to keep a tight squeeze on its habit of solid and respectable wealth.

'My school wasn't far away from here,' Osman said. 'This was the big city. When we came here the masters imagined that we were coming to the art galleries and museums or some bullshit like that. But most of the guys were after dope. I was after pussy. Great place for it. Full of little slappers from the valleys.'

'Gus used to come here,' Danny told him, remembering. 'He hated it. He said they'd built all this on the profits of slavery, then made out it didn't happen.'

Osman gave a sharp bark of laughter.

'You guys should forget about slavery,' he said. 'It's depressing.'

He turned off the main road and suddenly they were in a pocket of shabby terraces. The streets here had a furtive, lurking air, like a piece of territory airlifted in from some depressed area and plonked down in the swaggering heart of the city, hoping that no one would notice its presence.

'I'll show you this place I used to come and eat African food.' He grinned. 'Of course it was nothing like the food we ate in Lagos, but I didn't know that then.'

Danny nodded. He'd have preferred to go to a spot near the university where they would have been lost in a crowd of students, but he understood Osman's desire to revisit the places he used to frequent as a boy.

Osman parked outside a hairdressers, the window decorated with photographs of black women wearing various hairstyles. On the pavement lower down the street a crowd of black youths were squabbling, shouting at the tops of their voices. Osman locked the door of the van with ostentatious care and they walked across the street.

The restaurant they went into was a converted shop with half a dozen formica tables lining the walls, a couple of gambling machines standing opposite each other, and a small bar in the corner. Apart from five elderly Africans who were sitting round one of the tables playing a card game, the place was empty.

When the owner tore himself away from the game he brought them the only items on the menu: fried fish and fried plantain, rice and gongo peas.

'How come your brother was so friendly with a white South African?' Osman asked.

'Not South African. Zimbabwe she comes from.'

'Same thing.'

Danny shrugged. The same question had occurred to him, but Gus had said that Eleanor was different, that being born there gave her a right to her interest in Africa and African things.

'She's got no rights,' Osman said abruptly. 'Whites shouldn't have any rights in Africa. Not any more. They've had their fun. It's about time they left us alone.'

'You could say the same thing the other way round about us here,' Danny replied. He'd heard Osman say things like this before, and usually he didn't comment, but this time, for some reason, he felt irritated, up for the argument. 'I don't believe in all this territorial shit. If I've got rights here, what's wrong with her having rights in Africa? Anyway, it's a bit weird you saying that when you're living in England.'

'That's different.'

Danny shook his head and laughed at him, and in a moment Osman began laughing too.

'All right,' he said, 'I know that's illogical, but there's something that gets on my tits about these white people who reckon they know more about Africa than I do or see themselves as Africans or some shit like that. It's like they're trying to take away from you the last thing that you've got.' He laughed again, full of glee this time. 'Some guy told me a story about that once. There's this Nigerian living next door to an Englishman and they start talking and one day this English guy starts going on about Livingstone, and the Nigerian says, "Who's Livingstone?" I mean, he knows, but he's being funny, right? So he says, "Who's Livingstone?" and the English guy says Livingstone was an explorer who discovered Lake Victoria and all the rest of this stuff. So the Nigerian says, "What do you mean he discovered it? There were people living there all the time." So the English guy says, "Yeah, but he was the first white man to go there." "Oh yeah," the Nigerian says, "have you heard of Oladapo?" So the Englishman says, "No – who's he?" The Nigerian says, "He's one of my ancestors who discovered Blackpool." The Englishman starts laughing.

"He never discovered Blackpool," he says, "there were people living there all the time." "That's right," the Nigerian says, "but he was the first black man to go there." '

Danny had heard the story before, but he laughed obediently, enjoying Osman's pleasure in it.

'Yeah, well, you're making my point for me,' he said. 'That's how dumb the whole business is.'

In the street outside it had begun to rain, a soft drizzle which the windscreen wipers cleared with a lazy swipe. There was still no reply when they knocked on the door of Eleanor's office, but there was a typewritten notice pinned up which said that Dr Hutchinson had cancelled all her appointments for the day. Osman read it and swore loudly.

'What we gonna do?' he asked Danny. 'No way I'm hanging around here for another day.'

'Don't worry,' Danny told him. 'I've got an idea.'

They went down to the lobby and borrowed a phone book from the receptionist. There were several Hutchinsons, three of them with the title Doctor, but there was only one Dr E. Hutchinson. The address was in Clifton, and it stirred a distant memory in Danny's mind. Gus had talked about Clifton.

'This is her,' he told Osman.

She lived on the ground floor of a house set in a Georgian terrace which curved in a crescent round a leafy communal garden. Even in the rain, which was now beginning to fall in a steady downpour, it looked like a scene from the front of a postcard. Danny pressed the bell and when there was no answer, pressed it again.

'I'll wait in the van,' Osman muttered, but as he moved to walk away, there was a crackling sound from the grille next to the door and a woman's voice asked who was there.

'Gus's brother, Danny.'

There was a brief silence, then a buzzer sounded and Danny pushed the door open. They were in a spacious hallway, tiled in black and white. Against one of the walls a china vase of red lilies and blue asters rested on a spindly wooden table. Next to it was a wooden coat stand with a solitary raincoat hanging above a neatly furled red umbrella. On the opposite wall was a line of watercolours. It was a scene of quiet and elegant domesticity to which both Danny and Osman responded by carefully wiping their shoes on the doormat.

Eleanor was standing in the doorway at the end of the hall.

'Please come in,' she said.

She was a short, wiry woman with a pretty face, round blue eyes fixed wide open like a doll's, and a mop of curly iron-grey hair. She was wearing a black sweater and black jeans and her feet were bare. Her skin was pale and puffy without the protective colouring of makeup, and the dull pink shade of her eyes seemed to show that she'd been crying.

She sat them down in armchairs in the sitting room, and brought them coffee in delicate white cups. Danny and Osman sipped awkwardly, the discreet and ordered prettiness of their surroundings putting them on their best behaviour. Through the window they caught glimpses of the rain slanting down fiercely. In different circumstances, Danny thought, he would have enjoyed the feeling of being locked in an oasis of peace and order, keeping the elements at bay.

'When did you last see Gus?' Eleanor asked.

It had been a matter of months, Danny told her. He had gone down to London to spend Christmas Day with his brother, and they'd spent two nights and a day talking, mostly about Danny's life at university and his prospects. Gus kept saying that he'd spent too many years pushing at closed doors or travelling up cul de sacs. But the prospects for a young black man had changed. Not by a lot, but there was movement. Danny's chances were better than his had been, Gus said, but he had to be clear about what to do next.

It was the kind of conversation Danny imagined he'd have had with his father if he'd been alive. Eleanor nodded.

'He talked about you a lot,' she said. 'He wanted you to be happy and successful.' She paused. 'Especially successful.'

She said this with a solemn and reflective air which made Danny feel as if he was already in church attending Gus's funeral. She was avoiding his eyes, her hand cupped round her mouth, her gaze directed at the floor. He hoped she wasn't going to cry, because he suspected that if she did he would find himself breaking down too. Casting about in his mind for a distraction, he remembered that Gus had left the day after Christmas because he was going to spend the rest of the holiday with Eleanor. He couldn't imagine it, though, the two of them here together in this neat, pristine space, sparkling with polish and the scent of flowers.

'He sent me a mask. I know what it is. It came with a letter that he wrote me,' he said. 'Do you mind reading it?'

She gave an involuntary start when he mentioned the mask, then she looked him in the eye, her mouth set tight.

'Why?'

'He said you would know what to do.'

He held out the letter, but she hesitated before she took it, looking straight at him now. In that moment he thought he saw something. A flash of anger, perhaps. She read the letter carefully, her expression blank, controlled.

'I was the one who told him about it.' She didn't look away from the paper in her hand, and it was as if she was talking to herself, uttering her thoughts into an empty room. 'They asked me to take a look when it was offered to them. It was certainly made in West Africa and it's round about the right time, but no one can say for certain what it is. I told him that, but he was already convinced, even before I saw it.' She folded the letter, then unfolded it again. Her hands trembled. 'It was the legend really that began to obsess him, I think. They said that when the Oba danced he had dreams about the future, and when he wanted to bring on these visions he wore this mask.' She shrugged, and looked up for the first time. 'It's likely, but the story only surfaced after Brandt smuggled the mask out of Africa. It's possible that we'll never really know what it is.'

'So what's the big deal?' Danny asked. For the moment he was distracted. 'Why is it so important?'

'Because it's something special. You can tell just by looking at it.' Danny remembered the feeling the mask had given him, holding it in his hands, and he nodded slowly. Beside him he felt Osman stir. 'Then there's the legend. Perhaps great works of art always become myths, or perhaps myths achieve their expression by the emergence of great art.' She folded the letter carefully, pressing the creases flat between her fingers. 'What matters is the period and the region. No one actually knows very much more about most African art objects.'

She looked at him, studying him for the first time. Distracted by his resemblance to Gus, she could hardly recollect what she'd been saying, and she found herself focusing carefully, trying to escape the feeling of dislocation brought on by the sense that she was speaking to a younger version of the man himself. Occasionally she found herself wanting to say, 'but I've already told you this'. Watching him now she began to take note of the differences. He was a little taller than Gus had been, and his skin was smoother, a soft ochre highlighted by the dark smudge of his emerging beard. He hadn't bothered about shaving today, she thought, and the next idea to flash through her head was that if she'd had a child with Gus this might have been how he would look when he got to Danny's age. Tall, handsome, a serious face with the promise of a mischievous grin round his mouth. When she first met Gus she had still been young enough, and she'd imagined that having a child with him might be possible, but his cool reaction when she left Jack had convinced her that their relationship could only survive if it continued to be a series of raids in the dark. The thought of her being his partner and the mother of his child would have frightened him off. Even so, she had briefly considered taking her chances and getting pregnant without telling him.

'I'm not bothered about the mask so much,' Danny said. 'What I can't really understand is how he got mixed up with Doctor Okigbo and all these other guys.'

Eleanor had warned Gus about Okigbo. Years before, when

she'd been married to Jack and they were both teaching at Kano, she had got to know about men like Okigbo. In those years, just after the bloodshed of the riots, they had sometimes been confined for weeks to the lecturers' compound where they lived. Their housekeeper, Yusuf, a Hausa from a village nearby, had paced the yard dolefully, his fussy manners subdued, his normally cheerful features drawn into lugubrious lines. His brothers had been killed, Jack told her. That night she lay awake, racking her brains about how to express her sympathy without appearing patronizing or condescending, how to make him believe that she felt his pain. But in the morning Yusuf had disappeared and she never saw him again. It was round about this time that the university held a reception for the senior army officers in the town. Politics was how Jack described it. Cynical and opportunist sycophancy, she replied, and she refused to attend. At that point she still thought of herself as having a future in Africa, and the issue became part of the interminable agony of bitterness which began to grow between them. For a long while she dreamed that the rage would end after they arrived in Europe, but when they finally settled in Bristol it gradually became clear that it was Africa that had been holding them together. That was before Gus, or any of the others.

'I told him about Okigbo,' she said, 'but he brushed it off. He got quite angry about it.' Unable to stop she told Danny about how Gus had met Okigbo and recruited Rodney. 'I refused to help him at first, but that just seemed to make him more determined. I offered him the money he wanted, but he wouldn't take it.'

Danny was struggling with a sense of having been let down.

What Eleanor was telling him accounted for the hassle he'd been getting from Okigbo, and for Rodney's involvement, but none pointed in a specific direction or made it any easier to decide what to do.

'He said you'd know what to do,' he repeated, a note of helplessness in his voice.

In a quick movement Eleanor held the letter out to him, as if rejecting the responsibility he was implying.

'The plan was that he'd leave it with me, and then do whatever it was he intended. He talked about circulating photos at the Commonwealth Prime Ministers' conference and starting a diplomatic furore, but I didn't want to be involved in that. Only Gus knew what he was going to do next. My part was to hide it for him.' She paused, and when she resumed her voice wavered a little. 'I'll still do that if you want. I promised him.'

'I don't know where it is,' Danny said. 'It's gone.' Her head came up quickly and she gave him a stare of blue-eyed surprise. When she did this she looked even more like a painted doll, her long eyelashes glued together by her tears and sticking out. Danny found himself suppressing the impulse to giggle. 'A lot of strange things have been happening,' he continued.

Rapidly he told her about his experiences during the last few days, culminating in the theft of the mask, and his kidnapping by Okigbo's henchmen. She listened with one hand pressed against her bosom, her lips parted in an expression of shock.

'Could those boys you talked about have followed you?' she asked as soon as he'd finished. 'Apart from Okigbo, they were the only ones who knew about it.'

'There was someone else,' Danny said. He hesitated, uncertain about how she would take it if he mentioned Justine. Seeing his eyes turn away from hers, Eleanor understood immediately.

'A girl?'

Gus never talked about his girls with her. Equally, Eleanor avoided revealing anything about other men. Such talk, they had found out early on, stirred up emotions which their relationship couldn't accommodate.

Danny nodded reluctantly.

'Justine Oyebanjoh.' He told her briefly about his meeting with Justine and what she had said about Gus. Before he'd finished, though, Eleanor interrupted.

'Oyebanjoh, you said?'

'That's right.'

'Wait a minute,' Eleanor said.

She got up quickly and left the room. Osman touched Danny on his arm, and raised his eyebrows in a question.

'What's going on?'

Danny shrugged. 'No idea.'

Eleanor came back into the room. She sat down again and opened the book she was carrying, flipping through the pages with impatient fingers. As they turned, Danny saw that it was a photograph album, the earlier photos in black and white and then a blur of colour. Eleanor stopped and turned the book towards him.

'Look at this,' she said.

The photograph to which she was pointing was of an African man in his shirtsleeves standing on a lawn, a riot of red trumpet-shaped flowers forming a background behind him. Next to him and holding his hand was a mixed-race teenage girl. The face was rounder, and she had a plump look which she had lost, but the resemblance was unmistakable. Justine.

'Is that her?' Eleanor asked.

'Yes.'

Eleanor slammed the book shut.

'Damn. Damn.' She looked at Danny, her face creased up as if a sudden pain was shooting through her body. 'Did she tell you if she knows Okigbo?'

'She said she'd never met him.' Her manner had affected him and he was beginning to feel a shiver of apprehension about what she was going to tell him.

'Damn it,' Eleanor said. 'This is Doctor Oyebanjoh. He was Okigbo's doctor for a while and they were good friends. Okigbo was like her uncle. She knows him all right. She lied to you and she must have lied to Gus.' She stopped, her breath catching in her throat. She thrust the album away from her, knocking it off her lap and on to the floor, photographs spilling out of the covers as it sprawled open. Her eyes screwed up, and a sudden flood of tears began to flow down her cheeks. 'Bloody Gus,' she stammered, swearing from between her clenched teeth. 'How naive can you get? Bloody Gus.'

Chapter Nineteen

On the way to her meeting with Okigbo, Justine thought about her father. She had seen him last when they parted in Lagos. As she turned to wave goodbye he had been putting away his wallet. Beside him an official, the uniformed man who had flipped through her passport, was holding a bundle of naira which she guessed had come from her father. They were both smiling broadly. This was how she remembered him; at the centre of an aura of mystery and threat, his expression cheerful and untroubled. When she tracked backwards through her memories of him it struck her that she'd always felt this way.

For instance, when they arrived back in Lagos he had taken her to St Mary's for an interview. At first she thought this was an odd choice because neither of her parents had ever been Catholics and she knew nothing about the religion, but when she mentioned this to her dad, he'd simply smiled and said, 'Don't worry.' They had gone to the school without discussing it any further, but once past the wrought-iron gates she'd felt a change in him. He seemed to have become bigger and more jovial, with an air of command which had been weaving itself about him since they'd got off the plane. Justine had noticed it before on the second day when their chauffeur was late and her dad had spoken to him in a peremptory tone she had never heard him use in England. She was just getting used to the idea of having a chauffeur and cook, looking at them timidly and wondering how they would react if she dared ask them to do anything. Her father, by contrast, seemed to have no inhibitions whatsoever about ordering them around, clicking his tongue and looking about impatiently if they were out of earshot of whatever requests he wanted to make. On the day of the interview she felt this impatience about him as he sat behind her facing the nuns, an uneasy vibration in the air, like a dam about to burst.

There were two of them, a black woman dressed in black robes and a white woman in a blue dress who spoke with a French accent and had sly green eyes. The nun, who she later learned to call Sister, asked simple questions about her schooling, but she kept looking at Justine's dad. The French woman, who also turned out to be a nun, said nothing, but she, too, kept her eyes on Dr Oyebanjoh. Later, Justine grew accustomed to people treating him with a certain obsequiousness, which he called respect. Sometimes, when she was with him in a village outside the capital, men would come to the house and lower themselves to the floor as if about to do push-ups at his feet. The first time she saw someone do this, she remembered that her father was some kind of hereditary chief, but when she asked him what it meant he laughed and told her it was meaningless. The people who called him chief, he said, were a tiny sub-group within a larger population and they had long been scattered, their villages dispersed even before the

Civil War. His own father, along with the rest of his closest relations, had been killed in one night of disorder during a distant election campaign. There had been nothing left, not even the land. These men who bowed down before him were old men, he said, who had known his father and wanted to pay him respect.

Justine had, in any case, been intrigued, but unworried. When her father talked about these events it was clear that they were history, and sometimes, she knew, she even felt a kind of relief that there were no close relatives to accommodate. In England, when her father had broken the news that he had been offered an important job back home – as he called Nigeria – and that they were going to live there, she had felt as if a great jagged tear was about to rip through her life. One of the fears which haunted her all the while they were preparing to go away was that, isolated in this foreign place, she would be unable to remember or think of her mother. The images which crossed her mind were of herself picking a path along jungle trails or squatting, shoeless, in a dusty village street, but it had been nothing like anything she imagined. The convent had been a place of grass, flowers and the sound of water, verdant behind the high walls which kept out the baked earth and dust of the town. Her classmates, she discovered, were also mainly the daughters of big men, one or two of them Government officials, at whose names faces stiffened and went blank. When she walked through the busy streets or in a market she felt armoured, protected by the uniform of navy blue and white which declared her to be from St Mary's, the child of an important family. Within a matter of months she had forgotten all her previous fears, and the dust, the heat, the sun's glare which had begun to burn a dark film into her flesh, all seemed as normal as an English autumn.

Her father's pleasure at the speed with which she settled into her new life was immense, and they grew closer and more familiar than they had ever been. Sometimes he came to watch her playing hockey. The field was bordered by a tall wire fence, and whenever the girls played there would be a line of spectators along the fence. Among them were the permanent fixtures: a couple of stallholders and half a dozen beggars, tin cups clutched in hand, working through the crowd which the schoolgirls' presence delivered to them twice a week. Most of them were men, transported by the sight of the schoolgirls' bodies, which, in that place, had the exotic, foreign look of magazine models, slim and hardened as they were by the convent's regulated diet and the constant bouts of exercise.

Justine's father was one of the few parents who ever came to watch, stepping out of his car by the side of the street, and preceded by his chauffeur, officiously brushing the spectators aside to create a space where the doctor could stand and view the play, undisturbed. At such times the volume of noise would drop suddenly, as if someone had turned a knob. The catcalls of advice, jokes and howls of lust would be replaced by silence for a few minutes, and, when the noise returned, it would be at a quieter, more subdued level which, on the field, was more or less drowned out by the thwack of the sticks and the shouting of the players. Afterwards Justine's father would take her to a hotel for tea or a glass of imported fizz.

Walking towards the middle of Waterloo Bridge, she thought now of the smell of her father's aftershave – something lemony, a fresh clean tang which always felt like standing under a shower, the long streamers of clear water smacking into her face until she threw her head back, gasping for breath. 'Oh Daddy,' she almost said aloud, gripped once again by the fear that she was too late, that all this would be for nothing.

Okigbo was already waiting, standing by the rail, his hands resting lightly on it, looking out over the river. He wore dark glasses, a black-and-white check jacket and light grey trousers. As usual, he looked immaculate. It was not long after lunchtime and in the chill sunshine there was a thin stream of people crossing the bridge on foot; several of them were tourists, who, as they trudged past on the pavement, risked a quick glance to see what it was that this elegant black man was staring at so intently. Okigbo ignored them, his pose as still as a statue, but as Justine approached he turned and smiled broadly. Tactful as ever, he didn't move or make any attempt to touch her in greeting.

'I'm glad you picked this spot,' he said. 'It's been too long since I came here. Earth has not anything to show more fair.'

She guessed that this was his way of teasing her. She had picked the middle of the bridge because she would be able to see in either direction so as to make sure that he was alone before approaching him, and she was certain that he knew this.

'That was Westminster Bridge,' she said automatically.

Okigbo laughed. 'Yes. They taught you well at St Mary's.'

'Oh leave off,' Justine cried impatiently. 'You wanted to talk. That's why I'm here.'

'I was hoping,' Okigbo said, 'that we could talk about your conditions.'

'You know what my conditions are. I want you to go to the

High Commission, or to those oil company friends of yours, and negotiate for me. I want to hear from my dad, a letter or something that will tell me he's alive, and then I want him out and sent to another country. Then you'll get the mask.'

'I'm not sure it can be done.'

Justine laughed harshly.

'I'm sure it can.'

They faced each other, Justine's stare defiant and angry, daring him.

'Why are you like this to me?' Okigbo asked. 'Your father and I were like brothers.'

That was true enough, Justine thought. The first time she met Okigbo had been when her father took her out after school. He had risen from where he was sitting on the veranda of the hotel and greeted her warmly, holding her hand in both of his.

'What a beautiful child,' he'd said. 'A rose.' Her father laughed, pleased at his compliments. 'Welcome,' Okigbo told Justine. 'Welcome to your home.'

Various relatives had been saying things like this for a couple of months but when Okigbo said it he made it sound as if he was making her a gift, and suddenly she had felt that it was true. This was now her home. Even when, later on, she set out for England, she had still been certain of her return.

'You wouldn't leave your brother sitting in prison for over three years,' she said.

Okigbo sighed.

'If you've got it,' he murmured, 'you can negotiate for yourself.'

'No I can't. You know I can't.'

More than three years must have passed since she'd received the letter from her father. He had written to say that he had been arrested and was about to be tried. In the rest of the letter he told her that he loved her, that he was proud of her and all she'd achieved. Then he warned her not to come, not to waste time trying to get him released, because it would be useless. The charges had no grounds, he wrote, and he would be released or not. Outside intervention would simply make things worse. That was the last time she had heard from him.

Disobeying his instructions, she caught the first plane she could. In her imagination she pictured herself talking with her father through prison bars. She suspected that what he had said in his letter was true, that there was nothing she could do, but at least she wanted to see him. Perhaps, she kept thinking, it had all been a mistake. Caught up in a flurry of arrests in the latest upheaval, he would perhaps have been released already, and he would be sitting in his car outside the airport, ready to scold her for doing exactly what he had told her not to do.

At the airport there was no one to meet her. She went to the house of her cousin Uma. He was a health inspector, a post which her father had been instrumental in obtaining for him, but he greeted her in a matter-of-fact way and showed no sign of distress or grief about what had happened. The charges against the doctor, he explained, were a result of his business activities. He had been involved with a group of investors in the North who were accused of embezzlement and corruption. There had, as yet, been no trial, and no one knew where he was being held.

During the next few weeks Justine made a tour of the Ministry, the British High Commission, and of all the important men she could remember her father knowing. Most of them refused to see her. When she went to see Okigbo she was told that he was out. When she returned on the next day she was just in time to see his car emerging from the drive. In the back seat he looked straight at her, smiled, and turned away.

By this time Justine was incapable of surprise. In fact she already knew that events of this kind hardly ever broke the surface of normal life. At St Mary's all talk of politics had been discouraged. During her classes on the French Revolution Sister Marie Redemption had told them firmly, more than once: 'Our business here is education – not political debate.' In Justine's second year at the school, a general whose two daughters were in her class had been arrested for plotting a coup. No one had spoken about it, and the two girls, isolated by their bewilderment and grief, began to take on the appearance of pariahs, wandering the corridors hand in hand, their group of friends dropping away until, a fortnight later, they vanished.

It was as if her father had vanished in the same way, diminishing gradually to a small dot in the corner of the picture to be removed some time later, casually and without reflection. Growing reckless, she haunted the Ministry, telephoned journalists and foreign advisers, visited the clubs and hotels where senior officers enjoyed their leisure. None of it did any good. What she heard was that most people believed her father's associates to have been thoroughly corrupt, but in that they were no different to many other men of business who were allowed to conduct their affairs undisturbed. The real answer, she began to believe, was that Dr Oyebanjoh had publicly committed himself to a campaign for free elections and a return to civilian rule. From that time on he was walking a tightrope. In the circumstances her efforts were bound to be in vain, and, running out of money, she had given up and flown back to England. It was a couple of years later that Okigbo had contacted her.

'You know that I can't negotiate with them,' she said. The point was that they wouldn't be able to take her seriously. She had no illusions about that. She was foreign, a half-breed, and a woman. Everywhere in the country she had met with warmth and welcoming smiles. People liked her, frankly curious and charmed by her pale colour and her exotic eyes. She threatened nothing and no one. If you were a visitor or had no serious tasks to perform this made for a pleasant and agreeable life. If you were interested in making things happen it was an immovable barrier. In the continuing cycle of conflict the real enemies were men who almost shared the same blood, and the other side of the coin was that, between them, they also shared the same pools of influence and fought over the same chances of power. In their hands the levers of the state were moved and shaken. Okigbo was one of these.

'If I can get a message from your father . . .' he said.

'I want to see his handwriting,' Justine interrupted. 'Then I want him out and in another country. Benin, Togo, Ghana. Even Chad will do.'

Okigbo screwed his face up. 'I don't know.'

Justine's patience was gone.

'I know you can do it.' Her voice was shrill, carried by the wind, and a little group of fat white Americans, strolling ponderously past, turned to look. 'You still have that much power,' she continued, bringing her voice under control. 'Perhaps if my dad was really important it might be impossible, but I don't know what happened. He's just a fucking number who got lost, and they're too embarrassed or uninterested to let him go, or there's some petty provincial sadist whose idea of fun this is. You know that. You've done as much yourself.'

He frowned, looking past her over her shoulder, and she spun her head rapidly to see whether one of his men had come on to the bridge, but there were no black faces there, no one except the usual plodding file of white office workers and tourists.

'You don't need to be nervous,' he said. 'You can trust me.'

Those were more or less the same words that he'd used when he telephoned her that first time at her office. He had taken her to dinner at a hotel near Oxford Circus, where a uniformed flunkey had leapt to hold the door open as they stepped down from the car. She was as impressed as he intended her to be, and over dinner he told her that he had a plan to get her father out. It required her help, he said, but he would have to withhold the details until he was sure of her complete commitment. Halfway through the dessert he told her what he wanted. He had always liked her and she would have to sleep with him before he would continue with his proposition.

Justine had received such proposals a number of times from various men, including her cousin Uma, during her ordeal in Lagos. The difference about this one was that she believed it, and she believed, too, that Okigbo's vanity and his sense of self-protection required this guarantee. It was only later that she realized that he needed to know how far she would go.

She had walked out on him that night, but by that time she was, incredibly, twice as desperate as she had been two years previously, and at their second meeting she agreed. She had gone to bed with him reluctantly, forcing herself to relax as he touched her, with the thought that she was doing it for her dad.

A couple of hours later Hadida knocked on the door and came in with a tray of tea steaming with the scent of jasmine. Calmly Okigbo remarked that it was her custom to watch over him through the half-open door when there was a guest present in his room. While they drank tea Okigbo told her about his plans for the Dancing Face and explained that he wanted her to become Gus's companion so that there would be no prospect of the mask escaping his grasp. That was several months ago, but hearing him repeat the phrase about trust reminded her again about how much she had begun to hate and distrust him.

It wasn't as if she'd ever quite seen him as trustworthy, but the strength of her present resentment was recent. It dated back to a couple of months previously, after she had found out something which altered everything about the way she felt towards him. It had come up while she was having lunch with one of the attachés at the High Commission, a brother of one of the girls with whom she'd been at school in Lagos. Talking about a reception he had attended the night before, he had mentioned seeing Okigbo. 'Your father's good friend,' he'd said, giving the words a sarcastic twist. She had asked him what he meant by his manner, and when he tried to shrug it off, she persisted. He'd looked over his shoulder, as if to make certain he wasn't overheard, then he told her. 'Okigbo was a director of the business that your father invested in. He was one of the big boys who got away. It was the small fish, like your father, who got caught in the net.' He gestured. 'That's how it is.'

'Why did no one tell me before now?' Justine asked. She thought of her cousin Uma and the conversations they'd had about her father's trouble. He had never mentioned this. If he knew. The attaché looked embarrassed. 'Everyone thought you knew.'

She understood. Truth was what emerged from a balance of various forces and interests. Everyone had assumed that she was engaged in complex negotiations about her father's fate, and to rub her nose in inconvenient facts would have been impolite and perhaps cruel.

It was after this that Justine decided to make her own arrangements for the mask.

'I don't trust anyone,' she said mechanically.

She looked at her watch. Three o'clock. Along the river Big Ben began to chime the hour.

'Our original agreement,' Okigbo told her calmly, 'was that I would get him out when I got back, and for that I need the Dancing Face.'

'But you don't need it to get my dad out. I don't want to wait any more, and I don't trust you. If I give it to you now you've got no incentive, have you?' She remembered something. 'That day in Lagos, you saw me, didn't you? You drove right past, you recognized me and you smiled, but you wouldn't even talk to me.' She saw from his face that she was right, and all of a sudden her rage and suspicion boiled to a climax. 'Well, screw you. You get me my dad and I'll bring you the mask. Otherwise no deal.'

A taxi drew up alongside the pavement next to her and the driver reached out to thrust open the door as he stopped. She turned, stepped away from Okigbo, and got in. This was exactly how she had arranged it, and even though the taxi was a minute late she felt a lift of elation at how smoothly it had worked. As they pulled out into the traffic she glanced back to see the look on Okigbo's face, but he had turned away and was standing still once more, staring out over the river.

Chapter Twenty

Rodney had been waiting for over half an hour in front of Justine's flat before he began worrying about whether he'd got it wrong. He had trailed her to Waterloo and watched her meeting the African. He had assumed that she was going home immediately, so he simply drove up to Shepherds Bush, but when he got there and rang her doorbell there was no answer.

Sitting in the Escort opposite Justine's flat, Rodney kept his eyes open, scanning the street for any sign of the little red Peugeot that she drove. In his head he was dreaming.

Years ago his mum had taken him on a trip to the island she had come from, back in the seventies, the old days when work was plentiful, you could get a job just by walking along the street and looking at the notices in the shop windows. Things were different now. His mum wouldn't understand, he thought. Somehow she couldn't get it out of her head that the way you made it was to get some crap job and work your way up to the second rung on the bottom of the ladder. The memory of his mum's moralizing gave Rodney a momentary jolt of irritation and disturbed the pleasant

daydream he'd been building. As bloody usual, he said to himself, which was why he tried not to think about her. The last time
they'd been together was just before she'd set out in a mini-van
to preach the word of God in Cardiff. When he went to see her
off in Seven Sisters Road it had been difficult, at first sight, to pick
her out from the group of middle-aged black women dressed in
white and huddled together on the corner. These were the sisters
of the Church of God's Last Testament, the church which had
taken over his mum's life. The minister, a lumbering black hulk
with a white beard, angry red eyes, a glittering gold chain round
his neck and a Bible in his hand, had waved them into the van,
glaring up and down the street as if in urgent expectation of a
satanic invasion. That was the last Rodney had seen of his mum
for over a year. 'Nutcase,' he muttered to himself, 'nutcase,' but
alongside the anger he felt when he thought about her, and hidden
somewhere inside him, there was still a tiny place, shimmering
with heat and light, white sand and waves which broke in creamy
patterns of lace and little multicoloured fish darting around in
pools of water clear as glass.

By the time he gave up, the last glimmer of sunshine had vanished. The street had become a dark and gloomy gauntlet, broken
up by patches of light from the streetlamps. In the buildings opposite, all the windows, except for Justine's seemed to be glowing.

Rodney wound down the window, turned on the heater, and
wheeled the car back towards Ladbroke Grove. At first he'd
intended to stop and get himself a snack and a drink before going
back to check on whether Justine had got home, but once he found
himself driving down Ladbroke Road he gave in to the urge

which had been growing inside him and pushed the car, speeding in and out of the lanes of traffic, towards Harlesden where Janet and her mum lived. Perhaps, he thought, she would have eased up a little by now. In his heart he knew that it was a foolish hope, but he couldn't help it.

The first thing he heard when he rang the doorbell was Janet's mum running her mouth as usual. He grunted in disappointment and turned his back. The house was in a giant estate near Harrow Road, a mixture of low-rise apartment blocks and terraced houses. It was one of those estates which the council had been making a big effort to humanize, with rows of shrubs and pots of flowers sprouting along the paths. If you looked closely you could see that the pots were littered with fag packets and silver paper and Kentucky Fried boxes, but at this time of night, with the dustbins lost in pools of shadow and the lamps throwing soft globes of light along the front of the houses, it looked clean and pretty.

He had been hoping that Janet's mum would be out, because he knew that if he could get her on her own for a while, listening to him, he could change her mind, or at least persuade her to come out with him and bring the baby. As it was, when he heard Mrs Welsh rattling the chain on the door he knew he was in for the sort of kicking he'd had from her before.

'What do you want?' she snapped at him when she saw him standing there.

She was a tall, light-skinned woman with a scornful look about her, like she was something special. Dressed in a pleated skirt and flat-heeled shoes, she put Rodney in mind of a social worker, which, in a way, was what she was. Her real job was something in the housing department down the Town Hall, but most of her spare time was taken up with organizations like the tenants' association or the homeless shelters in the district. With another kind of mother, Rodney thought, even a religious nut like his own, he and Janet might have stood a chance, but Mrs Welsh had never liked him, and once Janet had run back with her face bruised and telling crazy stories about his gambling and drug-taking, the mother had treated him like some kind of animal with an infectious disease.

'I want to see Danielle,' he said.

Somewhere in the house he could hear the little girl babbling and screaming. He imagined that he heard Janet's voice too. His heart gave a leap.

'Let me explain something to you,' Mrs Welsh said sternly, looking down her nose at him. 'We have an injunction against you coming here and making a nuisance of yourself. I could call the police right now.'

At first Rodney used to think that the only features Janet shared with her mother were the marmalade-coloured eyes she had flicked at him the day they'd met in the college canteen. She was seventeen, just out of school, but she'd defied her mother to set up house with him, not far away, in Neasden. Her mum had been so mad about it that she hadn't come round until the baby was born. Janet's reaction had astonished and shocked Rodney. One week she was telling him what a bossy cow her mum was, the next week she was ringing her up every day and having long chats on the phone with the bedroom door closed to stop him overhearing. It wasn't long before Rodney began to wish that Mrs Welsh had stuck to her principles and kept away. Looking at her now he had the feeling that she had always been standing like this between the two of them, her angry eyes blazing defiance.

'Cha,' he told her, 'what's this "we"? If it wasn't for my daughter I wouldn't come near you. Just tell Janet I'm here.'

He knew she wouldn't, but he couldn't help himself. In response Mrs Welsh's face contorted with rage.

'Get off my doorstep,' she shouted, 'or I'm going to call the police right now.'

She was always threatening him with the police, and if he had known she was like that, he thought moodily, he would never have gone so far with Janet. The trouble was that she had inherited the same kind of mentality as her mother. He hadn't fully grasped this until he'd come home one day and, nipping into the bathroom for a quick piss, found the little plastic sacks empty and lying like abandoned skins on the floor of the bathroom. He knew what had happened immediately, but he couldn't believe it – until he confronted Janet and she told him straight out that she'd dumped the lot down the toilet. Rodney's entire being evaporated into one explosion, an aeration of fury. Before this time, when he slapped Janet, he had put a curb on his temper, doing it merely to correct her headstrong ways, show her who was boss. Now he was incapable of restraint and he'd given her a good slapping, then dragged her to the bathroom and flushed her head in the bowl. Afterwards he'd tried to explain what she'd done. This was the chance he'd been waiting for. Top Cat had let him into the ring of important dealers. They'd been in the same class, mates on the football field and side by side facing up to the Triads and the Moroccan gangs after school. When the baby came and he had to drop out of college for a succession of crap jobs, he'd gone to Top Cat, who'd fixed him up with a deal worth ten grand, nothing up front except the trust between brothers. What she had emptied down the toilet, he told her, wasn't cocaine. It was his life.

Looking at Mrs Welsh's contorted features he knew he'd never make her understand. There was no point trying, so he walked away from her and got back in the car. All that was left now, he thought, was to do the business. When he had some money, and he was back at college, she'd be able to see that this had been just a difficult phase in his life, and then they could sort things out.

He was still angry and agitated by the time he got to Shepherds Bush, but he felt a kind of relief when he saw the light shining in Justine's window. He got out of the car, walked across the road and rang the bell. He was hurrying as if driven by some force inside himself, not thinking about what he was going to do next.

She looked surprised when she opened the door and she didn't invite him in.

'I want to talk to you,' he said, without preamble.

'What about?' she asked.

He put his foot in the door in case she tried to close it.

'Not out here.'

She backed away reluctantly and he followed her in, shutting the door firmly behind him.

'You've got your money,' she said.

She was giving him a condescending look which reminded him

of Janet's mum, and which started a slow burn of anger somewhere inside him.

'A grand? That's peanuts. You know that.'

'Two,' she came back, 'and that's what we agreed.'

'That was split with Baz,' he said. 'I had to take it, but now it's just you and me I'm telling you it was peanuts. Gus said that thing was worth a million.'

'It would be if you could sell it. But you can't.'

'What about the African? How much is he giving you?'

The question shocked Justine.

'What are you talking about?'

'Don't bullshit a bullshitter,' Rodney said. 'I saw you meeting up with the guy.'

'Have you been following me?' Justine snapped, angry now.

'Good thing I did. Everybody making a big profit out of this thing except me.'

Justine stared at him feeling a flicker of apprehension. Rodney had been her secret weapon ever since Gus had brought him to the party and introduced them. When she contacted him later he'd been ready enough to do what she asked, grabbing the money she offered with both hands. As it turned out, the plan she'd conceived, of hijacking the mask after the robbery, hadn't worked, mainly because Gus had got rid of it faster than she'd anticipated; but when she found out that it was in Danny's possession she realized that Rodney would be the perfect tool. She had offered him all the money she had left to go up North and steal the mask back from Danny, and it had seemed generous enough to buy his silence. At the back of her mind she had imagined that he might, at some point, try to blackmail her, but by then, she thought, the matter would be settled.

'It's not about money,' she said, staring at him coldly, trying to suppress the fear swelling inside her.

'As far as I'm concerned it is.'

Rodney hadn't missed her confusion when he mentioned the African, and now he was convinced that he was right.

'I don't know,' Justine told him. 'Maybe I can raise some more money.'

'How much?'

'I don't know.' She looked away from him and shrugged her shoulders. 'Why don't you come back tomorrow?'

Rodney laughed.

'That's not good enough. I take a big risk. Now I want my share of what you're getting.'

'Your share of what?' Justine exploded, her voice pitching itself high and shrill. 'I told you this isn't about money. I'm not selling it. If I make you an offer that's all there is.' She took a deep breath and forced herself to speak calmly. 'I think you'd better go now. Come back tomorrow and I'll see what I can do.'

Rodney watched her, grinning. It was Janet's mum all over again, thinking she could dismiss him like some kind of servant. While he waited and watched he'd been thinking that he would be happy sharing whatever Justine got for the mask. Now it struck him that he could take it away from her and go to the African himself. There was nothing she could do about it.

'Where is it?' he asked.

'Get out,' she replied. 'Just get out of my flat.'

The contempt in her voice stung Rodney. He brushed past her and pushed open the door to the bedroom. He went in without a pause, opened the wardrobe and started throwing the clothes out.

'I'm ringing the police now,' he heard her shouting.

He ignored her and tipped the bed over with a crash. It wasn't there. There weren't any other hiding places in the room and he came out, heading for the kitchen. She was still standing in the sitting room, but he noticed that she'd put the phone down.

'It isn't here,' she snapped at him. 'Will you go now?'

Still ignoring her he walked into the kitchen and opened up the cupboards. When he came out she was sitting on the sofa, glaring at him.

'Are you satisfied now?' she said. 'Please go.'

He looked around the room, uncertain what to do next. He'd been watching her ever since he'd handed over the mask, and until she met the African at Waterloo she hadn't gone anywhere special. He had been sure that it would still be in her flat. Suddenly a new idea struck him. The boot of her car. He looked round for her bag, and saw it lying on a table next to the window, but as he went in that direction she darted in front of him grabbing for it. He pushed her away, but she came back at him, scratching and hitting out, until he finally lost his patience and gave it to her, a powerful slap across the face, then, as she cowered away, her hands over her face, he hit her with a righthander in the belly. As she crumpled to the floor he heard an explosive grunt which turned into a jagged wheeze. Rodney bent over her, hauled her upright and pushed her back on to the sofa. Her shirt had come apart during the struggle and he tugged it the rest of the way off, ripping it up the back, and tied her hands behind her. She started struggling again while he did this, but it was feeble in comparison to her previous efforts and he held her down easily. She wasn't wearing a bra, and he stared at her breasts, suddenly fascinated by the contrast of her big dark brown nipples against her creamy pale beige skin. Drawn as if by its own volition his finger went out to touch one of them. She cried out and began scrabbling into the sofa to get away from his hands. Carried away by his excitement, Rodney went after her, wrapping his arms round her to squeeze at her breasts. Aroused beyond control, he pinned her down with the weight of his body and reached between her thrashing thighs.

The doorbell rang, a long concentrated burst of sound. Rodney froze. Justine, her face buried in the sofa gave a muffled shout, then turned her head, took a deep breath and opened her mouth to scream. Rodney clamped his hand over her face and she bit him, crunching her jaws tight and worrying at his flesh like a dog. Rodney snatched his hand away feeling the skin rip and tear, but before she could do more than draw breath, he had covered her mouth with his palm.

The doorbell rang again. Justine whined through her nose, but Rodney kept her pinned almost motionless while they listened. After a couple of minutes they heard the sound of footsteps departing. Rodney eased himself off Justine and got up.

Justine screamed. In the confines of the flat it sounded loud enough to alarm the entire street and, panicking for an instant, he jumped at her, clapping one hand over her mouth, then, tearing off a piece of the dangling shirt with the other, he gagged her. As he crouched above her Justine huddled her body into a ball and burrowed once into the sofa, as if trying to escape through the back of it. But Rodney's excitement had gone. The interruption had brought him to his senses and reminded him about why he was there.

'Don't flatter yourself,' he said, moving away from her.

He went back to the handbag and opened it, dumping the contents on the floor. Looking for the car keys, he almost missed it. Tangled with the key chain was a locker key with a red plastic handle, and in a flash he knew where the mask was.

'Got it,' he told her.

His mind made up now, he picked the phone up and rang the African's number. All the while Justine's eyes followed him, dry and murderous. When he was finished on the telephone, he smiled at her, walked back into the kitchen and returned holding a tube of instant glue which he'd seen earlier in the cupboard under the sink. Ignoring her attempts to kick him, he hauled her off the sofa and lay her down on the carpet near the wall. He uncapped the tube of glue, smeared some of it on the wall, then grabbed her feet and planted them firmly, holding on as she twisted and turned, feeling the movements of her body with an excited and vibrating tension that was almost like sex. After a few minutes he let go. When he took his hands away, Justine's feet were bonded tight to the wall, and as she twisted, trying to free herself, she gave a cry of pain through the gag. Rodney grinned at her. She could free herself in a while, he thought, but it would take a long time. By then the deal would be done.

'I'll phone in a couple of days,' he told her. 'I don't want you to starve. If you don't answer I'll ring them people at your work and tell them you're trapped in your flat.' He laughed, contemplating her half nude body, bound and helpless. 'They'll enjoy that.'

He went to the door and, with his hand on the handle, turned round to tell her something he'd been thinking.

'You know,' he said seriously. 'That stuff is completely useless for anything except sticking your skin to something else. You shouldn't waste your money on it.'

Chapter Twenty-One

Back in his flat Dr Okigbo sat drinking tea and reflecting on his options. He had waved Hadida away impatiently when she came to join him, an indication of how angry and disturbed his meeting with Justine had left him. Usually, when he was in the flat at this time she would talk with him about what she'd been doing during the day. She was a frequent visitor to the mosque in Regents Park, and sometimes she would walk down to Edgware Road with some of the Arab women she met there to shop and listen to the gossip that circulated round the cafés. Somehow she had made herself a part of a network about which he knew little. For instance, she had been asked to assist in the instruction of a group of Englishwomen who had embraced the teachings of the Prophet, and once a week she would return giggling and full of stories about the strange ways of the English.

In normal circumstances Okigbo was entertained by Hadida's tales, but on this particular afternoon he was in no mood to listen to her chatter. It took more than an another hour before he could restore a degree of order to his thoughts, and once he had calmed his rage, he began thinking about his prospects of recovering the mask quickly. Justine had been overestimating his power to make things happen, but, looking at it from her point of view, that was understandable. In fact he knew no more than she did about where Dr Oyebanjoh was being held or whether he was alive. He had ways of finding out, but it would take considerable sums of money to locate the man, even before he could begin thinking about how to effect his escape. Of course it wasn't the money that mattered. The problem was that all this would take a long time. It could take months, perhaps longer, and while he sat in London dangling on the end of a string held by a stupid girl too many things could change. The solution was to use more direct methods. Briefly he considered kidnapping the girl and forcing her to disclose the whereabouts of the mask, but this was an option he rejected almost as soon as it occurred to him. In Africa he would have had no hesitation about doing whatever was most speedy and convenient, but he knew that in Britain things could very easily get out of hand. In any case the whole idea was distasteful. He was no torturer. It was true that he had caused such things to be done in the past, but that had been at the end of a long chain of intermediaries which he could disclaim. He had more than once willed the end, he knew, but he had always refused to be involved with the means that his subordinates employed. There was a line he would not cross. Trickery was his only recourse, he thought, and he began calculating his moves with a certain enjoyment, like an expert player facing a complex problem on the chessboard.

The telephone rang. As he recognized the voice on the tape his irritation returned, and he was just about to reach out and switch the machine off when it struck him that he had nothing to lose by listening.

'I have something you want,' Rodney's voice murmured. 'This is a new ball game. If you want it you talk to me. You think she's got it, but she don't. This time you don't talk to me, you buggered, all right?'

Okigbo picked up the phone.

'I don't understand. Who are you? What are you talking about?'

'You know what I'm talking about,' Rodney said, 'and you know who I am. If you want that thing you deal with me. You understand that?'

Okigbo's instinct was to tell the boy to get lost, but there was something about Rodney's voice which struck him as more self-confident and knowing than when they'd spoken previously. Besides, if the boy knew about his dealings with Justine it meant that he must have some contact with her, and this implied that he must know something about the whereabouts of the mask, even if he didn't have it in his possession.

'What do you want?'

On the other end of the line Rodney gave a self-satisfied chuckle.

'Not on the phone. Meet me later on.'

The meeting place Rodney dictated turned out to be Waterloo Bridge, the spot where Okigbo had met Justine a few hours earlier. Okigbo found this disturbing, because it demonstrated that Rodney felt confident enough to play with him, jerk him around by showing up on the same stretch of pavement where he'd recently suffered so much abuse. To make matters worse, there was no one waiting on the bridge when he stepped out of the car. It was nearly midnight, and the pavement was more or less deserted except for the occasional straggler. The view now had a fairy-tale quality. The surface of the river looked like a still dark mirror, reflecting the glowing strings of light on the path down below. Across the water Big Ben hovered, its pale round face luminous as the full moon.

On any other occasion the radiant quality of the landscape might have held Okigbo's attention, but at this particular moment it seemed to be a mere distraction. He turned his back on the river, searching the shadows at the end of the bridge. He had instructed Chris to drive past at ten-minute intervals, and he'd hardly set foot on the empty pavement before he decided to get into the car and leave when the chauffeur made his first circuit.

He was looking at his watch when he heard the footsteps and saw the boy walking towards him. Okigbo recognized him at once, not so much because of any distinguishing features he could pick out, but because Rodney represented a type which he had already identified from the voice on the phone and fixed in his mind. As it happened, Rodney's appearance was exactly as Okigbo had pictured it. He wore a long black overcoat and thick-soled white sneakers. His head was shaved close to the scalp, giving him an air of bullet-headed aggression. As he came nearer the look he gave Okigbo was scowling, angry. Okigbo smiled warmly and held out his hand.

'Rodney?' he asked.

Rodney kept his hands in his pockets.

'This is business,' he said.

Okigbo put on a disappointed manner and let his hand drop. That is precisely why I'm smiling, you fool, he thought.

'What do you want?' he asked.

'Money,' Rodney told him.

He watched the African closely. He had waited on the steps below for half an hour before the big black BMW arrived and before that he'd made a couple of tours round the bridge, so he was fairly certain that the African was alone and unaccompanied, as he'd requested. On the other hand, he knew how tricky these guys could be. As he climbed on to the bridge he'd found himself wishing that he had let Baz in on the rest of it, but the truth was that either he could handle this on his own or it couldn't be done. Besides, splitting the duns cut the profits down so much that it was hardly worth the risk.

'What for?' the African asked.

He was still smiling. No reason why not, Rodney thought. The guy was a millionaire. Thief so much money from his own people he could afford to smile. Rodney took one hand out of his pocket and gave the African the photograph.

Okigbo studied it closely. It was a photograph of the Dancing Face, almost identical to the one Justine had sent him, with the same newspaper propped against the mask, and, as far as he could make out, taken with the same camera.

'What's this?' he asked.

Rodney made an impatient sound. 'Cha. Talk sense, man.'

'This doesn't prove anything,' Okigbo said. 'What do you expect me to do?'

'I want thirty grand,' Rodney told him.

He had calculated the sum carefully. It would pay off his debt to Top Cat, and it would allow him to resume his career as a student without the penury which had forced him to these lengths. Once he had the money, he thought, he'd be free and clear. After this his life would take a clean upward course.

'Thirty thousand pounds is a lot of money,' Okigbo replied, 'and this is not proof. You could have found this or you could have stolen it.'

He held out the photograph disdainfully, between the tips of two fingers. Rodney waved it aside.

'You keep it. In a coupla months you can look at it if you want to remember what the real thing looked like.'

Okigbo smiled appreciatively. This was one of the very few things he admired about the blacks in Britain and the USA. They possessed, almost invariably, he thought, a kind of verbal speed and dexterity, which had allowed them to take the language and produce a network of idioms which were recognizably their own. He noted, too, that the boy's accent had changed. Now he sounded like any other well-spoken Londoner.

'I want to believe you,' Okigbo spread his hands in a gesture of sincerity, 'but all this is very sudden. First one person says they have it, then another. I don't even know how you're connected with all this. Before I can believe you, I need to know what's going on.'

Rodney felt himself relaxing a little to match Okigbo's accommodating manner. He'd expected that explaining what was going on would be part of the deal, and he could live with that, as long as the guy finished up by forwarding the duns.

'I helped Gus capture the mask. It was my idea really.' This was an embellishment that somehow he couldn't avoid adding, and the African gave a little nod, as if noting its significance. 'But Gus's woman phoned me. She said that his plan was crazy, and she told me about you and how you were financing the whole deal.'

Okigbo nodded again. Damn her, he thought. Aloud, he confined himself to a polite murmur. 'Good.'

Rodney's face creased up and he pointed his finger, his manner suddenly intense and angry.

'I was supposed to be his partner and Gus never told me, man. Nothing about the money side of things or how much he was getting. You're a millionaire, right? I knew he was keeping a lot for himself.'

Okigbo kept his face straight. He had the suspicion that if he told Rodney how small the sum of money that he'd given Gus was, the boy would refuse to believe it.

'Surely he paid you,' he said, pretending astonishment. 'We budgeted for your assistance.'

'Peanuts,' Rodney exclaimed. 'Fucking peanuts, man. That's why I went in with her. We never sussed that Gus would send it out of town, like he didn't trust us. Then he had the accident and the brother showed up. She just called me late that night and gave me an address, told me to go and pick it up.'

'Ah.' Okigbo was feeling a surge of respect for Justine. She had betrayed both Gus and himself, and she had almost got away with it. 'And now she has it?'

'No, man,' Rodney said. 'Listen to me. I took it away from her. If you want it you have to deal with me. Thirty grand is the price.'

Okigbo paused for a few seconds. He frowned, pretending to

consider the situation. He believed Rodney because it all fitted, and listening to the boy he could barely conceal his pleasure at how well things had begun to fall out.

'What guarantee do I have that this isn't a trick?'

'Talk sense, man,' Rodney said again. 'I bring the mask. You bring the money. We exchange. Goodnight campers.'

Okigbo smiled openly now.

'That sounds reasonable,' he said.

Chapter Twenty-Two

It was still rush hour, and the motorway was crowded. Osman drove faster than usual, switching lanes and overtaking with a recklessness which, at any other time, would have made Danny cringe with terror. On this occasion, however, Osman's driving fitted with Danny's mood, and he hardly noticed the speed. All the way to London he kept trying to ring Justine on the mobile. When the machine answered he cut the connection. He felt desolate, angry and sad and betrayed, all at the same time.

'What are you going to say to her?' Osman asked.

Danny shrugged his shoulders.

'I don't know.'

They'd been through this sequence repeatedly. Once it was clear that Justine had been lying about her relationship with Okigbo, it had occurred to all of them that she also must have been deceiving Gus too. The other thing about which they were all certain was that the Dancing Face was now in Justine's possession. The knowledge lay inside Danny's chest like a stone, weighing on him, dragging his mind down into strange new depths, and the idea which made him shiver when he thought of it was that Gus's accident had been set up in some way by Justine.

If that was how it was, he thought furiously, he would find a way to make her pay for it.

The oddest part of all this, the part which made Danny feel sick and guilty, was the fact that, in spite of what he was thinking about Justine, she still inspired in him a secret and furtive desire, and now he sensed that ever since they met he had cherished a bright little nugget of hope about his prospects with her.

When they arrived outside her flat he experienced such a feeling of sick dread that if Osman had suggested waiting or had driven off again he wouldn't have objected. Instead, he threw open the door as soon as the van came to a halt and, without a word to Osman, he got out and raced across the pavement. He gave the bell an angry stab with his finger and, after a couple of minutes, when no one appeared, he did it again.

'Nobody in,' Osman said behind him.

They retreated to the pavement and looked at the windows. In Justine's flat the curtains were drawn and there were lights shining behind them.

'She can't have gone far,' Danny muttered. 'We'll wait.'

They got back in the van. Danny sat with his back to Osman staring at the windows. In his imagination, he saw her sitting opposite him in the candlelit restaurant where they had met. While they talked he had kept recognizing emotions and mannerisms that were like his own, and he'd understood immediately why Gus had been in love with her. Perhaps, he told himself, she had kept quiet about knowing Okigbo because she wanted to reject her background. Perhaps she'd wanted to avoid the prospect of anyone identifying her with the class of men who started wars and burned villages. He almost began to say this to Osman, then stopped himself, because he suspected that when he tried to put this idea into words it would sound stupid.

Across the road a door opened. A man came out. There was something familiar about the way he moved. Then the light gleamed on his head before he shut the door behind him. For a moment Danny thought he must have been mistaken, and he was still trying to make up his mind when the man walked along the pavement and got into a white Escort. In the back window a red light glowed as he switched on the engine.

'See that guy just got into the Escort?' Danny asked Osman.

'What about him?'

'I think that's one of the guys who fronted me up at Gus's flat. Rodney, he said his name was.'

The Escort pulled away and sped past them. In the glow of the streetlamps Danny saw the driver clearly.

'That's him.'

'So they're all in on it,' Osman said. 'They stitched Gus right up, you know.'

Danny didn't answer. He was angry with himself again. At the point when Rodney emerged he had been trying to find excuses for Justine.

Osman shifted restlessly.

'I reckon she's in there.' He chuckled. 'Maybe she's in bed recovering.'

He made an obscene gesture with his fist.

'Shut the fuck up,' Danny shouted.

He flung the door of the van open and jumped out. He didn't look back, although he wondered for an instant whether he'd offended Osman. Then it struck him that he didn't care. Oz should have known better than to say something like that, he thought furiously.

He gave Justine's bell a long ring, then when she didn't answer he rang the bell above. When the entryphone squawked, 'Who is it?' he said, 'Justine.' 'She's the bottom bell,' the voice said. Danny stuck his finger on the next button, and this time when he said 'Justine', he added hurriedly that he knew she was in but that her bell didn't seem to be working. There was a moment's hesitation, then a buzzer sounded and he pushed the door open.

There was another bell beside the door of the flat and when he pressed it he could hear an echoing chime. Osman pushed past him and put his ear to the door.

'I can hear something,' he said. 'There's somebody in there.'

The thought that Justine had been entertaining Rodney and was now refusing to open the door to him infuriated Danny. He pressed his ear against the door and listened. There was a sort of bumping sound he couldn't identify. Then he heard a muffled howl.

Osman had heard it too. As they listened they heard it again, and again.

'Move,' Osman said.

He stepped back to give himself room in the narrow corridor, then launched himself in a stiff-legged kick, slamming his heel against the lock. It didn't start to give until the third kick, then they both hurled themselves against the door until it sprang open with a crash.

Danny spotted Justine immediately. At first the fact that she was lying on the floor and almost naked made him think that she must be dead, but that couldn't be true, he realized in a flash, because her eyes moved as she looked at him over her shoulder, which was turned away in what seemed like a futile attempt to hide her body.

'Justine,' a woman's voice called out from the top of the stairs. 'Justine, are you all right?'

Danny guessed immediately that, having let them in, she'd heard the door being smashed and started worrying. Quickly, he bent down, untied the gag which covered Justine's mouth and pulled it away from her face. She coughed and her mouth worked silently.

'Justine,' the voice from upstairs called out again.

There was a moment of silence, then Justine seemed to gather herself together and shouted back.

'I'm all right. The door stuck. Sorry about the noise.'

Silence again, then they heard footsteps retreating. Osman laughed.

'There's a dressing gown in the bathroom,' Justine said. 'Can you give it to me?'

In the circumstances her voice sounded remarkably calm and controlled.

'Are you all right?' Danny asked her.

'Apart from the fact that I've got my hands tied behind my back, my feet are stuck to the wall and there's man I've never seen before leering at me,' she said, 'I'm fine. Now can you get me my fucking dressing gown?'

'I'll get it,' Osman said. He was grinning, and Danny could hear him laughing all the way into the bathroom.

'What happened?' Danny asked her.

She looked away, not answering for a couple of seconds. When she spoke her face was still turned away from him.

'Untie me, can't you?' She paused. 'No. There's a pair of scissors in the kitchen. Just cut it.'

Danny went into the kitchen, found the scissors, and came back. Osman was draping the dressing gown over Justine. Neither of them spoke. Danny bent down, fumbling under the cloth, and, trying to conceal his disturbance when he felt the heat of her body, cut her bonds with a few awkward strokes. Justine stretched her arms out under the dressing gown, raised her head and looked at her feet.

'Can you scrape me off this wall?'

'I suppose so,' Danny said uncertainly.

Behind him Osman clicked his tongue impatiently. 'Get her to tell you what happened,' he said.

Justine turned her head to look at him.

'Who are you?'

'This is Osman,' Danny told her. 'He's my friend.'

'Now we've had the introductions,' Osman said, 'what about that guy Rodney? What was he doing here? Why'd he do this to you?'

'It's none of your business,' Justine replied. 'Look. Either help me get loose or get out of my flat.'

Her tone was contemptuous, defiant, and Danny felt a kind of admiration for her being able to sound like that, lying on the floor half-naked with her legs stuck to the wall. At the same time, he noticed that her face was bruised and swollen. Oddly enough, instead of increasing his sympathy for her, the sight hardened him, as if the marks on her face were an outward symbol of her secret corruption, a sign that she was damaged and tainted goods.

'What happened with Rodney is your own business,' he said. 'But I want to know why you lied about Okigbo. I've seen photos of you and him and your father larking about.' He was lying about the photos, but he was also ready to bet that such things existed. Thinking about it he felt himself beginning to be transported with rage, standing over her and jabbing his finger at her face. 'I bet Gus never saw those,' he shouted. 'I bet he had no idea that you knew either of those guys.'

Suddenly, and without warning, Justine gave a sob and began to cry, the tears flowing down her face. Danny moved to do something, he didn't know what, but he heard Osman move, and when he looked round he saw him flop on to the sofa, his legs stretched out, his face turned towards the ceiling, eyes closed. Danny guessed that this was a signal about how to react. He hesitated, then he went over to the box of tissues he saw on the bookcase, set them down alongside Justine without touching her, walked over to the sofa and sat down beside Osman.

After a little while Justine stopped crying, took a tissue from the box, blew her nose and dried her eyes.

'I suppose,' she said thickly, 'you think that I stabbed Gus in the back.' She blew her nose again. 'But I didn't. I didn't.'

'So why did you lie?' Danny asked. It was hard not to believe her, but every time he found himself softening he remembered that her sincerity had only been a facade.

'I went with Gus because of Doctor Okigbo,' she said. 'All right, but I had to. It was my father. He promised to get my father out.'

'What's it got to do with your father?'

She looked round at him, as if startled that he didn't know, then seeing his blank expression she began to explain about her father and about what Okigbo had promised. As she talked she gathered the robe around her, hunching herself into it as if the room had turned colder.

'I wouldn't have hurt Gus. Maybe if I'd told him at the beginning it would have been okay, but he was so determined that it shouldn't go back to the government that I couldn't tell him right away why I wanted it. Then after a while I couldn't anyway. He trusted me, but I wouldn't have done anything to hurt him.' Her voice was pleading, anxious to convince Danny, or perhaps herself. 'The thing was that as far as Gus was concerned it didn't matter what happened to the mask. He just wanted it to disappear so he could make a political point. I thought that if I took it and helped my father I could tell him later. It wouldn't have mattered to him.'

Her voice trailed away towards the end, as if she wasn't sure she believed what she was saying. She blew her nose again. Danny waited, trying to contain the anger he felt. He wanted to shout back at her, to scream that she'd been a bitch and a traitor to Gus, but he couldn't trust himself to speak.

'Rodney was helping Gus,' she continued. 'That's how I met

him. When I found out you had it, I sent him up to your place while you were in London.'

So that's why she'd slept with him, Danny thought bitterly. To give Rodney enough time to get the mask away.

'So I suppose he's got it now,' he said.

She squirmed under the robe. Her hands urged at it as if she felt the desire to pull it up over her face and disappear.

'I left it in a locker at Euston Station. He took the key.'

Danny looked round at Osman, but he didn't have to say what was on his mind.

'No point,' Osman said. 'He'll have gone by now.'

'Can you get me out of this?' Justine asked. She paused. 'Please.'

For a moment Danny felt like leaving her to it, then it struck him that if Okigbo turned up she'd be helpless. Whatever she was like, he told himself, he couldn't do that to her. Revenge seemed pointless now. He shrugged at Osman.

'Let's do it.'

They soaked the wallpaper with water and hacked at the plaster until it came away, leaving Justine's feet caked with chunks of plaster. She groaned, stretched, sat up and pushed her arms through the sleeves of her robe. Then she began picking and scraping at her feet.

'What are you going to do about your father now?' Danny asked her.

'I'm going to get it back,' she said.

'Uh oh,' Osman's voice went. 'Let's get out of here.'

Danny ignored him.

'How are you going to do that?' he asked her. Inside him was the feeling that, after all that had happened, he couldn't simply give up and walk away from the thing that Gus had started, and which had cost him his life.

Justine swivelled round, her arms wrapped round her knees. Bundled up in the robe she looked a bit like a small girl waiting to go to bed.

'I heard him on the phone arranging to meet Doctor Okigbo. He wouldn't have taken it with him. He's not that much of an idiot. I don't think he would have got it out of the locker yet.' She paused, her eyes narrowing as she gazed at Danny, the tone of her voice hardening. 'If you come with me, we can go there and wait till he comes to get it.'

Behind Danny, Osman grunted contemptuously.

'You can't trust her, Dan.'

'You do what you want,' Justine said. 'I'm going anyway. I want to see that guy again.'

She got up, scraping her feet against the carpet, walked into the bathroom and slammed the door shut.

'You can't trust her, man,' Osman repeated. 'You don't know what she's planning.'

'I've got no choice,' Danny told him. He paused, thinking about it. 'Besides, I've got my own plan.'

Chapter Twenty-Three

It was about midnight by the time they got to Euston, and at this hour of the night half its lights had been turned off. In the gloom the station had a dull, murky air, which gave it the feel of a site where mysterious assignations might take place.

Osman drove past the front along Euston Road, then turned right and parked near the side entrance to the station.

'What do we do now?' he asked.

Danny had been thinking about this.

'We'll have to wait until he turns up, if he ever does. The best thing is if you go inside and keep an eye on the locker. He doesn't know you, so he won't panic if he sees you.'

'So what happens when he turns up?'

'We catch him coming out and take it off him.'

'Just like that?'

'He's not going to like it.'

'There's two of us.'

'Three,' Justine said.

Osman looked round at her and laughed.

'You really want to give him a good spanking, don't you?'

'He deserves it,' Justine said.

Osman reached under the seat and pulled out something metal and shiny. At first glance Danny thought it was a big spanner and he was going to tell Osman he didn't need it and to leave it where it was when he realized that it was a gun.

'What the fuck is that?'

'It's a nine-mil Centurion,' Osman said calmly. 'Same as the Beretta. US army and police. Eight inches long. Automatic or single shot. Fifteen shots in the magazine. This will get his attention.'

In the back of the van he heard Justine draw her breath in sharply and he felt her scrambling to take a look. In the next moment she was leaning over the back of his seat. He could smell her, scented from the shower, her warm breath tickling his neck. At the same instant he was conscious that having her so near had given him an erection. He ignored it and stared at the gun, trying to conceal his fascination and excitement at seeing it.

'Where'd you get it?'

'Dave took it off that other bloke. He didn't tell Cynthia, but he didn't want it around. He gave it to me.'

'Sometimes I wonder about you, Oz,' Danny said. 'Are you crazy? You go in the station with that, some cop stops you and searches you, what do you think is going to happen?'

'Let me ask you a question,' Osman came back at him. 'This time of night who's more likely to get searched? A nice, well-spoken African student who's missed his train, or a mixed-race couple sitting in a transit outside the station in the dark?'

It was a toss-up, Danny thought, but Osman was probably right. He had the edge.

'Why don't we just chuck it away?' Danny said.

'Now you're kidding. All right. Maybe I'll get rid of it tomorrow, but right now if we're going to take the thing off this guy I feel better holding it. Don't worry, it's not loaded.' Suddenly he pointed it at the windscreen and pulled the trigger. Danny tensed himself, but all he heard was a click. Behind him Justine let out a sibilant explosion of breath. Osman laughed. 'See?'

He slid the door open, still chuckling, got out, and looked back at them.

'Don't do anything I would do,' he said.

As he walked away Justine clicked her tongue in annoyance. She began climbing into the front of the van, and, automatically, Danny shifted over to the driver's seat so she could sit next to him.

'He's a complete lunatic,' she said. 'Nuts.'

'He's okay,' Danny told her. 'He probably saved my life a little while back.'

She took this in without comment, and they sat in silence for a couple of minutes.

The traffic was still flowing steadily up and down Euston Road, but it was light enough now to be able to distinguish the sound of individual engines as they stopped and started at the lights. Ahead of the parked transit, the street which ran beside the station was empty, deserted. There were no houses or offices bordering it, and at this time of night only the occasional vehicle rolled past.

'I think this mask might be my dad's only chance,' Justine said quietly.

Danny knew she was looking at him, but he didn't turn round to meet her eyes. The same idea had already occurred to him, but it had been followed by the thought that she didn't deserve his help. At the same time he remembered that he couldn't think what to do with the mask if he did get his hands on it.

'You can't trust Okigbo,' he said.

'Of course not. I don't intend to.'

Danny shrugged, thinking about the sense of power and authority he had felt radiating from Okigbo.

'I know that this probably doesn't mean much to you,' Justine said, 'after all that's happened, but I think Gus would have helped me.'

'Only you never told him.'

She flinched as if he'd threatened to strike her.

'I know,' she said. 'I wish I had.'

A pair of headlamps swung out of the Euston Road, momentarily lighting up the interior of the van. Danny was struck by a sudden premonition and he scrunched down in his seat quickly, gesturing at Justine.

'Get down. Get down.'

She crouched down. The car slowed behind them, the beam searching, then it swung over to the opposite side of the road and stopped almost in front of the stairs beside the station. The lights vanished, and, peering into the rear-view mirror through the bottom of his window, Danny saw that it was a white Escort. Rodney got out and, without looking around, trotted up the stairs and disappeared into the long arcade leading to the station. As he paced out of sight another pair of headlamps lit up the van from behind, and another white car rolled slowly across the road and parked several yards in front of the Escort. Danny recognized it at once. It was the Cortina in which he'd ridden with Ola and Ogu.

'Stay down,' he muttered to Justine.

As if to confirm his identification the taller of the two Africans, Ogu, got out of the car and stood on the pavement gazing at the station. After a minute or so he climbed back in and Danny saw the glow of a cigarette lighter flaring.

'Keep down,' he hissed at Justine.

His mind raced ahead to what would happen when Rodney came out of the station and down the steps. If he was carrying the mask, the Africans would probably do precisely what he had intended to do himself. He squirmed back in his seat and closed his eyes, grappling with the various possibilities. He had been confident enough about the idea of mugging Rodney and taking the mask away from him, but Ogu and Ola were a different proposition. One thing was certain: if the two Africans seized the Dancing Face, it would go straight to Okigbo and he'd never see it again. An unexpected anger rose up inside him at the idea. For this pearl his brother had paid a great price. It belonged to no one else.

'Who are they?' Justine whispered.

The question startled Danny. In his preoccupation he had almost forgotten about Justine, and in any case he hadn't known that she had never seen Ogu and Ola before. He started to turn and face her, but she had wriggled up behind him on the driver's seat to look over his shoulder. Now she was so close that when he shifted his position the movement pressed him back against her breasts. For a mad instant Danny felt an intense desire to turn and embrace her, drag her on to the floor of the van.

260

'These are the guys who work for Okigbo,' he whispered back. 'The ones that grabbed me.'

He felt her shudder. Her breasts moved softly against him.

'What are we going to do?'

'Shush,' he told her, 'let me think.'

Later on, talking about the events of the night with Osman, he was certain that if he'd had a little more time he'd have figured something out. As it was, what happened next had its own spectacular momentum.

'Look,' Justine whispered in his ear, 'look.'

He looked. In the distance, at the front of the station, Rodney had emerged, carrying a bulky package. He stood for a second or two on the forecourt looking around him. Watching him, Danny felt a flash of understanding. Walking through the approaches to the station at night he'd always felt oppressed and a little daunted by its sheer emptiness. The width and height of the glimmering concrete which framed the space seemed to have been conceived for beings many times larger than mortal men, and, as he passed through the forecourt, he would have the insistent feeling that somewhere, hidden in the dark patches thrown by the irregular glare of fluorescence, there were eyes testing his every move.

Across the road Ola opened the door of the Cortina and, crouching, got out into the road. Still crouched, and using the intervening cars as cover, he ran back to the Escort and squatted down beside it. Justine nudged Danny roughly.

'What are we going to do?'

Danny considered it. If he shouted or revealed their presence in some way in an attempt to scare off the Africans or warn their victim, Rodney might run, and if he disappeared with the mask there would be no way of catching up with him again. Whatever he was going to do, Danny thought, he would have to do now.

'Move,' he muttered to Justine. 'Move back. Give me room.'

She shifted. As she did so he could her panting, her breath coming and going in loud ragged gasps. He wound the window down slowly, and heard Rodney's footsteps echoing louder and louder as he walked down the arcade towards them. Danny sat up, released the handbrake, and put his foot on the clutch. The plan that had sprung into his mind was to cut in front of either car if it tried to move off. He had no idea what he would do afterwards, but he knew that he wasn't going to let the Dancing Face slip through his fingers without a struggle. Distractedly, he wondered where Osman was.

Rodney skipped down the stairs. He was holding the package in both arms in front of him, hugging it like a child with a teddy bear. He walked briskly to the Escort, and Danny could see the flash of his teeth, grinning. He stopped, put his package on top of the car and felt in his pockets for the keys. At the same time Ogu opened the door of the Cortina, got out and moved towards him. Rodney froze. Ola stood up from behind the Escort and faced him, then he moved round the car to get behind Rodney, who took a couple of steps backwards and put his back against the wall, his hand coming up to point a long blade which glittered in the reflected light.

'Fuck off,' Danny heard Rodney shout. 'Fuck off.'

It was like a performance, Danny thought as he fumbled with the catch on the door of the van. Ogu shrugged off his jacket and, holding it like a club, swatted at Rodney, who swiped back at him, giving Ola an opportunity to close in on the other side. It was over in a few seconds. The three men joined together in a clump of struggling limbs. Rodney gave a high-pitched scream and fell to the pavement. Danny, his initial plan forgotten, jumped out of the van and began sprinting across the road, shouting. He was halfway there before he remembered what he was doing, and he skidded to a halt, using the palms of his hands against the side of the Escort as a brake. Ola turned away from Rodney and came towards him, holding the knife chest-high, his arm half extended. Danny stared at it, hypnotized by the little movements it made, side to side, like a snake's head swaying.

'Hey,' Osman's voice said.

He was standing on the pavement at the foot of the stairs. Danny hadn't seen him until that moment, and he guessed that Osman had walked through the underground car park and made his way up the ramp where the cars drove in. He was holding the gun up by the side of his head, his posture straight and stiff like a soldier on parade.

'Take that thing and put it in the van, Danny.'

Danny slid the mask off the roof of the car and carried it across the road, breathing deep as he felt the unexpected weight of it. The Africans hadn't moved, and when he turned around Osman was saying something in their language. His voice had the authoritative bullying tone that Danny had heard him use back at the club that first time. In reply Ogu came out with a long burst of words. His voice sounded as if he were pleading and he moved towards Osman, his hands wide apart. Osman snapped his arm out suddenly, the gun pointing rock-like at Ogu's head.

'I don't give a shit,' Osman said, harsh and loud. 'Go now, before I have to shoot you.'

They went. As they walked back towards the Cortina, the impression they gave Danny was of moving like hyenas, slinking off slowly, looking around sullenly, as if ready to charge at the first unguarded moment. Osman didn't move. He had lowered the gun to his side, but he was still standing at attention, watching Ola and Ogu intently. In a minute they were gone, pulling quickly out into the road and accelerating away in a roaring burst of noise.

As the red rear lights on the Cortina receded, a taxi chuffed round the corner, its headlamps lighting up the scene: Osman standing straight up on the pavement, Rodney lying comatose at his feet, Danny by the door of the van. The taxi went past, then slowed down, and Danny could see two pale faces peering back at them.

Osman put the gun in his pocket, smiling as he turned round and called out to Danny.

'Let's get out of here.'

Just then Rodney moaned loudly and called out in a feeble quavering voice.

'Help.'

Danny ran across the pavement and knelt down beside him. Rodney was bleeding in a steady stream but he was alive, both hands clutching at his jacket, pulling it tight across the side of his chest where he'd been stabbed.

'He'll live,' Osman said.

'I'm going to drive him to the hospital round the corner,' Danny told him without looking up. 'UCH.'

'Stick him in his car then,' Osman said. 'I don't want him bleeding in my van. I'll meet you there. And hurry.'

He ran across the road, got into the van and slammed the door. In a moment Danny heard the engine racing. He hoisted Rodney up, trying, without success, to avoid the blood with which his clothes were completely soaked and which still seemed to be seeping out of him.

'Oh Jesus,' Rodney said, as Danny levered him into the passenger seat. 'Oh Jesus. Jesus.'

It was only a short distance up Euston Road and round the one-way system to the hospital. Osman's van was already there, sitting by the corner. Danny drove the Escort past and parked right in front of the hospital doors. Rodney was still conscious.

'I'm going to leave you now,' Danny said carefully. 'Can you make it inside?'

'Yes,' Rodney replied. His voice was tearful. He peered down at his chest fearfully. 'Look at how those bastards cut me. Jesus Christ.'

'You're lucky, man,' Danny said. 'You're not that good at this shit. I'd leave off if I were you. Keep it up and things could get worse.'

'Fuck off,' Rodney muttered. He plucked at the catch on the door trying, and failing, to release it. Danny got out on his side, walked round the car and opened the door for him, then ran back to the van. Osman already had the engine running and when he switched the headlamps on they saw Rodney fall out of the Escort, stagger to his feet and stumble to the door of the hospital.

'Told you,' Osman said. 'You can relax. The bugger's going to live.'

Chapter Twenty-Four

When Danny telephoned Eleanor, she simply said, 'It's okay. Come if you want to.'

The problem was that they had nowhere else to go. Danny didn't expect any more trouble from Rodney, but Okigbo was a much tougher proposition. This was the second time that he and Osman had made Okigbo's men back down, but he had the suspicion that if there was a third time the confrontation might turn out differently. What concerned him immediately was the fact that Okigbo knew where Justine lived. Going there would give him the opportunity to trace them, or even break in and seize the mask. Enough was enough, Danny told Justine and Osman. He needed time to think and, besides, he wanted Eleanor's help.

Justine had objected, but Danny simply told her that she could stay in London if she wanted, and after that she kept quiet. As they rattled through Hammersmith towards the motorway she sat in the back holding on to the package with one hand, as if she couldn't bear to be parted from it.

'You all right with this?' Danny asked Osman.

'Now he asks me,' Osman laughed. 'It's okay, I'm having fun. When it gets too serious I'll piss off.' He laughed again, the sound exploding in the interior of the van. 'Has it occurred to you people,' he said, 'that everyone who's had this mask has also had something bad happen to them?'

'Nothing will happen if you keep your eyes on the road,' Danny told him.

'Now that's the difference between you black people in Britain and America, and any African I can imagine,' Osman said. 'You grow up believing that you can control things which can't be controlled. Sometimes, I swear, I can't tell you apart from any white man, the way you think.'

'Don't talk bollocks,' Danny replied. He knew what was coming and he was half interested, half irritated by what Osman was saying.

'I'm serious,' Osman bellowed. They came up to the roundabout and the van canted sideways a little as Osman took the bends at speed, wrestling it up the ramp to the motorway. 'You've got this romantic mythology about blackness with Africa at the centre of it, and at the same time you've grown up thinking like Europeans. Every time you open your mouth a contradiction jumps out.'

Danny considered his response. Leaving aside the merits of the argument he understood that Osman was taking this tack because it put him on the defensive. Therefore he had some purpose in mind which would only emerge later. He sensed also that Osman was high on the adrenaline of the night, and when he was like this, it was as if theories and ideas were zapping through his head, emerging as a fluent stream of hallucinogenic oratory. In spite of himself, Danny sat back and fell into his accustomed role of straight man.

'You don't have to be superstitious to be an African,' he said. 'The continent is full of doctors, lawyers, scientists, sociologists and administrators who believe in scientific evidence and all the rest of it, same as Europeans.'

'That's what I mean. Right there,' Osman insisted. 'To you it's like some kind of heavyweight match between science and superstition. In your own head you've got to defend Africa by making out it's no different from Europe underneath all the weird customs, so as soon as your European mind comes across some bit it doesn't like it starts going: "Alert, alert, superstition alert!" ' Osman was mimicking a computerized and electronic voice. He glanced over at Danny, grinning, hugely amused by his own joke. 'Dig it,' he shouted. 'Danger. Danger. Archaic African traditions on screen.'

'Oh leave off,' Danny muttered. Suddenly he was conscious that Justine was sitting behind him, listening to the argument, and he was beginning to suspect that Osman was showing off for her benefit.

'It's like those black Americans' version of Africa,' Osman said, his tone calming into mere sarcasm, 'all nice and clean and dignified and exactly like themselves, only with funny accents. When they meet the real thing they're shocked.' He took one hand off the wheel and gestured. 'You ever noticed how when they do that roots thing they're always descended from princes and kings and beautiful princesses? None of the stupid, ugly peasants ever had any children.'

He laughed uproariously. Danny smiled, trying to figure out a way of returning Osman's attack. Listening to Osman, he never failed to be amazed by the confidence and cynicism with which he could produce his ideas about any and every subject that came up. His field was international law, although Danny had never actually noticed him working at it. On the contrary, the piles of books on the floor of his van were mostly novels. 'Excessive specialization,' he told Danny one time, 'is the curse of post-industrial society. It's crippled European minds.' Knowing something about everything was his fetish, but at the same time this was precisely why Danny got so much pleasure from their conversations, which would have been impossible with one of his white classmates. Not so much because they talked about race and Africa, but because when they talked about art or culture it was without reference or relevance to cultural gurus. At the centre of their arguments was a kind of struggle with their own identities; and instead of trotting out the opinions of newspaper columnists or fashionable movie directors or a favourite lecturer, as most of his fellow students did, Osman came out with stuff that emerged from his thoughts about his own experience and observation. The other thing that Danny loved about arguing with Osman was that they could be frank with each other, without a trace of the uneasiness he sometimes felt with his white friends, in whose eyes he could always discern a flicker of fear or embarrassment when the conversation got too close to truth.

Playing for time he turned round and looked at Justine.

'Are you hearing this? What do you think?'

'No use asking her,' Osman shouted. 'She's lived in Africa. She knows what I'm saying.'

'He goes on like this all the time,' Danny told her.

Justine shrugged.

'This is nothing,' Osman said. 'In my father's house they'd sit around for a couple of days and nights just arguing about one thing. That's what an oral culture is about. You start discussing anything seriously you need to quote twelve hundred cases and authorities to make your point. You can't just go and look it up in some book. You have to tell people. One time when my sister got married there was an old man there started comparing Roman and traditional African law. I went to bed, got up and he was still at it.' He paused. 'Of course we're addicted to the law. My dad can argue the rules of half a dozen legal and administrative traditions left over from the past, and all of them are supposed to have the same status. Turns into a vice.'

'What's all this got to do with the mask?'

Osman didn't answer for a little while, and Danny was about to repeat the question when he spoke, his tone sombre, reflective.

'Nothing. Except you ought to ask yourself the question most Africans would ask when there's trouble.'

'What's that?'

Osman glanced sideways, taking his eyes off the road for a second.

'The question is: Why are these things happening right now, and why are they happening to me?'

Along the sides of the van the wind muttered and howled. From time to time it struck with so much force that the vehicle shuddered under the impact. Ahead of them the road stretched away into darkness, illuminated only by the gleam of catseyes. Danny stared out into the rushing darkness, his imagination picturing the gleaming metal face squatting behind him in the van, hidden only by the cardboard in which Gus had wrapped it. The hairs rose on the back of his neck.

Halfway down the motorway they stopped at a service station for petrol. Lounging at the pump, Osman nodded at the van where Justine sat next to the mask.

'What are you going to do about her?'

Danny spread his hands, miming his puzzlement.

'I don't know.'

'Put it another way. Forget her for the moment. What would you do with that thing if it was up to you?'

Danny said the first thing that came into his head.

'Dump it in the sea. Blow it up. Something like that.'

Osman nodded.

'Exactly.'

They got back in the van. Osman didn't say any more on the subject, and Danny, sensing that he didn't want to talk about it in Justine's presence didn't pursue the comment. Pulling out of the service station Danny glanced over his shoulder to see whether Justine was asleep, but she was sitting bolt upright staring straight ahead, her eyes gleaming in the faint light reflected from the dashboard. Danny cast around in his mind for something to say to her, but the effort seemed too exhausting. Instead he leaned back in his seat, stretched his legs out and gave himself up to the night.

Chapter Twenty-Five

'If I were you,' Eleanor repeated, 'I'd try and do some kind of deal with them directly. I'm sorry, but if I had to make a judgement I'd say that all Okigbo's energies will probably be directed towards getting hold of the Dancing Face. You'll never be able to tell whether or not he was telling the truth.'

'I don't care,' Justine replied, 'as long as he does something for my father.'

That's the problem, Eleanor thought, and although she didn't say it aloud, she knew that everyone else in the room was thinking the same thing. What Justine proposed was littered with obstacles, dependent on unknown or non-existent factors. It would work if Dr Oyebanjoh was still alive. If Okigbo actually had the power to do what she hoped. If his agreement hadn't been a cover for some other scheme. If her intervention was to be a success, she would have to take all these matters on trust.

Justine shivered, her eyes fixed on the parcel which lay, unattended, on a table in the corner of the room. She hugged her coat, which she had still not taken off, tighter around her body as if to keep out the cold. It was, in fact, quite warm in Eleanor's flat, but Justine felt as though the cold had penetrated deep into her body during the ride down the motorway. Inside, she was still chilled and frozen.

They had reached Bristol at about four in the morning. Eleanor was fully dressed in black jeans and a black sweater, as if she had decided not to go to bed before they arrived, but Danny noticed that there was a nest of cushions on the sofa in her sitting room, squashed into the shape of her body, as if she had been lying there, dozing off while she waited.

At first, the way she greeted them had been warm and matter-of-fact, but when Danny introduced Justine she had looked at her with a mixture of suspicion and challenge. Without delay Danny began to tell her about what had happened since he and Osman had left her flat, starting with how they'd found Justine, bound and helpless. As he talked, Danny found himself elaborating a little, emphasizing the fact that Justine had been motivated by the desire to help her father, and pointing out that she too had been a victim of Okigbo's wiles. Throughout this narrative Eleanor watched Justine as if attempting to gauge the truth of what she was hearing, and as if she would have preferred hearing it from the girl's own lips. Suddenly, she interrupted and addressed Justine directly.

'Do you know what happened to Gus? Was it really an accident?'

Her tone was quiet, restrained, but the effect was as if she had screamed the words at the top of her voice. Justine flinched visibly.

'Of course it was.' She paused, thinking about it. 'As far as I know.'

Somehow this answer seemed to satisfy Eleanor. She didn't quite relax, but some of the tension went out of her body, and the atmosphere in the room eased a little.

'I know Doctor Oyebanjoh,' she told Justine, 'and I met you once when he brought you up to Kano. You don't remember?' Justine shook her head. 'You had just arrived in the country. He talked pretty freely in those days, but they left him alone.'

Justine shrugged. It had never occurred to her back then that the way her father talked might have been courageous or daring, and she had listened to him with the innocence of a child recently arrived from Britain, even repeating at school some of his scathing comments about corruption and inefficiency.

'I know he'd never do anything corrupt,' she said. Her eyes pleaded with Eleanor, the words aimed at Danny. He had to understand that her cause was just, and that doing some kind of deal with the Dancing Face might be her father's last chance. 'It's one of their jokes to charge him with corruption.'

Eleanor nodded. Faced with Justine's grief, she had lost her anger, and now she started to give her the best advice she could, remembering the girl she had met all those years ago, sticking by her father's side as if frightened to let go, head bowed, something bewildered and timorous about her glance when she looked up.

As he listened to them talking, Danny felt a sense of being dislocated, adrift from his moorings. The day before, he had set out, fired by the desire to call Justine to account and full of anger about her deceit. Now he was willing to give her everything she wanted, in spite of her lies. It was the same with Eleanor. Half a day earlier she had been venomous about Justine, calling her a little bitch who must have twisted Gus round her little finger. Now they were chatting like sisters. He looked round to see how Osman was reacting, but Osman had his eyes closed, his head snuggling into the back of the sofa.

'You must be tired,' Eleanor said, catching the expression on his face when he looked at Osman. 'We can talk in the morning.'

She took Justine to the spare room and came back with pillows, a sleeping bag and a duvet for Danny and Osman. She bustled around switching on lamps and offering them tea. Eventually she left, saying that they could sleep as late as they liked. In the morning they would talk. It was odd, Danny thought, in spite of everything there had been a gleam in Eleanor's eyes and an undertone to her voice which made him feel that she was full of pleasure at having them invade her flat in the early hours of the morning, and delighted, too, at the thought that they were staying, sleeping under her roof.

The night passed without dreams and even though, in his sleep, Danny was aware that the mask was lurking somewhere nearby, the fact caused him no disturbance. It was the women's voices, murmuring outside, which woke him. The room was still dark and shadowed, but when he looked, he could see from the thin gap between the curtains that it was already late in the morning. Turning his head he saw Osman lying smothered under the duvet, but his head was sticking out at the end, eyes wide open, watching.

'About ten o'clock,' Osman said, before he asked.

'I think I'm going to help her,' Danny told him. He must have made the decision while asleep, because when he woke up he had known that this was what he was going to do. 'That all right with you?'

'I don't know. I've been thinking about it. Leave Okigbo out of it. I've been thinking that it shouldn't go back at all.'

By some reflex Danny swivelled his head immediately to look at the package. From where he lay he could see it, still lying on the table, the perspective making it seem larger than he remembered, looming over the room.

'They're not exactly short of art in this country,' Danny said automatically. 'I would have thought you'd want it to go back where it belonged.'

Osman sat up abruptly. He grunted and coughed with the effort, swinging his legs, still covered by the duvet, over the side of the sofa. Peeping out, Danny could see the soles of his feet, a clean dusky pink.

'There isn't a place where it belongs any more,' Osman said. 'You keep thinking it's art. Like a thing. It's not. It's a piece of power and it doesn't belong to anyone. It never did. When they made it, they made it because that was the way they were. If you're going to talk about belonging, you have to reckon that it belongs with them in the past or in heaven, or wherever they've gone, and it's not like some urn you could stick on the mantelpiece and look at dear old granddad's bones. It's like if you could dig up the Oba himself and have him walking around with all his craziness and lust and strength. It wouldn't be good.'

Danny sat up in his turn, struggling to remember what Gus had written about this.

'It's got to be better,' he told Osman. His mind went back to the night before. It seemed a long time ago now. Apart from a few comments which bordered on the edge of sarcasm, Osman had hardly spoken to Justine. 'I don't know if Justine's father is innocent or what. But if the mask can help him and it goes back home it's better than what it is now. It's not exactly what Gus wanted, but it's better than nothing.'

Osman moved again, sliding to the floor so that he was sitting on a level with Danny.

'I don't know,' he muttered. 'It's up to you.' He looked across at Danny, frowning. 'I think I'll go back today.'

Before Danny could reply there was a brisk knock on the door, and Eleanor came in. She was wearing a long black dress, belted at the waist, a pair of black earrings dangled at the side of her head, but, in contrast with the funereal style of her clothes, she seemed perky and cheerful, a triumphant smile creasing her face. She was carrying a tray loaded with a teapot and a couple of cups, and she put it down on the table next to the package, then crossed over to the curtains and pulled them apart. The room flooded with morning sunshine. Standing with her back to the window, Eleanor was surrounded by a nimbus of light.

'We've been talking about it.' After the dark and silence of the night, her voice seemed excessively loud and exuberant. 'I know exactly what you should do.'

Chapter Twenty-Six

The trees sparkled in just the way Danny remembered them. Gus used to bring him to this place to visit the zoo, but what always stuck in his memory were the glowing colours, especially in autumn. Red, yellowish brown and a soft vivid shade of green which glittered in the sunlight, as if the landscape was a kind of stage behind which an army of careful technicians scurried around to produce a delicately graded effect.

Nowadays the bits of the zoo he could see through the railings looked rusty and uncared for, the furtive bustle of unseen animals muted. Unable to stop himself, he made a quick detour to see the wolves. The memory he retained from all those years ago, and which drew him irresistibly, was a silent file of great hairy beasts whose jaws seemed to be slavering with carnivorous lust as he walked past, but whose eyes revealed an aloof detachment, as if only barely interested in how a small boy might taste. Going past the fence which had guarded them he paused for a few seconds, but the wolves had either gone or they were lurking somewhere under cover, waiting for their moment to pounce.

The red-haired man was sitting alone at a table in front of the restaurant in the middle of the park. When Danny made the appointment he had named this restaurant because it was the only place he remembered in London, off the top of his head, where he could arrive and leave from a number of different directions and where he could make a quick reconnoitre before revealing his presence.

He walked past, turning off the road and across the lawn which led down to the lake. At the edge of the water he squatted down, pretending to feed the ducks, but when a couple of them waddled hopefully towards him all he could offer was an impostor's grin instead of the pieces of stale bread they were expecting.

'Next time, boys,' he told them.

Satisfied that there were no surprises in store for him, Danny got up, walked back across the road, through the nearest entrance to the gardens and, coming round the restaurant from behind the red-haired man, greeted him by name.

William turned sharply.

'You're Danny?'

'That's right.'

William didn't beat around the bush.

'Let's be clear about this,' he said. 'I'm meeting you because of Doctor Hutchinson. I know she believes you, but I don't know if I do, and if this is some kind of hoax you can forget it right now. I don't have the power to pay you anything. We wouldn't anyway. It's been tried before.'

'Did I ask you for money?' Danny asked. He pasted a look of outrage on his face. Behind it he was thinking that William was more or less what he'd expected. A young stuffed shirt, nervous as a cat, and at the same time excited to be in the middle of a secret negotiation. Eleanor had predicted as much. William had been a student of hers. In fact, it was at his suggestion that she'd been brought in as a consultant to the exhibition. So when she rang to tell him that she'd been approached by someone with information about the Dancing Face, he could hardly refuse to speak or to listen.

'I'm only a middleman myself,' Danny told him.

'We all are.'

'Exactly. So did you talk to the people?'

William looked at his watch.

'He should be here any minute now.'

William didn't like being a middleman. He didn't like the way that any of this had turned out either. When they'd sent him to Alexandra Palace with the money he had gone in good faith, unaware that he was clutching a briefcase full of worthless paper. Afterwards the thought which haunted him was that he could very easily have been killed. This time too, he had the feeling of not knowing what was going on. Dr Hutchinson had assured him that the man was harmless, that this wasn't some kind of hoax as far as she could tell, but he knew her to be a mere academic, unused to what went on out in the real world. He could take nothing on trust. But he'd had little choice, apart from doing what Danny asked, because, on the telephone, Danny had insisted that he wouldn't talk to anyone except a representative of the oil company which was funding the exhibition. Not to the insurance men, or the police, or even William himself. William had been astonished and angry; mostly astonished. 'I don't know what you mean,' he'd said. 'They're nothing to do with it. Nothing at all. I've never spoken to them myself. Someone else handles all that.'

'Don't worry,' Danny had told him, 'they'll talk to you if you call and tell them there's a chance of getting it back quietly without the flashing blue lights and the newspapers. Tell them you want the department that's been dealing with Doctor Okigbo.'

'Who's Doctor Okigbo?' William was completely bewildered now.

'Just ask.'

This had only been a few hours ago and William was still astonished at the speed with which he had been able to arrange the meeting. Without speaking to Dr Leonard he had rung the director who he'd met at the launch party. The man had listened to what he said without comment then put him on hold. After ten minutes of muzak, another voice had come on the line and asked him when and where he was meeting his informant.

That had been a few hours ago. During this time William had agonized about whether to call in the police, but in the end, he had decided that if it was all a hoax he'd look stupid enough. Besides, after the fiasco at Alexandra Palace he wasn't at all sure that there would be any point.

'How come you're into African art?' Danny asked abruptly.

Because it's the next big thing in my field and there's not a lot of competition, William thought automatically, and it was the sort of answer he might have given to someone he trusted, but, looking at Danny, he suspected that it would be the wrong thing to come out with.

'I studied it at university,' he said briefly. 'We're still learning a lot about it. It's an interesting field.'

He had also been born in South Africa, a fact which had given him an impetus towards the subject, but he didn't want to tell Danny that, either.

'Yes, but studying at university,' Danny said, 'what's all that about? It's different, isn't it? I mean Western art always goes in a historical context. You've got your classical period, your romantic period, realism and all the rest of it. I mean that's going to be what you have to learn in art history at university. It must be hundreds of years since Western artists were able to create anything without employing strategies to get round the fact that their audiences separate art from real life. Like nowadays it's got to the point where they're tormented by it. They're taking things out the gallery, subverting the gallery, turning everyday objects into art. Right? They're desperate because the first thing they understand is that most people think that art is not life, that it's somewhere over there in a place they don't want to go. And even if they wanted to go there's a barrier of knowledge or class or beliefs or some damn thing. To cross it you've got to buy a passport which says this is one of the kind of people who's permitted to enjoy art.' Danny paused and leaned forward. He'd started on this tack because he was nervous sitting there in the open, not knowing whether the man he wanted to see would turn up for real or whether a police car would suddenly appear and block the entrance. But once he'd got into it he realized that he was saying something that had been running through his mind for the last few days, and that William was exactly the sort of person to whom he wanted to say it. 'African art, I'm talking about traditional African art, may be contemporary too, but I don't know, that's not what we've got here. African art is different. It's about representing mythologies which are at the same time a way of turning the abstractions that people live by into reality. You know what I mean?'

William stared at him, frozen, his mouth slightly open in shock. He had assumed that Danny was some sort of petty thief, and the last thing he'd expected was a conversation about art. In different circumstances, perhaps if they'd met in the gallery or at the university, it would have been easier to reply, but somehow William couldn't get over Danny's physical presence on the other side of the table. Dressed in sneakers, jeans and a sweater covered with some sort of basketball logo he looked exactly like the kind of young black man William treated with caution, even before one of them had kicked him to the ground and plucked the briefcase out of his hand with no more effort or reflection than it would have taken to knock a dustbin over. He frowned at Danny, dislocated by the unreality of it all, trying to work out what he was saying and why.

'How does someone like you know?' Danny persisted, a strange urgency in his voice. 'How do you know whether what you're looking at is good or bad or rubbish and what it means? Maybe you see an African mask and what it is really is like one of those pictures of Jesus that some dumb peasant hangs on their wall with the eyes flashing and artificial blood dripping. Maybe it's really the Sistine Chapel. How do you know?'

William cleared his throat uneasily. It flashed through his head that the question might be some kind of test, but he still hadn't

283

made up his mind when a man in a suit walked up to the table, pulled out the remaining chair and sat down.

Neither William nor Danny had noticed his approach and, aware of their surprise, he sat back looking at them with an ironic smile.

'Let me guess,' he said. He pointed to Danny. 'You're Danny.'

He was the sort of middle-aged man you saw in expensive restaurants or standing in front of hotels in some posh part of town, chatting on the pavement while a taxi drew up. His greying hair was carefully styled and he had a fading tan which gave him an air of distinction. He grinned at them, as relaxed as though he were having a drink with a couple of his mates.

Danny watched him, trying not to show his excitement. Now the man was here he realized that he had never quite believed that it would happen. This was because it was actually Eleanor's idea. Once she'd heard all the details from Justine she had worked out a way of bypassing Okigbo.

'He won't be talking to anyone at the High Commission,' she'd said. 'For them he's a non-person, and all of them are too vulnerable themselves to be seen acting as his mouthpiece. Besides, he's better connected than most. He knows where the power is.'

His logical way in, she explained, was through the oil company which had been a major force in his own region, and with which, everyone knew, he had links which had been forged a long time ago. The ruling circles had a deep contempt for foreigners and outsiders, but the oil company executives were, in a manner of speaking, insiders, whose deep pockets ensured that they always had the ear of important men.

'It's the same thing here,' she'd said. 'Big money is the fetish of powerful men.'

Okigbo's disgrace and flight would have made no difference to the company. It had a long memory. Some of its protégés had started out in a mud hut or a prison cell. It had seen men cast down, like falling stars, into the depths and back again to the height of the tallest trees. If Okigbo had a useful proposition the company would help. It might have had to withdraw from him publicly, but at its heart it would not desert him until his usefulness was totally and completely at an end.

Remembering what Eleanor had said, Danny half expected to feel an aura of power and certainty radiating from the man.

'This is about Doctor Oyebanjoh,' he said quickly.

He hadn't known what to expect, but he could see that the name had produced an effect. The executive stopped smiling, then, instead of replying, he turned to William.

'I'm very grateful to you for coming,' he said. 'I think I can take this from here. I'll telephone you tomorrow and tell you where we are.'

He held his hand out for a handshake. William looked disconcerted, offended even, but he shook hands obediently with the oilman. Then, without speaking to Danny, he got up and walked away, his shoulders stiff and square as he stalked the passage to the street.

'What about Doctor Oyebanjoh?' the oilman asked. He hadn't bothered to introduce himself, and Danny had the feeling that it would be pointless asking his name. In any case, if they could make a deal, it wouldn't matter.

'If you can deliver Doctor Oyebanjoh,' Danny said, making it short and sharp, making it obvious that he wasn't going to beat around the bush, 'we can deliver the mask.'

The oilman raised his eyebrows. He smiled.

'I take it this comes from Justine Oyebanjoh.'

For a moment Danny was staggered, remembering what Eleanor had said about the long reach of the company. If the man knew this he must know a lot more.

Then he remembered Okigbo.

'You've been talking to Doctor Okigbo,' he said with an equal coolness.

The eyebrows went up again. Looking at Danny, Digby reminded himself not to underestimate the boy. The problem was whether to tell him, and when he did, how to move on from there.

'Are you related?' he asked. He didn't think so, because the shape of Danny's face and body were not at all reminiscent of Oyebanjoh's region, but the fact that the boy was mixed race might have been deceptive. He wanted to be sure.

'No, I'm just a middleman.'

Digby took a deep breath. There was nothing to be gained by putting it off.

'Doctor Oyebanjoh died a year ago,' he said carefully.

He had checked even before this latest approach, because Okigbo had asked him to do it a couple of days previously. In his pocket was a copy of the fax he had received only a few hours ago, telling him that Oyebanjoh was out of the picture. It was important, as he told Okigbo on the telephone, that everyone understood that. The whole affair was enough of a mess without complicating it further.

'Are you sure?' Danny asked him earnestly. The news didn't mean much to him personally, but one quick beat of the imagination told him how Justine would take it, and how difficult it would be to tell her.

'The source was reliable,' Digby said. 'As high up as we could go.'

We pay enough for information like this, he thought, even though it was actually a matter of public record. On the other hand, unless you had the right sort of authority it would be impossible to find out.

'I'm sorry,' Digby continued, 'but there's nothing we can do about that.' He leaned forward to stare intently into Danny's eyes. 'The important thing now is to save a precious element of African heritage. You understand that, don't you?'

Chapter Twenty-Seven

On the train back from London, Danny had been racking his brains, trying to figure out how to tell Justine. At the same time he was working out the problem of how to put their relationship on a more intimate footing. He'd been thinking about this, off and on, since they first met, and, to his surprise, even while he was reflecting on her father's death, he was also working out how to take the first steps. Walking through the square he was torn between his elation at seeing her again, and despair at the thought that his news would bring her pain.

It was Eleanor who opened the door for him, and, immediately, she interrogated him with a lift of her eyebrows. Danny shook his head to indicate failure. She gave a crestfallen grimace and led the way back into the sitting room. Following her through the hallway he could hear the sound of canned laughter from the television set, and for a moment he felt like an intruder. These surroundings were like a set his mind had called into being to describe the home he'd always wanted – the clean, shiny furniture, the glowing tints of the watercolours, the sound of laughter, even the imagined picture of

Justine sitting in front of the television, smiling as she waited for him. But instead of a welcome homecoming his role was to stain the colours dark, bringing news of death and disaster.

'Osman left this afternoon,' Eleanor told him, looking round, as if to see how he would take it. 'He said he would ring you.'

That's all I needed, Danny thought. He'd forgotten that Oz had declared he was going, and now he felt a kind of resentment at being deserted like this.

Justine looked up from the sofa and, when she saw him, switched the television off with a swift movement of her hand.

'Any good?'

She was trying to sound casual, but she was breathing quick and fast and her eyes glared at him wide and round. Intense.

Danny shook his head, unable to speak.

'What happened? Was it Okigbo? Something's happened.'

'Nothing to do with Okigbo,' Danny said. 'It's your father. It's not going to happen.'

'Didn't they go for it? What was wrong? Didn't they believe you?'

'They believed me,' he said.

'So why wouldn't they do it? What did they say?'

She was thinking, he could tell, that she should have gone herself, that it had been a mistake to let them persuade her that it was too dangerous, or that it would be a better strategy for Danny to pretend to be an anonymous middleman. Behind her impatience for the news, anger lurked.

'It's your father,' Danny said. 'Something happened.'

'What?'

Danny could see from the stricken look in her eyes that she had already guessed. He couldn't put it off any longer.

'They say he died a year ago.'

Her lips moved without sound.

'I don't know if that's definite,' he said hurriedly. 'This guy said that was his information.'

She was still gazing at him, her forehead creased, eyes narrowed, her lips compressed, her face frozen in a mask of agony. She spoke through her clenched teeth.

'Is that all they said? How did he die?'

Danny shook his head again.

'No. They'd just found out. They hadn't been told the details, except that it was natural causes. The guy said there was nothing they could do.'

'Maybe it's a mistake.'

She was clutching at straws and she knew it.

'I asked him that,' Danny said. 'He said they'd checked it and had it confirmed from a source which was as high up as they could go.'

He didn't tell Justine what the oilman had added, which was that once they'd made the announcement they would make sure it was true, and either way it was all up with the doctor.

Justine put her face in her hands. She gasped, drawing her breath in aloud. Danny sat next to her and touched her arm. She shuddered and wrenched away from him, got up and walked out of the room rapidly. In a moment the door of the spare room slammed. He looked at Eleanor, who was still standing, staring at him, her face an echo of Justine's expression.

'Leave her alone for a bit,' she said.

Danny sat back, leaning into the corner of the sofa. He felt as if he'd just run a marathon, and now he was exhausted, limp, without enough energy to think about what he was going to do next.

'What happened?' Eleanor asked. 'Was that all?'

'No.'

Danny remembered now that there'd been more. The offer the oilman made was straightforward. The best, he said, that they could do under the circumstances. Return the mask to the exhibition, and they would make sure that she learned every detail of what had happened to her father. They would take her there and help her to reclaim his body, even if she wanted to bring it back here for burial. They would give her everything she wanted, short of bringing him back to life; and of course, there would be a reward. Money was no object.

'I don't think she'll want to hear that right now,' Eleanor said.

The telephone rang. Eleanor answered, then handed it to Danny, mouthing the name, 'Osman'. Keeping his voice low, Danny gave Osman a quick summary of what had happened.

'I guessed that might be it.' He didn't sound shocked or even surprised. 'Are you coming back?'

Danny thought about it, realizing that what he was going to do next depended on what Justine decided.

'I don't know.'

The door opened and Justine came in. Her face was smooth and shiny now, expressionless, except for the feverish glare in her eyes.

'Can I use the phone?' she said curtly.

Danny told Osman goodbye and gave it to her. Justine took it without a word, went over to the table in the corner of the room and sat down, opening a little address book in front of her.

At the first number she rang she was answered by a machine. 'Doctor Okigbo?' she said clearly. 'This is Justine Oyebanjoh. I must speak with you urgently.'

She gave him the number of her mobile. After this the numbers she rang were in Nigeria. Her voice was calm, relentless, the undertone of desperation concealed. She called old schoolfriends she hadn't spoken to for years, distant relatives, minor officials she had once met, asking the same question over and over again. 'Have you heard anything about my dad?'

This must be costing a fortune, Danny thought. Then it struck him, incongruously, that there was a fortune sitting on the table in front of her, its golden gaze fixed, indifferent to either suffering or joy.

Eleanor, apparently unmoved by any worries about the massive bill that Justine would be running up, moved around softly. She put a cup of tea in front of Justine, and after it had remained there untouched for half an hour, she brought another. Danny refused her offer of food. He'd only had a sandwich on the train, but he wasn't hungry. In fact he felt a kind of revulsion at the thought of eating. Time went by, the quick, restless muttering of Justine's voice fading into the background. Eleanor murmured that she was going to bed and disappeared. Danny rolled back into the sofa, put his feet up and stared at the ceiling. Then he was asleep. He knew he was asleep. He was in a cellar, facing a brick wall. It was actually a prison cell, he understood. As he studied the brickwork, looking for a door, the walls began to close round him. Summoning up all his superhuman strength, he smashed at the wall and finally broke through, the bricks collapsing round him. On the other side was another brick wall. Gaining momentum he smashed that one, too, only to be faced by another, and another, and another. His hands began to bleed. He held them up in front of him, looking at them with horror, and the scene faded, leaving him in the dark. His eyes were open and he sat up with a jerk. He was still lying on the sofa, but the lights were out, only a faint gleam from a chink in the curtains gave him enough illumination to make out the shape of the room. He lay back with a moan of relief, then he remembered Justine. He wondered for a moment whether she had found out anything, or whether her grief and fatigue had eventually defeated her. He thought of going to speak to her, to comfort her somehow, but he guessed that if she was asleep the last thing he should do would be to wake her. Hesitating, he went to sleep again.

When he woke it was morning. There was a swish as Eleanor pulled the curtains apart, and the sunlight hit him like a fist in the face. He covered his eyes with his hand and through his fingers saw Eleanor coming towards him.

'Danny,' she said urgently. 'Wake up, Danny. Justine's gone. She must have left early. She's gone.'

Chapter Twenty-Eight

'It's got to be Okigbo,' Eleanor said. 'He's the only person who might know for certain, the only one she can reach. He didn't return her calls so she's gone to confront him.'

'She wouldn't do that.' Danny shook his head. It was too risky, too stupid to believe. 'She knows there's no point.'

'No, she doesn't. Anyway, even if he can't or won't tell her anything, she can accuse him, scream at him, kick him in the balls. At the moment he's the closest she can get to her father. We're not involved. We're no good to her. Not the way she is now.'

Danny felt a brief thrust of pain when she said that.

'What do you think I should do?' he asked. 'Maybe I can go up to London. See she's all right.'

'I wouldn't,' Eleanor advised. 'She'll be back, or she'll telephone. There's nothing you can do.'

He knew she was right, but the knowledge that Justine might be in some kind of danger crawled in his brain. They'd been discussing her for over an hour now, but talking about it only seemed to make things worse.

'Tell me about yourself,' Eleanor said. 'Gus never talked much about his childhood. It must have been difficult.'

Danny tried to focus on the question. The problem was that he had nothing except fantasies with which to compare his experiences. At times during his childhood he remembered being haunted by a picture of a family which used to appear on advertising posters and in newspapers. There were two children, a boy and a girl, flanked by two grown-ups. Their faces glowed as if they were standing in front of a fire which, unseen from the bottom of the picture, radiated warmth and comfort. They were all smiling with delight at being together. He couldn't remember what product they were selling, but whenever he thought of a family he thought of this picture, and whenever he had to think about what had been missing from his life, his mind called up this warm glow. At the same time, the homes he'd lived in had been full of kids abused and abandoned by their parents, and he knew that this picture was only a dream, like the memories he had reconstructed from things Gus had told him, of himself lying in a cot, his parents hanging over him smiling proudly, and Gus standing beside the rails, shaking a rattle at him.

'When we lived with Lucy,' he said, 'she wanted to adopt us both, but then she had an accident and she couldn't look after us.'

They'd split them up then. Gus, fifteen years old, had decided he was big enough to look after himself, and he went to live in a house supervised by an eccentric old man, who, the younger boys said, touched them in bad places. Danny had gone to stay with a nice couple who thought they might want to adopt him, and smiled at him kindly until they decided he was too much of a handful. He could still remember walking to the car, holding Miss Foster's hand, the other hand clutching a book about the big cats of Africa, and wondering what would happen now. 'Bastards,' Gus had snarled when he came to visit.

'It's hard being a child in this country,' Eleanor said. She was wishing now that she hadn't brought the subject up. Sometimes she had tried to talk to Gus about her own childhood, riding on the farm or sitting on the veranda watching the hawks and listening to Solomon reading Shona poems from the newspaper. Every time she did so, however, he would tell her to shut up.

She was remembering this, and half listening to Danny, when the doorbell rang.

'Maybe that's her,' Danny said. He followed her out to the hallway, but when she opened the door it was Osman standing there. He gave Eleanor a big smile, but, instead of coming in, he peered past her at Danny.

'You want to go for a walk?' he called.

'Why don't you come in?' Eleanor asked. 'Have some coffee.'

'Maybe later,' he told her. 'I've been driving for a couple of hours. Stretch my legs, you know.'

Coming back into the hallway, carrying his shoes, Danny watched them talking to each other, smiling with easy enjoyment, as if the events of the last few days had left them untouched. It seemed strange, and it suddenly struck him that Osman might fancy Eleanor. Hopping about in the hall, levering his foot into a shoe, he considered the idea. Eleanor was at least forty, so old that the thought of her doing it seemed rude, a little perverse, but he could see that she had something. Perhaps it was her eyes. They were larger than most, giving her that doll-like look he'd noticed before, and when she stared directly at him, the sight of her wide, round pupils made him feel uncomfortable, as if there was an exchange going on that revealed too much.

Osman gave Eleanor a final grin as she shut the door. Getting into step on the pavement beside him, Danny wondered whether to mention that Eleanor must still be mourning Gus. In the circumstances his friend's manner hadn't seemed quite right.

'Justine's gone off,' he told Osman.

Osman paused in his stride, looking at him.

'Where?'

Danny shrugged.

'Don't know.'

He explained quickly how they'd found her gone and his fears about what she was doing. Osman listened without comment, and when he'd finished they walked on in silence. Up ahead Danny could see the top of the bridge rearing up into the sky.

'See that bridge?' Osman asked. 'The way it sticks up in the sky it's like it's telling you something.'

'It's telling you it's there,' Danny said.

'Very droll.' But Osman didn't smile, instead he gave Danny an irritable look.

'Get your head round it, man. I don't know what it felt like when they built it, but now it's like it was always there. It's like that everywhere I go in England. You look at the countryside, it's like some kind of big garden that someone's caring for, watering the flowers and all that shit. Even the places that are a bit wild it's like you know that if they stuck a couple of bulldozers in and let go some dynamite they could change the look of it in a few days. The things that hit you in the eye, the really impressive unforgettable bits, are things that somebody stuck up there, like this bridge or the buildings in cities. See, it's different in Africa. Walk in the bush, you keep coming across things that people built covered with plants, trees growing through the middle of them, ruins eaten by the ants – everything dead. Animals, buildings, rocks, it all gets eaten up or changed into something else. They never build them right in the first place. We know that nothing lasts.'

'That would be good, in a way,' Danny said, swinging into the rhythm of the thing. At the back of his mind he wondered, without urgency, where this was going. 'But the fact is that rainforests are shrinking all over the place. Africans can destroy the ecology as efficiently as white men. Just give them some time.'

Osman laughed.

'Destruction's different. That's not my point. My point is that in this landscape it's people who are boss. In Africa you have to go with the flow. Let Nature do what it wants instead of imposing your own image on it.'

Danny had no answer, but in any case, there was something else which interested him more.

'What made you come today?'

Osman took his eyes off the bridge.

'I wanted to talk to you.'

Danny felt a little lift of triumph. He'd known there was something.

'Talk.'

'It's about the mask. I've been thinking.' Danny could feel him looking. They turned a corner and found themselves in a Georgian crescent. A perfect curve, it shone in the sunlight with the pale beauty of a white cliff face. Osman gestured. 'In a place like this you'd think nothing bad could happen.' He hesitated, looking round at Danny. 'When I was at school I saw this kid being raped. I thought it was rape. I wasn't sure at first. I came round the back of the pavilion for a smoke and saw these two boys holding a kid over a tree trunk. The guy holding his arms was the captain of the second eleven. He looked up and said, "Piss off, Oz." I didn't know the kid, he was new, only young, so I pissed off. I felt guilty about it afterwards, but he turned out to be a right little catamite so I guessed it was okay.' He paused. 'The thing is, I felt bad about it for a long time.'

Danny watched him in silence. He'd heard of such things happening in posh schools, but he'd always thought of the rumours as mostly myth.

'I think I should have done something,' Osman said. 'I had this fantasy for a while, about going back to the past and doing the right thing. But that was nothing to how I felt about going back home.' He paused, gazing round again, but Danny had the feeling that his eyes were focusing on something a long way beyond the buildings round them. 'When I went back I wanted to reclaim myself. I had this idea that the military would always be power-brokers, which was right, and I thought having been an officer would be the perfect base for whatever I wanted to do there. Which was right too. I was in the cadets at school, army training. Did I tell you that?'

Danny shook his head.

'Well, I was. I'd had enough of drilling and training, but I was pretty good at all that. I think I could have gone right to the top.'

'Why didn't you?' Danny asked.

Osman sighed loud enough for Danny to hear him above the background of traffic noise as they turned back into the main thoroughfare.

'Something happened. It wasn't a complete surprise. It was my reaction to it that was the problem. I think they left me here too early and too long. I'm not going back, you know. Maybe for a visit, but I can't imagine going back.'

This was the first time Danny had heard Osman say something like this. Somehow he felt a spike of alarm as if Oz had suddenly gone crazy and was likely to run amok.

'How come? I always thought you were kind of marking time here.'

For a few seconds Osman didn't answer, looking up at the spires of the bridge, his face screwed up as if puzzling over something.

'I rang my dad last night. Asked him about Doctor Oyebanjoh. He said he'd heard the rumours. But it was nothing to do with him, he said. Oyebanjoh was part of the gang that wanted to pillage the North, and the cannibals were simply eating each other, he said.'

'Shit,' Danny muttered.

Osman clicked his tongue.

'The thing that happened, I talked to him about it, and he said he understood, but he didn't. After that I had to leave. No way I was going to become a general.'

'What was it?' Danny asked. It had taken a while but eventually he'd sensed that Osman wanted him to ask.

'They sent my unit to the North, patrolling up and down: Sokoto, Katsina, Kano, Kaduna and back again. There was always something happening up there especially when governments changed. Send the army out. They were soldiers anyway. We knew we had to keep order. I could deal with that. You always know how terrible the alternative could be.' He paused, frowning. They turned another corner, oblivious to the direction. 'The elections were coming up and there was some kind of campaign going on. Trade unions, electoral registration. You name it, somebody was doing their nut about it.' He glanced sideways at Danny. 'You have to understand that I was young, very junior, a new arrival, still learning about the country. Then they'd move you around, keep you out of places where you might have family ties. The local issues were never very clear when you came marching in.' He paused again, thinking about it. 'One day we were camped somewhere near Zaria, I think it was, doing an exercise, and a major I'd never seen before turned up. He was from a special unit, and he said he needed to borrow my men. I didn't like it. I rang the colonel in Kano. He knew my father. He said to do what the major told me. Then he was weird. He said, "Of course, you're exhausted. Take a couple of days' leave." I retired to my tent and went off the next day. But I didn't entirely miss the fun. That night I could hear the guys getting pissed up on the major's booze, then they left in a couple of lorries. They didn't come back till the morning, kind of staggering, you know, like drugged. They were wearing civvies, too. I drove down to Kano and hung out for a couple of days before I came back, and then it was all over.'

'What happened?' Danny had been literally holding his breath.

'I didn't want to know,' Osman said, 'but that day I heard that the headquarters of the local opposition in a ring of villages nearby had been broken into, everyone inside beaten up, women raped, fires started. They used sticks and knives and rocks. Three men were killed. I knew who'd done it, and I knew that there was nothing I could do, apart from keeping out of it, but what got me, what really blew me away, was that my men were normal young guys. Not like hard cases; most of them had never seen any action. We used to sit around talking at night. A couple of them knew my family. They used to play the guitar and make up songs. They wanted to be famous like Fela. I saw them coming back that morning, laughing and joking, like they'd had a good night out.'

They turned another corner and found themselves back in Eleanor's street.

'So what are you trying to tell me?' Danny asked. 'What's this got to do with the mask?'

He was affected by Osman's story and at the same time genuinely puzzled.

'What it is,' Osman said, 'is that they don't need all this tradition shit. Like they've got enough of that already.' He gestured, squeezing the thought out. 'It's something that keeps people going, but it's also like a burden on their backs when they're trying to put a different spin on their future, and that's not at all like anything you know. In this country you've got the soul of life in a cage, and to prove it you can drive a spike through the heart of the countryside, pin it down with monuments like that bridge. All the forces of life, nature, spirit – call it what you like – are sort of tamed, cut down to utilities you can keep in a box. When you want, you open the box and take out a bit of tradition or a bit of art or a bit of religion, use it and put it back. It's different in Africa. It's like Pandora's box is already open and all this shit is roaming round loose. They don't need it any more.'

Danny frowned.

'I don't understand you, man,' he said. 'It sounds like you're saying it's evil.'

Osman shook his head violently. He stopped and faced Danny. They were in front of Eleanor's door.

'Not evil. Both good and evil. But that doesn't matter. What it is, is too much. You keep thinking about it like it's about identity or culture or some bullshit. What I'm telling you is that Africans live their history and their culture, except there's always someone interfering. You put that thing back in the equation there's no way you can tell what will happen next.' He put his hand on Danny's arm. 'Monuments like this are like transmitters that the dead can use to send messages, to impose the disasters of their time on the future. Leave the dead alone. Sometimes they're angry and vicious and mean you no good at all. The best thing you can do is drop that mask off the bridge or blow the fucker up. Get rid of it and stop all this.'

Before Danny could answer, or even be certain of what he was going to say, the door opened, and Eleanor looked out.

'There you are,' she said breathlessly. 'I was going out of my mind wondering when you'd get back. There's a message for you about Justine. She's in trouble.'

Chapter Twenty-Nine

'Justine is with me,' Okigbo said. On the telephone his voice was clear, relaxed and authoritative, as if he was resigned to reasoning with someone who wasn't very bright. 'I want you to bring the thing from wherever you are and give it to me.'

'Why should I do that?' Danny asked.

'I want to keep this short,' Okigbo told him, 'so don't be stupid. Let me give you a hint. If you don't, you'll be sorry. You certainly will.'

'Bollocks,' Danny said. He was playing for time, because he had no doubt that Okigbo was deadly serious. 'I don't even know if what you're saying is true.'

'Wait a moment.'

There were a few seconds of muffled silence, then Justine's voice.

'I'm sorry about this.' She sounded as if she were apologizing for being late or dropping a teacup. 'Just don't listen to anything he says. It's all a bluff. Pay no attention.' Suddenly her voice rose to a shriek. 'Tell him to fuck off.'

Her voice was cut off abruptly as if someone had put a hand over her mouth and dragged her away. Danny gripped the phone tight, imagining the scene precisely. Out of the corner of his eye he saw Osman and Eleanor move towards him, both of them with the same anxious frown on their faces. Something began boiling in Danny's head.

'Okigbo. Okigbo,' he shouted at the top of his voice as if trying to make the sound carry all the way to London. 'Leave her alone, Okigbo.'

'Calm down,' Okigbo said quietly. He sounded amused. 'She's not hurt.'

Danny lowered the phone and took a couple of deep breaths. He knew he had to think fast, but his brain was a whirlpool of confusion.

'What do you want?' he asked.

'I told you,' Okigbo said. 'Bring it to me today.'

'And if I don't?'

'There's no reason why you should not,' Okigbo said. 'All I want to do is take it back where it belongs. That's what everyone wants.' He paused. Danny couldn't think of a reply. At that moment he didn't know what he wanted apart from seeing Justine. 'I want to bring this to an end today, one way or the other,' Okigbo's voice took on a hard and peremptory tone. 'If I don't have it by tonight, I can't be responsible for what happens to her.' He paused again. Danny could hear him breathing. He wondered whether Justine was in the room listening, but he still couldn't think of a reply. 'Tonight she'll be staying with my friends. They're very angry about what happened at Euston and the other time. Humiliated, I would say. They'll want to assert themselves. They have very conventional ideas about women.'

Danny found his voice at last.

'I could ring the police right now,' he threatened.

Okigbo chuckled softly.

'For your own sake, I hope you don't. But I'm not interested. Call me back in the next hour and I'll tell you what to do.'

Danny slammed the phone down when he heard the dialling tone.

'What's the difference?' Osman asked. He was sitting by the table in front of the mask, not looking at it. 'You don't know what to do with it.'

'Maybe he's bluffing.'

He told them quickly what Okigbo had said.

'I think he means it,' Osman said. 'I don't think he'll hurt her himself, but if he leaves her with those guys she's in trouble. I'd ring him back and do the deal. What's the alternative? Even if you called the cops you'd have too much explaining to do. He could deny everything or say it was all a misunderstanding. At the best we'd be back where we started. At the worst . . .' he hesitated. 'If I were you I wouldn't take the chance.'

Danny tried to think about what Gus would do. His brother had done everything he could to keep the mask out of Okigbo's hands and he'd trusted Danny with it. Now he was going to let him down.

'I don't know what Gus would have done,' Eleanor remarked as though she'd been reading his mind, 'but the fact is that he's gone. He left it up to you. You can do what you like with it. He wouldn't have wanted Justine hurt anyway.'

Danny picked up the phone.

'Wait a minute,' Osman said. 'Tell him midnight.'

'Let's get it over with.'

Danny was thinking now about Justine with Ola and Ogu. If Okigbo wasn't there to protect her, anything could happen.

'Midnight,' Osman repeated. 'I've got an idea. It will take time.'

'What?'

'A bug.'

'A bug?'

'Yeah, a bug.'

He could plant a bug inside the mask's wooden backing, Osman explained. Then they could track it wherever Okigbo took it.

'If we knew where it was we could tell your man at the gallery. Imagine Okigbo's face when the cops walk in and take it away from him.'

'Can you do that?'

Osman shrugged.

'It's easy. Dave has access to all that stuff.'

Okigbo's instructions were simple. They were to bring the mask to London and exchange it for Justine. When Danny told him midnight, he laughed.

'That's about the right time,' he said.

Osman left almost immediately, his manner urgent and secretive. Privately, Danny didn't care whether or not his plan worked. The important thing was to get Justine away from Okigbo, and after that he doubted that he could summon up enough energy or interest to carry on worrying about what happened to the mask. He had already failed in whatever it was that Gus had wanted him to do, and that was enough.

'Don't feel too bad about all this,' Eleanor told him. She was on her way out to her office. To collect her mail and do some odd jobs, she said. 'Gus had a plan, but that was his decision. It wasn't a legacy.'

Danny spent the rest of the afternoon wandering around the flat, watching television, hoping the phone would ring and it would be Justine. Nothing happened. He avoided looking at the mask. When he caught sight of it, the lips seemed to be twisted in a slight smile, as if it sensed and was amused by the emotions its presence had released. His fingers itched to cover it with something, blot it out of his sight, and eventually he closed the cardboard box, taping it with Sellotape, so that it was once again a simple package.

The evening had closed in by the time Osman returned.

'I'll take it out to the van,' he said. 'This is a delicate operation.'

Danny helped him carry the mask out. Curiously enough, he could now understand the revulsion Osman had displayed when he first saw it. The box felt heavier, as if the thing inside were exerting an inert downward pressure. He heaved it onto the floor of the transit with relief. On the carpet there was a tangle of thin black wires and a couple of boxes with what looked like walkie talkies poking out.

'Go back in and give me some room,' Osman told him. 'This is complicated.'

Danny left him to it. He'd lost whatever interest he'd had in

Osman's plan and he hadn't the heart to reveal the depth of his defeat by declaring that he had no intention of doing anything about it once they got Justine back. As far as he was concerned it was all over bar the shouting. Later on he would tell Osman.

Eleanor had fussed around, urging him to eat. Eventually she and Osman had gone out for an Indian takeaway. He'd bolted some, hardly tasting it, and afterwards he couldn't remember what he'd eaten. At the door Eleanor pressed his hand between hers and made him promise to ring her and let her know what had happened. He agreed listlessly, thinking that it would be pointless.

They reached London with half an hour to spare. Osman drove with an unusual circumspection. Coming off the motorway, they trundled through Shepherds Bush then through the West End and past Holborn. On Farringdon Road they followed the signs for the Barbican. Halfway there they saw the arch which marked the site of the old Smithfield Market. The metal beams stretched away from the light into obscurity, giving the structure a deserted, neglected air, as if it were waiting to become a ruin. Even at this time of night, there had been a steady stream of traffic as they drove through the streets, but now it was as if they had suddenly been transported to another, older city, charmed by some magician's wand into a frozen tableau of silence and decay.

The van slowed, as if startled by the abrupt change of scene. Osman drove deliberately through the archway, turned round and parked so that they were pointing back in the direction they'd come from. It was a few minutes before midnight.

'They'll have to come that way down the one-way street,' Osman said.

Danny nodded. He'd hardly spoken to Osman since they set out from Bristol, and Osman, usually impossible to shut up, seemed to have entered into his mood, keeping silent for most of the long journey. Osman reached under the seat and brought out the gun he'd used at Euston. He looked at Danny.

'It's loaded,' he said. There was a touch of challenge about his tone, as if he were expecting an argument.

'Okay,' Danny told him.

'Any trouble,' Osman said, 'we're ready to kick ass.'

With an effort Danny smiled. He had nothing to say. He had expected to feel wound up, nervous. Instead he felt cramped, listless and miserable.

On the dot of midnight a pair of headlights swung round the corner. Danny, shading his eyes with his hand, recognized Okigbo's BMW. Behind it another pair of headlights which he guessed to be the Cortina.

Osman blinked his lights and the BMW stopped near the other end of the arch.

'I'll take the mask,' Danny told him. 'You get Justine.'

He wanted it the other way around, but something inside him said that it was his role to offer up the final surrender. He got out, opened the back door and lifted the mask. It felt much heavier now, almost too much to lift, and he grunted with the effort. When he turned he saw Justine standing by the Cortina, flanked by Ola and Ogu. He began walking towards the BMW as Osman went past him, holding the gun in plain view by his side.

As he reached the BMW the rear door swung open.

'Put it on the seat,' Okigbo said.

'Tell them to let her go,' Danny told him.

Okigbo grinned. He swung open the driver's door and got out. Without speaking to Danny he unpicked the top of the box and ripped the cardboard away from the face. In the reflected light of the car's interior the surface gleamed.

'Beautiful,' Okigbo breathed.

He waved his hand above his head, and Danny heard Justine's footsteps stuttering towards him, the heels banging on the tarmac and echoing through the archway. He eased the box on to the back seat of the car and stood back.

'Thank you,' Okigbo told him. He got back into the car. 'All this was unnecessary, you know.' His tone was conversational, easy. 'We could have done this in the first place.'

'Fuck off,' Danny said. He turned and walked back towards the van, hearing Okigbo chuckling. Osman came towards him.

'Get in the van, quick,' Osman said.

Danny hesitated, staring at him.

'Bloody move,' Osman shouted.

He ran past Danny and tapped on the window of the BMW. By the time Danny reached the van and got in, Osman was running towards him.

Behind him, Justine put her hands on the back of his neck.

'Thanks for coming,' she said.

Danny's heart leapt. He turned to look at her, reached back and gripped her hand in his. He wanted to kiss her, but he wasn't sure how she'd take it.

'You all right?' he asked.

'Yes. What's going on?'

Looking past Osman, who had almost got to the van, he saw Okigbo get out of the BMW and bend over, scrabbling in the rear seat, then he backed away and ran over to the Cortina. Osman jumped in next to Danny, the van rocking with his weight as he hit the seat. He switched the engine on, reversed swiftly, and drove away, the wheels spinning on the surface of the road as he accelerated.

'What's going on?' Danny shouted.

'I just told him,' Osman said, 'that he had two minutes before the Dancing Face blew his car into small bits.'

'What are you on about?' Danny asked, then he remembered the equipment in the back of the transit. It had all been too much for a bug, he guessed, and Osman had driven as if he was balancing an egg on top of his head. 'Jesus Christ,' he shouted. 'Stop. Stop.'

Osman pulled over to the kerb and stopped. Danny pulled at the door. Osman gripped him round the neck, pulling him back.

'It's too late,' he said. 'There's nothing you can do.'

There was a rumbling roar. It came from the direction of the archway. Danny threw off Osman's arm and peered out of the window. Along the street, nothing seemed to have changed. There was only the fading echo of the explosion. Osman put the van in gear and drove carefully towards the Barbican. Behind him he heard Justine sobbing. He stared at Osman, too full of rage to speak. Osman glanced round at him.

'There won't be much of it left,' he said. 'I reckon Okigbo got away in time. Not much he can do about the BMW though.'

'Stop the fucking van,' Danny said.

Osman stopped. They were in Old Street. A thin stream of traffic flowed past as if nothing had happened.

'That was a bomb you brought back?' Danny asked.

Osman nodded.

'That's right. I told Eleanor about it. She was cool. She said do it.'

'What's the matter with you?' Danny said. 'Why didn't you tell me?'

'You wouldn't have agreed.'

'You're bloody right, I wouldn't,' Danny shouted. 'That was one of the most important works of art to come out of Africa. Do you know what you've done?'

'Don't tell me what it was.' Osman was angry now. 'It mattered just as much to me.' He stopped, making a conscious effort to calm down. 'I kept trying to tell you. What we have to do is confront the past, not resurrect it. I come from the same life as the Dancing Face did. I know what it was. It was more than art. It was my history.'

'Jesus,' Danny said. 'You know that, so how could you do it?'

'It wasn't a choice,' Osman said. 'I turned my back on history. After that it was easy.'

313

Chapter Thirty

The phone didn't ring until Danny and Simone were walking out of Flegenhauer's class. Danny was grateful for the interruption because Simone kept asking him what he thought of the paper on the Baltic republics that she'd delivered that morning. His answers were vague, because he hadn't actually been paying much attention. In normal circumstances he could easily have faked being interested and impressed, but for most of the preceding three hours, while she talked about the role of nationalism in determining what happened between Russia and the Baltic states, he had been thinking about Justine.

It had been almost two weeks since the night of the bomb. Afterwards, in the back of Osman's van, Justine had been silent, her face, caught in the flashes of reflected light when Danny looked back at her, set and brooding, a mask of sculpted pain.

'Take me back to my flat,' she'd said, her voice so faint that Danny almost missed it.

He'd tried to talk to her then, asking whether she was okay, and whether he should stay with her, but she didn't seem to be listening.

'Just take me back to my flat,' was all she would say.

Since then he had tried to telephone her repeatedly, and without success. He'd left her half a dozen messages about the arrangements he'd made for Gus's funeral, but she hadn't replied. On the day of the service, although he had kept looking round, half hoping that she would be somewhere in the chapel, she had been absent. Afterwards, as Osman drove out of the cemetery gates he had scanned the street intently in the hope that she might be standing there, but she was nowhere to be seen.

Desolate as he was Danny hadn't entirely given up the prospect of seeing her again, but he also had the uneasy feeling that, for Justine, he belonged to an episode in her life that she would want to put behind her and forget. For his part he was trying to think about her in precisely that way, but however hard he tried not to wonder what she was doing and why she hadn't been in touch he would find himself drifting into a daydream, in which they embraced, whispering in the dark.

'Maybe I should have made more out of the comparison with the Islamic republics,' Simone was saying in a worried tone, just as Danny's mobile began ringing.

'No, no, it was okay,' he reassured her, although he couldn't, for the moment, work out what she was talking about.

He put the phone to his ear, giving her an apologetic smile.

'This is urgent,' Osman's voice said. 'Meet me in St Osric's.'

Before Danny could reply the connection went dead.

'I've got to go,' he told Simone. She raised her eyebrows, and he thought in that instant that she was going to accuse him of not listening to a word. Instead, she smiled and shrugged.

'See you later,' she said.

Watching her walk away, Danny felt the sudden urge to go after her and apologize. He wasn't sure why, because there had been no formal declarations between them and, apart from sex, he wasn't sure, either, how Simone felt about him. When he told her about his brother's accident, she'd been warm and sympathetic towards him, but her manner had the self-consciously caring tone with which she talked about her close friends and relatives, as if the two of them had never been lovers. Somehow he had the feeling that when the term came to an end it would also signal an end to their relationship.

The way Danny felt about it, the term was already over, but there were several long weeks to go, and he didn't want to think about that, because he dreaded having to decide what to do with himself when the vacation arrived. Osman was planning to meet his father and go to New York with him, so he would be alone. At times like this he was suddenly aware of his isolation, and the feeling that he was branded and driven, a rat scrambling its way out of the sewer, would return. This year it would be worse. The absence of his brother would make sure of that. He knew there'd be a job waiting for him, delivering pizzas down at the Kashmir Pizza Parlour, but that was the job he'd done the previous summer, and everything that had happened to him recently made him feel that it was time for a change, that he had to take hold of his life and move in new directions.

Osman's van was sitting in its usual place at St Osric's, but there was no one in the driver's seat and the doors were closed. He banged on the side, his frustration guiding the blows. A familiar rusty screech, the door slid open, and Justine was sitting there on the floor looking at him.

Danny couldn't speak.

'I phoned you a couple of times,' she said, 'but you weren't in and I didn't know your address, so I remembered what you said about Osman and I came down here. He'll be back soon.'

Danny couldn't remember what he'd said about Osman and he didn't care.

'I was going to come up and see if I could find you this weekend,' he told her.

She smiled. A rueful look.

'That's why I came,' she said. 'I'll be gone tomorrow.'

'Where?'

'I'm going back there. See about my dad.'

But he's dead and buried, Danny wanted to tell her, then he remembered that she already knew that.

'Why?' he asked instead.

'I don't know. For myself. I have to find out if it's true. I have to find out all I can.'

'How long?'

She pressed her lips tight together and spread her hands in a don't know gesture.

'I don't know,' she said. 'That's why I came. I didn't want you to think I didn't care.'

He wanted to ask whether that meant she cared about him or about Gus or about the events in which they'd been involved, but, suddenly, he was afraid that the answer might reveal Justine's indifference to his feelings about her.

'Did you hear from Okigbo at all?' he asked.

She shook her head.

'He's got enough troubles of his own. I expect he's gone off somewhere. I haven't heard anything about him.'

Danny cast about in his mind for something to say, some appeal that would hold her.

'I'm going now,' she said. 'I'm driving over to see some people in Brum, then I'll go back to London.'

For the first time Danny noticed her car, parked next to the van.

'I wanted to tell you,' she said. 'I thought a lot about the things you told me, about being ourselves. I don't know what I feel about all of it right now, but I think it's important. I admire the way you're trying to work it out.'

Flabbergasted, Danny watched in silence as she climbed out of the van and walked over to her car. With her hand on the handle of the door she turned round and looked at him.

'Tell Osman I said goodbye.' She paused, considering. 'The way it worked out was probably best in the end.'

Danny nodded. After his first moments of anger at what Osman had done he'd come to accept that it had probably been for the best, and since then he'd been too numb and full of grief to think sensibly about what it all meant. When she said this, though, he remembered the relief he'd felt afterwards, the clear sense that Osman's act of destruction had taken a weight off his back.

Justine put the car in gear and it began to move before Danny could work out what he wanted to say. He knocked on the window, and she stopped and wound it down, her eyebrows raised, looking a question at him.

'Please come back,' he said firmly.

Justine frowned, then she smiled, and she gazed at him, a hint of sadness in her expression. Without speaking she put her hand out and grasped his.

'Don't worry,' she said. 'I'll contact you here when I get back. I'll write to you.'

Danny watched the car speed out of the driveway and turn into the street, then it was gone. Maybe she meant it, he thought, but if things went the way they had all his life he'd never see her again. His eyes prickled as the thought rushed at him, but then, remembering that he had determined never again to be overwhelmed by his feelings of helplessness and despair, he shook his head and suppressed the tears. Turning to the van, he slid the door open, got in and sat on the floor, looking out over the park and waiting for Osman to come back.

BLACK BRITAIN: WRITING BACK
Curated and introduced by Bernardine Evaristo

MINTY ALLEY / C. L. R. JAMES

It is the 1920s in the Trinidadian capital, and Haynes's world has been upended. His mother has passed away, and his carefully mapped-out future of gleaming opportunity has disappeared with her.

Unable to afford his former life, he finds himself moving into Minty Alley – a bustling barrack yard teeming with life and a spectacular cast of characters. In this sliver of West Indian working-class society, outrageous love affairs and passionate arguments are a daily fixture, and Haynes begins to slip from curious observer to the heart of the action.

Minty Alley is a gloriously observed portrayal of class, community and the ways in which we are all inherently connected. An undisputed modern classic, this is an exceptional story told by one of the twentieth century's greatest Caribbean thinkers.

WITHOUT PREJUDICE / NICOLA WILLIAMS

Lee Mitchell is a thirty-year-old barrister from a working-class Caribbean background: in the cut-throat environment of the courtroom, everything is stacked against her.

After she takes on the high-profile case of notorious millionaire playboy Clive Omartian – arrested along with his father and stepbrother for eye-wateringly exorbitant fraud – the line between her personal and professional life becomes dangerously blurred.

Spiralling further into Clive's trail of debauchery and corruption, she finds herself in alarmingly deep waters.

Can she survive her case, let alone win it?

BLACK BRITAIN: WRITING BACK
Curated and introduced by Bernardine Evaristo

THE FAT LADY SINGS / JACQUELINE ROY

'That is the glory of being a mental patient, nothing is impossible.'

It is the 1990s, and Gloria is living in a London psychiatric ward. She is unapologetically loud, audacious and eternally on the brink of bursting into song. After several months of uninterrupted routine, she is joined by another young black woman – Merle – who is full of silences and fear.

Unable to confide in their doctors, they agree to journal their pasts. Whispered into tape recorders and scrawled ferociously at night, the remarkable stories of their lives are revealed.

In this tender, deeply moving depiction of mental health, Roy creates a striking portrait of two women finding strength in their shared vulnerability, as they navigate a system that fails to protect them. Life-affirming and fearlessly hopeful, this is an unforgettable story.

BERNARD AND THE CLOTH MONKEY / JUDITH BRYAN

When Anita finally returns to London after a long absence, everything has changed.

Her father is dead, her mother has disappeared and she and her sister Beth are alone together for the first time in years.

They share a house. They share a family. They share a past.

Tentatively, they reach out to each other for connection, but the house echoes with words unspoken. Can they confront the pain of the past together?

Dazzling and heart-breaking, *Bernard and the Cloth Monkey* is a shattering portrait of family, a rebellion against silence and a testament to the human capacity for survival.

BLACK BRITAIN: WRITING BACK
Curated and introduced by Bernardine Evaristo

INCOMPARABLE WORLD / S. I. MARTIN

In the years just after the American Revolution, London was the unlikely refuge for thousands of black Americans who fought for liberty on the side of the British.

Buckram, Georgie and William have earned their freedom and escaped their American oppressors, but on the streets of London, poverty awaits with equal cruelty.

Ruthless, chaotic and endlessly evolving, London forces them into a life of crime, and a life on the margins. Their only hope for a better future is to concoct a scheme so daring it will be a miracle if it pays off.

Pulsating with energy and vivid detail, *Incomparable World* boldly uncovers a long-buried narrative of black Britain.

THE DANCING FACE / MIKE PHILLIPS

University lecturer Gus knows that stealing the priceless Benin mask, The Dancing Face, from a museum at the heart of the British establishment will gain an avalanche of attention.

Which is exactly what he wants.

But such risky theft will also inevitably capture the attention of characters with more money, more power and fewer morals.

Naively entangling his loved ones in his increasingly dangerous pursuit of righteous reparation, is Gus prepared for what it will cost him?
